The End Was Not the End:

Post-Apocalyptic Fantasy Tales

The End Was Not the End:

Post-Apocalyptic Fantasy Tales

Edited by
Joshua H. Leet

SEVENTH STAR PRESS

Cover art and design: Bonnie Wasson
Cover art in this book copyright © 2013 Bonnie Wasson & Seventh Star
Press, LLC.

Editor: Joshua H. Leet

Published by Seventh Star Press, LLC.

ISBN Number: 978-1-937929-07-7

Library of Congress Control Number: 2013936659

Seventh Star Press
www.seventhstarpress.com
info@seventhstarpress.com

Publisher's Note:
The End Was Not the End: Post-Apocalyptic Fantasy Tales is a work of
fiction. All names, characters, and places are the product of the author's
imagination, used in fictitious manner. Any resemblances to actual
persons, places, locales, events, etc. are purely coincidental.

Printed in the United States of America

First Edition

Dedication:

This anthology is dedicated to the ideas inside of us that just won't die, no matter the events that change our worlds.

Acknowledgements:

First and foremost, I'd like to thank Stephen Zimmer, commissioning editor for this project and author of the Rising Dawn Saga and Fires in Eden series. Stephen and I have been developing this project for several years, and he landed me a gig as editor for Jackie Gamber's *Sela* and Steven Shrewsbury's *Overkill* along the way. I know he is as excited about this collection as I am.

Many people have played a part in leading me into editing and writing, family, friends, employers and teachers, but my first actual editing work of any kind was for the website Wotmania.com when I was in college. Wotmania was a fansite for the book series The Wheel of Time, by the late Robert Jordan and Brandon Sanderson, his successor. I'd been a reader of the series for years, and I don't even remember how it happened, but the site owner Mike Mackert, aka wotmania, saw fit to make me admin (editor) of the Fan Fiction and Humor sections. It was a volunteer position, but it was the first time I would work with authors, including Nathen Gallagher, whose work appears in this anthology. Wotmania is gone now (the fansite absorbed into Dragonmount.com, the community reborn at readandfindout.com), but I'll always remember fondly my time there.

Finally, it's a cliché but nevertheless a blessing. I'd like to thank my mother, Karen M. Leet. She's always been loving and supportive, but she's also played a major role in my writing and editing career. She made the introduction to Stephen (she edits for him), and she co-authored my Civil War book, *Civil War Lexington, Kentucky: Bluegrass Breeding Ground of Power*. She's always willing to help, including answering obvious editing questions I have no business asking, and having a writer for a mother is the reason I first even considered getting into this business. Thanks Mom.

CONTENTS

Introduction

by Joshua H. Leet

Now begin your journey upon broken roads passing through dying lands. Huddle around sheltered fires with cloaked refugees and beware dark shadows at your heel. Desperately brave the dark woods in search of food, and if you're lucky, kill and feast upon that which hunts you. If you are unlucky, the beast survives to struggle another day. The world has ended, and the roads are no longer home only to mighty adventurers. Now all manner of men, women, and children are forced from homes by dancing earth, dragon's fire, dark curse, marauding monsters, and other dire threats. These are tales of worlds' ends, and what comes after.

This anthology explores stories of the post-apocalypse in a fantasy setting, both those settings one expects with castles, dragons, and swords, but also you will find tales set on a world very much like our own in times to come, where monsters or magic reclaim the world that has been broken. The anthology was conceived of by Stephen Zimmer at Seventh Star Press, author of the Rising Dawn Saga and the Fires in Eden Series, and me some years ago. As fans of fantasy and of the post-apocalypse genre, we realized these two elements are rarely seen together. Fantasy tales typically follow the quest to prevent calamity, and those that are in fact set after disaster are so often set in the distant future, where the disaster is spoken of as part of another age. We wanted to show more of the raw impact on a world of men and monsters and magic. We wanted to show the times after the hero failed, but before another hero has beaten back the darkness.

Many authors answered the call with a wide range of stories, and in this collection you'll note particularly the popularity of Norse themes, demons, wastelands, and rare but powerful magic. Our authors hail from England, Canada, and across the United States and drew from a variety of traditions to offer action, suspense and horror in their works.

The first story The Halls of War explores the impact of the fall of a kingdom on an unlikely hero and the drive that keeps them alive. Blood and Fire follows with a group of warriors hunting a dark foe, their home shores threatened. Next Make Way for Utopia shows that the young know not the depth of their peril. After you've been driven from your home, make Twenty Year Plan your cautious guide to reemergence. But planning is powerless against Nightmares and Dragonscapes, the terrors of the night and day, and be wary of how you grasp The Stone-Sword, lest you find yourself the wounded. You may then seek shelter In the Hills Beyond Twilight, but in the darkness there can be no peace, so light your way with the Blade of Fire and prove your worth. But know your limitations and know your escape before you find yourself Waist Deep, like the young man Ben, who is haunted and hunted, but finds some hope. Through all

Introduction

these tales you may journey in your mind, but there is no better place to witness the world shattered than upon Story's End, a flight through the darkness that will light up your imagination.

One of my favorite authors, Robert Jordan, famously wrote of endings that were truly beginnings in his Wheel of Time, a cycle of destiny. But what of tales of the end, when destiny failed? The end of kingdoms and kings, of war and warriors, of magic and mages. What of the worlds that were not saved, or perhaps not saved just yet? In these tales of endings, happiness isn't guaranteed, but even still, even when the world has fallen and all hope seems to be lost, sometimes the end was not The End.

-Joshua H. Leet

The Halls of War

by Deedee Davies

Chapter 1

I am Vronn, and I am a slayer of men.

It is only in the perfect stillness after battle that I can find a moment's rest from the pain that plagues and maddens me. In those fleeting moments, when the blood haze rises and the death cries are stilled, I can recall his face and his voice. I can remember the path of victory he carved through the eastern lands, the seats of power he took for himself, the days of dark splendor that were ours. For my love was a bringer of change to the barbaric lands of Nemea, while I stood beside him as empress and counsel.

Our empire was vast. In seven great countries along the southern coast of the Nemean Sea, our dominion held sway. Though we may have taken the lands from their former rulers, we brought order and civilization to their people, and taught man to live side by side with his fellow in peace. Our vision and determination built countless towering edifices: halls, temples and palaces, unparalleled in all the ages of the earth. Their stature and beauty was said to be such as to rival the home of the gods themselves, and the jewel in the crown of our empire was Aryssa, where we two finally laid down the sword and made our home.

Although our time together was dominated by the demands of our empire, the bonds of our love were true, and the hours we spent together—whether in the thick of some wild mêlée or in the dark opulence of our bower—were the happiest of my life. Our occupation of the East took us to lands undreamed-of, and brought us wealth and influence beyond measure. There were those that called us demons, and cursed the lands of the setting sun for sending us forth, but most accepted our rule as fair and just, and tributes and homage were paid to us in equal measure until we were almost sated.

Then, little more than a year ago, our reign was ended in a blaze of flame and thunder. The earth was wracked with titanic quakes, the like of which sank Atlantis, and the heavens opened to rain fiery death from above. Bedrock was sundered, the seas boiled and the skies cracked. Aryssa, the finest of the great cities we had built was swallowed as though it had never been, and a thousand souls were lost in the cataclysm. When the dust settled, our lands lay in ruin, and a cloud of black ash pervaded. It cloyed the senses, stifled crops, and cloaked the land in darkness and gloom. Once-proud spires lay in shattered pieces upon the barren ground, and the great paved roads we had worked so hard to build were cracked asunder, cutting one

The Halls of War

town off from another.

And worst of all, my love was lost to me, his life ended in plain sight of our subjects by a single thunderbolt from above.

Without his leadership, the civilizations we had fostered fell into chaos, turning brother against brother, child against parent, and all men against me. For I had become a living symbol of our downfall: a reminder of our invasion of the stricken lands, the symbolic cause of the disaster, and therefore a target for the hatred and fear of all men.

It pleases humankind to be able to apportion blame for the horrors that befall them.

Some believe that we were thrown down from power, our empire damned and subsumed in flame because we had angered the gods with our ceaseless conquest and bold ambition. Others believe that I am the curse that holds this land in the depths of hunger and despair, that by killing me they can regain the lost days of glory and undo the great catastrophe that plunged us all into darkness and ignorance. Still others believe that I fight only for myself, in desperate defense of my foul and unworthy life—but for me the world has lost all luster. Were it not for the fact that to end my own life, or to allow another to take it would forever keep me from his side in the Halls of War, I would surely have ended my struggle long before now.

And so there I stood once again, a lone she-demon, maddened by undiminished pain as the members of yet another lynch mob rose against me. They thundered towards me in a great wave, bristling with weapons and other makeshift implements of war, the air ringing with their cries for justice.

"Die, demon, so we can regain what was lost!"

They were but lambs to the slaughter.

I met them head on, my own demonic blood, tempered and set alight in the flames of battle driving my blade to sever and slice. My enemies erupted in fountains of crimson blood and splintered bone even as they attacked. I accorded them no mercy, for none had ever been shown to me. The word itself was alien to my ears. At last, only one remained. We circled one another, feinting and thrusting amidst the bodies of the fallen, looking for an opening.

It is said that grief can do strange things to a person. It can turn lovers into murderers; make the most staid person rash, the most cautious person careless. I was all of these things, a lethal combination, birthed of grief, which could ultimately lead to only one possible outcome. I struck recklessly, driven by sorrow and anger, my blade swinging wide in a powerful arc intended to take off my opponent's head.

Few things in life are inevitable—I count only birth and death among them—and I had seen far too much of the latter to be sorry for the end that was now served to me at the tip of the enemy blade. There was pain as the steel drove home, of course, but it paled in comparison to what I had suffered walking this world alone.

I had avenged my lover's death a thousand times over and spilled the blood of countless men in an effort to redeem myself. I would die with honor, in the thick of battle as I had always desired. I prayed only that it was enough to earn me a place in the Halls of War, and a seat at his side.

The Halls of War

The death stroke I expected did not fall. It was my enemy's head that rolled, not mine. It mattered not. With a length of metal through my gut, I was done for. However, I had to admit that a spark of curiosity still stirred within me. With friends and allies alike long gone, who would intervene on my behalf?

I was dimly aware of a massive form that blotted out the moonlight sinking to one knee before me, and a flicker of recognition energized my cooling blood. Few were the figures that compared to his in stature, and his long, straight horns—which put my own to shame—glinted in the moonlight with the adornments he sported upon them.

It is not unknown for the gods of war to send down friends or family to greet loved ones who die with honor, and it seemed that Fate had chosen to favor me in my final hour. With tears caused in equal measures by my mortal wound and my wonder at seeing him again clouding my vision, I somehow summoned the strength to speak.

"Have you come to show me the way to the Halls of War, my love?"

Before that day, I never knew that words had power: that even a single syllable, spoken aloud, could cut as effectively as any blade.

The answer was "no".

Chapter 2

The darkness mercifully took me then, and I was glad. I did not want to experience the reunion I had coveted through hundreds of lonely days, only to be rejected.

My dreams were deep, plagued with nightmares and morbid visions of the darkest day of my life: the day when the sky was riven with lightning and his life was ended before my very eyes. Had a mortal enemy attacked, I could have stood and fought at his side, but against the forces of nature itself, I was utterly powerless. It is this very helplessness that keeps me awake at night, that drives my arm in frustration to cut down my enemies, as though doing so might assuage my horror at my impotence.

Abruptly, I was thrown from sleep, thrust rudely back into a world I thought I had abandoned the last time I closed my eyes. Gasping, I clutched at my body, at the place where the fatal wound was made—and found nothing. My thoughts whirled as the true path of events tried to reassert itself over the vestiges of the dream. I should have been dead, yet I lived, and it appeared I was not the only one to be afflicted with unexpected life. Silhouetted against the fire, a great figure kept vigil, one whose outlines and contours I saw every time I closed my eyes. My heart gave a leap, as though in a bid to be free from my chest, and I hurled myself from the bed with his name on my lips.

"Achoris!"

An instant later, my arms enfolded him, and found I could not hold him close enough to satisfy the need that had

The Halls of War

dwelt unsated inside me for a full year. It did not matter. At that moment, I cared not where he had been, or what wondrous twist of fate had returned him to my side; all I knew was that we were together. The world could have ended then, and I would have been complete.

It is strange, how the mind can fool us when we are ridden with grief, how it can blind us to truths we know to be incontrovertible, how it can tempt us to cling instead to false hope. Eventually, all illusions faded, and by and by a sense of unease intruded on my blissful state. There was an insistent prickling feeling that scratched at the base of my spine and the back of my neck, and a sick feeling of dread that permeated the pit of my stomach. Something was horribly wrong. Though I stood upright with my arms flung as far around his great shoulders as they would reach, it was a one-sided embrace.

He was not holding me.

"What is it, my love?"

I withdrew slightly so that I could look into his eyes, where always I had found my answers in the past. What I saw and felt at that instant sent me stumbling backwards, crashing to the ground in blind terror. Until now, I had only seen him in the gloom, but the bright firelight revealed all. There was no recognition or welcome in his eyes, glowing as they were with some vile green luminescence. His body clearly showed the ravages of the worm, his once-bronzed skin cold and grey. Most horrifying of all, on his chest, gouged from flesh that I was certain knew not the thud of a heartbeat nor the rush of blood was a symbol so unholy that no sane creature would dare invoke its power.

"Achoris?" I gasped.

"That name no longer has any meaning for him."

I had thought us alone, and had been grateful for the fact. Now I was glad that I was not cloistered with him in privacy. At that moment, I was too frightened, too uncertain of what was real and what was not to face that situation.

The creature who spoke was female, lavishly—if scantly—accoutered, and accompanied by two men who also bore the unholy symbol of the Dharmek, chaotic god of pestilence and suffering, on their breasts. The truth was instantly clear to me. This witch, for such she must be, had raised Achoris from his eternal rest to serve her.

"You did this to him!" I cried. Although it seemed a pointless statement, it felt good to say the words aloud, to lay blame and accusation for the horror I saw before me.

Her response was a shrewd and appraising smile. Every step that brought her closer to my lover twisted at my innards and sent powerful feelings of proprietorial hatred pulsing through my veins. For the moment, I bided my time. My circumstances were still too new, too confusing, for me to take any direct action. Even when the witch draped her arms about him from behind—eliciting not the slightest response from his motionless form—I kept my peace, though my nails were drawing blood from my palms.

"Indeed. I brought him back, gave him new life, and as such he is mine, body and soul."

"To what end?" I forced the words out from between jaws

that seemed wired shut. It was hard to concentrate on anything but her proximity to him—but I had to know her intent.

The witch's smile became devious, and her hands began a seductive dance about the great lines of Achoris' chest and arms, while her lips edged closer to his cheek. "Use your imagination."

I have felled men twice her size with ease, so I saw no great challenge ahead when I vaulted to my feet and hurled myself, fists first, at her mocking face.

Some moments later, I recovered, face down on the far side of the bed, my entire body twitching and jerking as though some residual current of energy still passed through it. When I managed to heave myself to my knees, I noted to my chagrin that she had barely moved. Her trick cost her little effort, apparently. I was offered the opportunity once, long ago, to learn this arcane rite: to harness the great natural energies of the world and release them, offensively. But I live by the sword. Let those who have not strength enough to wield steel fritter their time away with the pursuit of such artifice, I thought.

I cursed the irony of hindsight.

"What do you want from me?" I asked, averting my eyes from his empty face, and keeping them on the object of my rancor.

"Your deeds over the last few months have not gone unnoticed. These Summoned serve me well enough in their way, but for the task I have in mind, I need a killer." She paused to run a long-nailed finger along my love's jaw, its honed edge cutting but drawing no blood, while her gaze bored into my forehead. "One with a brain."

My suggestion as to what she might do with herself may have been a physical impossibility, but it did have the merit of wiping the smug smile off her face. It was quickly replaced by a cold sneer that I estimated was far more natural to her than any pretense of humor.

"At my command, he will rip the still-beating heart from your chest."

She had not moved from Achoris' side, but she might as well have been holding him on puppet strings, for her control was complete. As the suggestion was made, the luminous green pits that passed for his eyes centered on me, and though not a flicker of emotion lit his countenance, there was a tension and a readiness in his posture that I found deeply unsettling. I had no doubt he would blindly carry out the order.

I had lost count of the times over the previous few months that I had prayed that death would seek me out; but now I found that the prospect of meeting it at his hands—changed as he was—was even more abhorrent to me than living. To have the life crushed from me by arms that once held me close in rapture, to see his noble face twisted in ignorant rage as he delivered the death-blow—surely I would harbor those memories through the afterlife and beyond.

A year of self-sufficiency in the face of adversity had given me undeniable strength and force of will. Nevertheless, I had no desire to spend eternity tortured by images of my own death at my lover's hands.

"Who do you want me to kill?"

The Halls of War

Chapter 3

There is an old adage in my country that says a leopard cannot change its spots. My way has ever been to strike first and strike hard, to leave no room for counterattack and to face every challenge head-on. The errand with which the witch—Felain by name—had tasked me went against every martial instinct and every honorable sensibility I had. I was to sneak into a nearby town, relatively untouched by the cataclysm, breaching its stout walls not by means of steel and wit, but via the sewers that emptied into a small watercourse on its southern boundary.

While readying myself for the mission, I had familiarized myself with the comings and goings of the Summoned, and the witch's own daily habits. Since she did not fear me with so many of her faithful lackeys around, and safe in the knowledge that she could incapacitate me with a twitch of her fingers, she made little effort to contain me. Consequently, I saw much of her domain. The upper levels of her tower were opulently— even decadently—appointed, and a group of recently deceased Summoned toiled there incessantly about menial tasks. Some even went so far as to linger on comfortable couches as though awaiting her arrival, their faces blank of all knowledge save the emptiness of the abyss. It pleased and sickened me in equal measures to suppose that some of the less worm-eaten she had taken for her consorts.

On several occasions, I tried to engage Achoris in conversation, holding his rotting face close and speaking words that always provoked reactions in him in the past: words of endearment, words calculated to strike at his pride, words of hurt and provocation. I might as well have berated the ground beneath my feet, for he was as cold and unresponsive as stone.

So I had continued my exploration, and found that the tower deteriorated rapidly as I descended. Through battered doors, streaked with rust from ancient nails, I perceived dank dripping walls, moldering furniture, and boarded casements. At the nadir of the tower, I found the pit where the witch birthed the horrors that served her. Its walls were splattered with unholy symbols, graffitied in blood; its floor was a foul mire of mud and entrails, and its light source was a wan and greenish firefly glow. I wondered what payment the vile god of pestilence demanded in return for her trucking with him. I hoped it was extortionate.

My mind returned reluctantly to the present and my odious surroundings. Before the fall of our empire, this city would have had sentries at every postern, and the sewer entrances would have been barred and guarded. I resolved to return and teach them a lesson in vigilance once my business with Felain was concluded. My heart sank as I saw the extent of the decay and neglect that afflicted the town, one of many that had prospered under our rule. Between tumbledown cottages and crumbling buildings, brigands and thieves lurked in the shadows, taking advantage of the lawlessness that now abounded. The cobbled alleyways, with their haphazardly-scattered stones were treacherous in the light rain, and everywhere was the all-pervading ash that no amount of brushing or cleaning seemed to remove.

I entered the run-down mansion house unchallenged, and stood eventually above a sleeping form partly obscured by blankets. A tuft of dark gold hair was the only visible evidence of the sleeper beneath. I drew my blade. My heart quickened, my self-loathing deepened. I wondered if I might at least give the sleeper a chance to defend himself. After all, I needed only to return with his heart and retrieve the item the witch desired. She did not need to know that I challenged him and fought him to the death. A nod to myself, and my decision was made. I poked the sleeper's shoulder with the tip of my blade. When nothing happened, I poked him again. Eventually my efforts were rewarded with a low mewling and a small upheaval as the form rolled over. One glance at me and its movement was stilled, to be replaced by a marked trembling. My patience thinned. I wondered at last what sort of man she had sent me to kill and what her reasons were for wanting him dead.

"Get up," I rasped, eager for it to be over quickly. "Get your weapon and defend yourself."

The figure responded with an even more frenzied shaking. The last of my patience vanished. "Do it now, or die in your bed!" I threatened.

This last seemed to have an effect. The figure stumbled out of bed and ran in a huddling crouch to the window, where a small array of weaponry was stacked. When he turned to face me, struggling to withdraw a sword he obviously didn't realize was held in by a buckled strap, something about his silhouette against the grey night struck me. The outlines of a human figure vary widely from person to person, and factors such as race, gender and age enable warriors to make judgments about who they face on a darkened night. As such, I have learned to identify the nature of my opponents in poor light, and I can recognize a child when I see one. I lowered my sword.

"Step into the light," I advised him soberly.

He did, and my suspicions were confirmed. Although tall, his form was gangly, and I had serious doubts that he was old enough to shave.

"P-please...." he said, this terrified child, "Please don't. Have mercy."

Mercy. No one had asked mercy of me in many months. My death-dealing had been too swift, too uncompromising, my reputation too heartless. This child, however, had no idea who I was and as such, no reason to believe that I would not accede. With that single word, my soul was thrown into turmoil. My actions over the last year were brought to light in lurid detail, and at last I saw myself as others must have done: a blood-crazed demon bent on death. My sword tip brushed the reed mat at my feet, and my eyes glazed, seeing only visions of darkness and murder. How much of it was necessary? How much was self-defense and how much my own senseless bloodlust, falsely justified?

I sank to my knees amidst a rush of feet that heralded the arrival of the rest of the household: a man in a nightgown and cap with his rotund and shrieking wife, a gaggle of siblings and two of the house guard, red of eye and bristly of cheek, but nonetheless awake and ready to answer the call. I made no protest as they disarmed me and removed me from the chamber. I could hear the boy's tremulous replies to his parents' queries fading as we descended.

The Halls of War

The interrogation was poor, by my own standards. I would have extracted the information in a matter of minutes—but these people were civilians, unused to violence and coercion. I envied them that. For a while, I sat and endured the threats from the house guard, and the angry cries of the parents while trying to ascertain my own place in things.

At length, when the provocations of the mother and the empty threats of the father both failed, they decided to call in the town guard to see what they made of me. Although I had no concern about fighting my way out of the situation, I found myself caught. I could not kill the boy, that much was certain. Yet if I returned to the fortress without his heart, and the other item she had tasked me with retrieving, I risked the witch's wrath, and I had no doubt she would have Achoris destroy me.

I looked up at the group of people surrounding me as though for the first time, and wondered if they could in fact help. I awaited a likely window in the conversation.

"Fetch them, Horace, fetch them now. Tell them we have some half-naked demon in our house trying to kill our beloved son."

"All right, Muriel, give me a minute, I have a few more questions before I go and bother the town guard...."

I let their debate continue for a while, and at a suitable lull, I spoke.

"I was sent here by a witch to kill your son. Do you not wish to find out why?"

Muriel and Horace stared at me as though the carpet had spoken, and the house guard at once made their presence felt, looming one at either side of me.

I stood, shrugging off their attempts to push me back in my seat, and locked eyes with the father. It struck me then that it had been a long time since I had talked to anyone, my brief bargaining with the witch and my one-sided attempts at conversation with Achoris aside. It felt alien, to try to resolve matters by talking. There was a time when I would have been the one to counsel against rash action, to urge rational thought and temperance in place of open violence. By the gods, how far had I fallen?

Every journey starts with a single step, it is said, and so I began mine by offering information about Felain, and the hideous errand with which she had tasked me—to kill Tomas and collect an arcane item he would have about his person. When I had finished, four pairs of eyes stared at me in blatant disbelief, and I was aware that the children of the house were watching furtively from the stairwell.

"This is preposterous," puffed Muriel, her prodigious chest jouncing as she bustled across the room, sweeping her progeny back up the stairs with a wave of one meaty arm. "He's our little angel. Never put a foot wrong in his life. Why would some witch want to...." She spotted the youth in question hovering on the landing, and dropped her voice to a stage whisper. "Kill him?"

"Maybe we should ask him," I suggested, which was met with open hostility from Muriel and mild protests from Horace. The two house guards, however, were nodding quietly, apparently more in tune with my own thinking, and unaffected by the distorted view a parent often has of their child.

The Halls of War

"Maybe young Tomas does have something to tell," averred the first.

Tomas was ushered down the stairs with the sort of care one normally accords delicate china, and settled in a seat as far away from me as possible. His mother clucked over him protectively for a time, while I tried to remember what it felt like to have someone watch over me. I dismissed the thought as weak, and locked eyes with the boy's own furtive ones. Instantly, I saw something I recognized from my days as arbiter of justice in our empire—guilt.

Ignoring the father's entreaty to go easy on the boy, I demanded, "Why would the witch send an assassin to kill you? This item she wants—do you have it?" And then, more shrewdly, "Did you steal it?"

Tomas shrugged, averting his gaze and keeping silent.

"There are many lives at stake here, not least your own," I reminded him.

This seemed to have the desired effect. He withdrew a tattered rag from within his night clothes, a thing apparently of such value—or of such sensitivity—that he kept it on his person in bed.

"Well...I did borrow this from her." At his parents' horrified gasps, he blurted, "But I was going to give it back— honest!"

I took it from him, and in unfurling the cloth quickly realized that it was skin. Opening it, I glimpsed an unfamiliar script, daubed onto the skin in a hue that suggested the contributor of the writing surface had also supplied the ink.

"Can you read this?" I asked of him. The youth, trembling, replied in the negative.

"Then why did you steal it?"

Tomas' voice was almost lost beneath the ensuing chorus of denial as his parents refused to accept that the boy had done such wrong.

"I wanted my uncle back."

The conversation ceased, and all eyes centered on him.

"What in the name of the gods does that paper say?" whispered Horace.

"You stole a <u>spell</u>?" Muriel's eyes rolled back in her head, and for a moment I thought she might topple like a felled oak. Her anger got the better of her.

While his parents' voices escalated again in admonition, I examined the writing, taking into account the context and what I knew of the witch's necromantic predilection. I was able to recognize a few words that were corruptions, or perhaps the predecessors of an eastern script of which I could read a smattering. Straining to discern the faded lettering through the many crease lines that contrived to keep the document's contents secret from me, I eventually made out the words for "life", "soul", "dead" and "return", along with another that might have been "heavens" or something similar. My heart pounded in my breast as my mind took a leap to the conclusion I most desired. Could this incantation provide the means to restore a lost soul to a corporeal shell?

The argument by and by intruded on my thoughts. I cut across it with a single word, and all fell silent at the urgency in my tone.

"How did you plan to use this?"

His answer caused a sickening hope to flare in my chest. A man, a necromancer, not far away, skilled in the lore of the dead, willing to work miracles for a few copper coins....

I lost track of the rest of the conversation, my eyes blinded to reality by an impossible fantasy, wherein Achoris was returned to me, whole and hale. We would resume our lives together, and the last year would be wiped clean, as though it had never been. I resolved to seek out the necromancer that very evening, demand the secret from him, pay his meager fee of copper coins and promise a king's bounty should his incantations lead to my lover's restoration.

"The man's a charlatan," growled one of the house guards. I shook myself from my reverie and stared searchingly at him, noting again his red-rimmed eyes, the growth of stubble on his cheeks and the despair that hung about him like a pall.

"Peace, Gerrard," murmured his companion in a low tone.

"No, let him speak," I snapped. If the man had something to say about the quality of the necromancer's work, I wanted to hear it.

Gerrard grimaced. "I lost my Cathy two years ago this spring. I couldn't bear the thought of life without her, and I heard tell of this man who could raise the dead. I paid my coins for the man to work his magic, and work it he did, but what came back...."

"Time for bed, children!" Muriel announced suddenly, to

a chorus of disappointment from the youngsters, in equal parts horrified and curious about the guard's story. They were ushered back up the stairs with great sweeps of her wing-like arms, no doubt to huddle in the shadows at the top of the staircase and eavesdrop.

"What came back?" I demanded, when the noises from upstairs had ceased.

"Something…unnatural. He raised the dead all right, but without a soul or a mind. It was just a body, a thing that looked like my Cathy."

"What happened to her?" I asked, hardly wanting to hear the answer.

"I…put her back in the ground. Paid him handsomely for it, too. It's better this way. She's at peace. That thing that walked around wearing her face had a black soul.…" He broke off, his voice cracking. His companion grasped his shoulder awkwardly, his eyes entreating me to cease my line of questioning.

I did. My mind was awhirl with possibilities. No doubt Gerrard had asked the necromancer for the wrong thing—he had asked him to raise the dead, and this had he done. With the spell the boy had just transferred to my possession, I could persuade the necromancer to restore my love's heart, mind and soul to his body, I was sure of it.

"Yes, yes, we're all sorry about Cathy. We went to her funeral. Both of them, in fact," huffed Muriel. "But that doesn't help us decide how we're going to save my poor little Tomas, does it?"

"We've caught ourselves the huntress," said Horace.

The Halls of War

"With her safely in the city jail, surely there's no longer a threat to our boy?"

"If I fail to return, she'll just send one of her undead lackeys." I warned. "Just one of them could kill the entire household."

Gerrard, the grief-stricken house guard regarded me warily. "If she has an army of the dead at her beck and call, why did she send you?"

I laughed mirthlessly. "It is a simple matter for the dead to be tasked to kill. However, more refined or specific errands—such as finding and retrieving a certain item—are often less successful outside her immediate sphere of influence." So much had the witch imparted to me, but even then I suspected that she savored the hold she had over me, and she derived some twisted pleasure from seeing me do her bidding against my will.

"So what now?" asked Horace.

"We stick to our decision: call the captain of the guard and put her in jail." The other house guard leaned on me as he spoke, impressing his presence with a heavy hand on my shoulder. The touch sparked a painful memory. Had Achoris seen an enemy lay hands on me in the days of our reign, the guard would have been missing the offending appendage in the blink of an eye.

"Were you not listening?" I demanded. "If I do not return with the boy's heart, she will send the undead for you, and one of her lackeys to hound and destroy me, one who—" my voice cracked.

"What do we care what happens to you?" asked Muriel. "You tried to kill our son!"

"She's afraid, mistress, can't you see that?" asked Gerrard.

"The undead won't be able to get her in jail," snapped Muriel.

I laughed aloud at that. Even alive, I had yet to see a barrier Achoris could not overcome by dint of brute force and wit. With the unholy strength of the undead at his disposal, I doubted there was a door in the land that could keep him out. I shook my head.

"Well, there's only one thing for it then," affirmed Gerrard.

Everyone looked at him expectantly.

"You take her back a heart."

The Halls of War

Chapter 4

It was so simple I wondered that I had not thought of it myself. I would take Felain back a deer's heart or a pig's heart. How would she know the difference? Part of me balked at the idea: a sorceress as skilled in necromancy as she would surely know the difference between a human heart and that of an animal. Would she perhaps even know the difference between one man's heart and another?

I dismissed the thought. My only goal was to return by the appointed time and leave her to her ritual while I stole away with Achoris to the old man who would restore him.

"Come on—I'll take you down to the salting room. There are some animal carcasses there that should provide what you need." Gerrard's resonant tones intruded on my thoughts.

I nodded my assent, following him out of the house and down some rough wooden steps into the house cellars. The man had spoken true: there were indeed several likely sized animals, and I busied myself in selecting one while Gerrard hovered nearby. Having chosen, I was about to make the first cut when he spoke, his voice bitter.

"He is a self-serving, evil-hearted little man. He has power, aye, but he knows the consequences of what he does, and has no qualms about piling further grief onto the hearts of the bereaved in return for his few coppers."

I looked at him askance, taking in the large, sad blue eyes, and the shock of dark, unkempt hair. "The necromancer? What makes you think I would have any truck with him?"

"I know that look," he replied, not unkindly. "I wore it for months after my Cathy died. If there's someone you're thinking of trying to bring back…."

"It's none of your concern," I snapped, and turned immediately back to the gruesome task of cutting out the deer's heart.

A moment later, he grasped my hand, not to prevent me from taking the heart, but to impress upon me the importance of what he had to say. I stared at it while he spoke, recalling for the first time in an eternity what it was like to experience human contact, and marveling at the warmth of his touch.

"It's hard …" Gerrard was saying, "… to lose the ones we love the most, but we have to believe they've gone to a better place."

I withdrew my hand, staring at him coldly. "And what if we <u>know</u> they have not?"

He had no answer for that, but his eyes entreated me to heed his words. I paid him no mind. I had more important considerations.

My task accomplished, Gerrard seemed reluctant for me to be on my way.

"It would be better to wait 'til dawn," he opined, indicating the shaft of wan moonlight that illuminated the cellar steps. "The city is a foul and lawless place by night."

"So much I have seen for myself," I responded, with a moue of distaste. "It would not have been so under our rule."

As Gerrard caught his breath, I wondered whether I had said too much. Having been recognized wherever I had walked in the past few years, it had never occurred to me that these people might not have divined my identity.

Instead of raising the alarm, he gave a slight shake of his head and a dry chuckle.

"That explains much."

An awkward silence fell. I could feel the usual tension growing inside me, the readiness to defend myself that kept me in a state of almost constant agitation.

With a quick breath, and another shake of his black-maned head, Gerrard continued, apparently dismissing my accidental revelation. "Should you make it out of the city, there are long stretches of open moorland before you. It is not terrain to be travelled by night."

"I can take care of myself," I countered uncertainly. It had been a long time since anyone had shown concern for my well-being, and given that he now knew my identity, I could not quite guess at his motives.

"I've no doubt of that," he replied with a wry grin. "I've seen your handiwork."

I watched him closely as he spoke, but I could sense no antipathy in him. My survival tactics depended on my ability to detect such things. If he had decided to turn me in, he appeared to be in no hurry to seize the opportunity.

As though attuned to my thoughts, he added, "My lips are sealed."

Assured of his silence, a dire urgency was pressing on me now: to return to Felain's tower, hand over the heart, and get Achoris to the necromancer without delay. With a curt nod, I bade him farewell. He grasped my hand again as I made to leave.

"Good luck, Vronn."

I had a feeling I would need a lot more than luck.

Some hours later, I was admitted to Felain's chamber, where her servants stood in orderly rows, attending the birth of yet another of their number. The poor wretch lay supine upon an altar of green malachite, its slick sides stained and streaked with the blood of previous victims. Two of the Summoned held him in place, and from his face, it was evident that he was both aware of his impending fate and powerless to avert it. I pitied him. Under other circumstances, I might have fought to free him, but it was imperative that I appear to be compliant, for a while longer at least.

At the witch's demand, I handed her the heart and the spell, which I had painstakingly copied to a new parchment to share with the necromancer. The witch opened the small blood-soaked drawstring bag and peered inside. She regarded me suspiciously.

"You had no trouble obtaining the heart or the spell?"

"I wouldn't say that," I replied drily. "The place was well-guarded."

Felain glanced back at the contents of the bag and humphed dismissively. Not wishing to tempt fate, I made my way back out through the gauntlet of zombies that stood between me and the door, and made my exit. As the door to the witch's resurrection chamber closed tightly, I swung about and raced up the stairs to the place where I knew Achoris was wont to toil through the long, lightless days.

The Halls of War

Moments later, I careened to a stop before him, took him by the hand and tugged with all my strength. His great form remained immobile, as though he were rooted to the spot, his gaze focused somewhere in the near distance.

"Come on!" I urged, begging and threatening when physical strength alone failed. Eventually, I resorted to desperation, and gritting my teeth, I cried: "Felain has ordered you to accompany me!"

I watched, sickened, as the words energized him and gave him purpose. There was a time when it would have been _my_ needs and desires that drove his actions, when he rejoiced in doing things for my sake. I prayed those days would soon return.

We were out of her tower, hastening across the open moorland when I noticed the pursuit. Far in the distance at first, a low, awful sound began. The noise grew as the undead approached, until I could distinguish the weird, inarticulate shrieks that passed for their battle-cry. With a shudder, I ushered him up to a high vantage point atop a rocky tor where they could come at us but a few at a time. And come they did. The army of the undead rose up around us, surging to cut off our escape on each side, leathery hands scrabbling at the rocks and clamoring for their prey. Even as they did so, I began to recall former days, before our empire came crashing down around us, when we two would have stood side by side and turned the tide by dint of steel and skill alone. It was then that it came to me: a heaven-born idea that nonetheless turned my stomach as I spoke the words I knew would compel my former emperor to carry out my plan.

"Help me—in Felain's name, fight!"

And so he did. Achoris turned on the undead that swarmed at us, and for a moment, we were reunited in battle, his axe cleaving and splitting, my sword chopping and slicing, and I could taste our success on the wind. The first went down when an axe cleft its skull in two, putrescent brain matter erupting from its head. The next found its innards spilling onto its feet, and while it stood in confusion, attempting to cram them back in, I took off its head. And so it went, each enemy meeting a death as swift and sure as the last, until the rock beneath us was mired in gore and entrails.

When at last the fight was over, the glory of days long past dazzled my mind, and replaced the nightmare landscape before me with the golden lands of Aryssa at the height of its beauty. I moved towards Achoris, expecting his arm to enfold me and crush me to him in delight at our victory.

To my bitter disappointment, I found that his giant frame was stilled now that the moment of battle was past, his eyes empty of thought or desire. He was dumbly awaiting his next command, as he would until the world turned to dust.

My excitement abated. Soon, I promised myself, soon the necromancer would restore him to me, and our world would resume upon its proper course. At my next command, we set off for the necromancer's home, and he fell into an easy stride at my side. I wondered at how simple it was to fool myself into believing the man loping along beside me was a living, thinking, reasoning being. From the corner of my eye, I saw only his familiar statuesque form, the points of his horns stark against the night sky, and in some odd way, my emptiness was lessened by his presence. I quickened my pace.

At length we arrived at the necromancer's hut. The makeshift door hung open, and a sickly green light emanated from within. As we drew closer, a buzzing noise, as of a swarm of angry locusts assailed my ears, and I found myself swatting in disgust at vile insects that rose in droves from the ground around the hut. They gave Achoris a wide berth, and though I suspected their aversion was more to do with a preference for live flesh, I allowed myself to think they showed deference to the honored dead.

Having rid myself of the worst of them, I glanced up to see the old man standing in his tattered robes in the doorway. I have met sorcerers and demons, emperors and kings aplenty over the years, and I was used to perceiving an aura of power in such individuals. This withered old sot had none. Still, perhaps those with the greatest power were those that hid it best, I surmised. Even then, I partly suspected that I was fooling myself.

When all three of us were seated cross-legged around the fire pit in the centre of the hut, and the few copper coins were jingling in the old man's hand, he spoke to me in a wavering, lisping voice.

"What is it you desire?"

"I want you to bring him back," I replied.

"He has already been raised from the dead, by the look of him," the old man observed. "What more could you want?"

I handed him the spell.

"Can you read this?" I asked.

The old man's bony fingers closed around the parchment,

and he shifted it with trembling hands until it was under his nose. He mumbled aloud for a few moments, before confirming that he could indeed read the incantation.

"And will it work?"

"Yes," he replied. "It will bring back his soul, heart and mind from the great abyss, and restore them to his body." At my concerned glance in his direction, he added, "He will <u>live</u> again."

I breathed deeply to steady my accelerating heart. We were so close. "Succeed in this and you will have a place of honor in our new empire. Whatever riches, possessions and companions your heart desires shall be yours without question," I promised.

The necromancer smiled and nodded, and with great effort raised himself from the floor.

"Wait here. I go to prepare for the rite."

Alone with Achoris again, I took his face in my hands and poured words of endearment and affection onto his deaf ears. I made rash promises of what we would do together when he was restored to me, of the new empire we would build, and the lives of pleasure that would be ours.

"I will never leave your side again," I swore, resting my forehead against his.

"Indeed you are right," came a cold voice, laced with derision. I swung about and was on my feet with sword drawn before she had finished speaking. Felain and the necromancer stood before me, a contingent of her undead flanking them. That I could be so completely unaware of their approach was a profound shock to me, and I cursed the moment of self-indulgence that had caused my distraction.

The Halls of War

At the merest flick of the witch's fingers, Achoris too was on his feet, and I found out at last what it was like to be on the receiving end of one of the sledgehammer punches I had seen him deliver to so many of our foes over the years. Floored, half-stunned and unable to move, I dimly perceived through a red haze that the witch was speaking again.

"This fool—" she indicated the necromancer, "—has neither the wit nor the skill to do what you ask."

At another of Felain's commands, I found myself seized and hefted aloft by the throat, my feet dangling freely above the ground. She stepped close, savoring my struggles as my love's decaying, calloused hands began to crush the life from me.

"But I do."

Her mocking laugh was the last thing I heard before the blackness took me.

Chapter 5

I awoke, sore and bruised in the pit at the bottom of the witch's tower, where preparations were well underway for the making of another undead servant—but this time, it was I who was on the altar. My chest was daubed in a stinking putrescent fluid forming the symbol of Dharmek, god of pestilence, and a number of rotting undead hands held me in place.

Felain approached me, a sway in her steps, and a triumphant smile on her lips. "Your true life ends here, demon, and what existence you have from this day forward will belong to me. Thanks to the spell you so kindly retrieved for me, you will be the first of a new breed of undead. You will remember everything of your former life, and be completely aware of all that befalls you—but utterly powerless to do anything of your own volition. You will knowingly serve me and pander to my every whim until such time as I tire of tormenting you."

I snarled in her face. "I hope your soul burns in Hell for all you have done, witch! You think your god works <u>for</u> you? He will have you pay in spades for his favors!"

Felain grinned. "Dharmek demands a high price indeed, but fortunately I didn't have to pay it. You see, Vronn," and here she regarded me with a sly smile, "The Kingdom of Aryssa was my birthright, so it was mine to give him in return for power over the dead."

My jaw dropped. At last I recognized her. She had been little more than a child when Achoris and I had stormed Aryssa and brought it under our rule. She and her family had been spared if they accepted exile. How damaged and twisted must the child have been to allow the destruction of her homeland in return for such power?

"And what better way to avenge myself on those who took my birthright from me than to force them to serve me in living death for all eternity?" she gloated.

"So destroying your own homeland was not enough?" I yelled, attempting once again to throw myself at her, to wipe the leering smile from her face, but the undead held firm and refused to release me.

"For what you and your ox of a man did to my kingdom and my family? No!"

"Do you have any idea how many people died when Aryssa fell?" I fairly roared at her. "<u>Your</u> people, Felain!"

"Those people were already dead!" she cried. "All those who willingly accepted your rule were damned the moment your dominion began." As she spoke, she drew a long, serpentine dagger from her belt, a blade that looked as though it would hurt as much on the way out as it did on the way in.

"And now it's time for you to join them." She grinned malevolently and raised the dagger, its wicked point aimed straight at my breast.

I struggled desperately against the undead arms that held me, but despite my greatest efforts, I could not move them an inch. It seemed as though I would at last face my end—not in battle, as I had hoped, but restrained like a sacrificial lamb. With an exultant cry the witch moved to strike, but before she could bring her weapon to bear on me, a dagger point erupted from her chest, spraying me in bright, frothy blood as the short length of steel sheared through her lung.

For a moment, the two of us stared dumbfounded at one another, and then hope flared in my heart—my love must surely have intervened! Her hold over him had not been strong enough to allow him to watch me die! As the witch sank soundlessly to the ground, I glanced up, my eyes eager to feast on the sight of Achoris standing proud in my defense.

Before me stood a tall figure with a shock of unruly dark hair and eyes as blue as the deep sea, a bloody dagger grasped in his hand.

"Gerrard!" I cried, and I wished I could have hidden the disappointment from my voice. A quick glance around showed that Achoris had not moved. He stood in line with the rest of Felain's zombies, obediently awaiting her orders. I sagged visibly.

Gerrard moved to release me, tugging at the hands of the undead creatures that held me, ready to fight to free me if he had to. Released from Felain's influence, they simply let go.

Rubbing my arms to restore the circulation, I examined Felain's body to ensure she was no longer a threat. The deathly pallor and glassy staring eyes were testament enough. It was a swift and ignoble end, perhaps, but no more than she deserved.

"Don't think me ungrateful," I began, turning to my rescuer, "But what brings you here?" I found myself warring with my own deep-seated suspicions. After all, he had discovered my identity.

"I followed you to the necromancer's hut." he explained. "When the witch took you away, I thought you might need my help."

"You knew I would make the attempt, despite your warning," I ventured.

"No-one understands your need better than I," he said, with a slanted smile.

Despite his words, my doubts about Gerrard remained. "But why would you help me? To your eyes, I am a demon who invaded your home and tried to murder one of your master's children."

Gerrard smiled. "You were coerced. Any fool could see you were acting against your will—Tomas would not be alive now otherwise."

My suspicions melted away at the earnestness of his response, and I did not doubt that he had kept my secret. Moreover, he seemed somehow lighter of spirit than before, as though he had accomplished something worthwhile. I liked that about him—it sat well on him, lifting years from the lines around his eyes, and bringing the ghost of a real smile to his lips.

"Everyone deserves a second chance, Vronn—even a creature like you." He said, with an appreciative grin in my direction. I did not know quite how to react to that. It had been a long time since a man had looked at me with anything but hatred or fear.

Turning to the motionless undead, Gerrard asked, "What do we do with them? Do we get the necromancer to bury them all?"

"No." I indicated the roiling mass at the centre of the pit. "We send them back whence they came."

He looked at the pit, and then back at me, his eyes filled with sympathy. "Do you want me to do it?"

"No!" I snapped, angrily. I would not be denied the opportunity for a final farewell. Then I caught myself, realizing that Gerrard meant only to spare my feelings. I managed a faint smile in his direction, the first in a very long time. "But I appreciate the offer."

The undead went in at our suggestion and physical insistence. They were as lost soldiers on their last march home as they shambled one by one to their ultimate dissolution. Although their passing caused pain, as their unearthly cries testified, it was over quickly.

Until at last, only my love remained. I muttered to Gerrard that I would like to be alone, and he gave a nod of understanding before ascending the tower stairs to wait for me above.

And so I stepped close to Achoris one last time, stealing a final embrace. His body remained cold and inert, waiting, as it ever would, for its next command.

It was brought home to me then with the force of a thunderclap that he was gone, and had been for an entire year. The witch may have animated his corpse, but his essence, his mind had never truly dwelled within it after his death. I had been deluding myself thoroughly to believe there was anything of him left, or that I could ever bring him back. A single tear escaped my eye and wound its way down my cheek.

"I have fought a thousand battles since you left me, my love, and even more before that in my time with you, but this is the hardest fight of my life—the fight against my own selfish needs. There is nothing I want more than for you to stay here with me, but I know that this is for the best. Your soul will be at peace at last."

"And so I will leave you now, my love. I know not if you understand any of my words, or the tale I have told you, or whether you know anything of what has befallen you, but I can assure you of this: we will meet again in the Halls of War, when it is my time."

I indicated the pit and uttered the single word that would end him.

"Go".

There was no recognition of what I had done. Achoris did not turn at the last moment and bid me farewell. There was no ethereal whisper that told of a love that would endure beyond death. There was only a corpse that walked obediently into the flaming pit, and a scream as the flesh was seared from its bones.

For a moment, I considered following him. I felt as though all my hopes and dreams had died in that one incandescent moment, but I could see at last that they were dreams of a lost future, one that could not possibly be regained. I knew that Gerrard awaited me in the tower above, a good man who had stood by me despite my faults and blindness.

The old empire was gone, leveled by cataclysm and scattered to the winds, and perhaps that was to the good. Although I did not know what the future held, I felt that I stood at the threshold of a new dawn, and that I faced it perhaps with a new friend.

The End

Blood and Fire

by Desmond Reddick

The man who stands

at a strange threshold

should be cautious

before he cross it,

glance this way and that:

who knows beforehand

what foes may sit

awaiting him in the hall?

...to be blind is better

than to burn on a pyre:

there is nothing the dead can do at all.

-excerpt from the Eddaic Viking poem Hávamál

Desmond Reddick

Father says the rain may spoil this year's crops like they almost did last year. Mother says the church will help us, but I know that Father will do everything in his power to get by on his own. We made it last year, by a hair's breadth. If they would let me help, the time would pass without worrying thoughts. But Father tells me that fieldwork is not for girls. So, I am left to let my fears of starvation and invasion take hold as I tend to the cooking fire.

Not since the barbarians came to the northern coast of our great island has there been such fear throughout the village. These awful men attack our farmsteads and take our food and any wine or keepsakes we have happened to gather. Once they made it very close to our village. I feared they would take my mother. Other children have had their mothers taken from them. Some children have even been taken. I have never been more frightened in my entire life that time they skirted our village and set fire to our church.

Never more frightened until now. The tattered black sail of the great dark ship nearing the shore can only be a bad omen….

***

Black smoke stings my eyes as I look out to the ocean. It is a clear day at sea but I am here, smelling the stink of burning flesh. This is the third time this has happened in the cycle of one moon and I am growing weary. There is no honor in this.

I had hoped to encounter our enemy here, but we are too late. My warriors grow tired of cleaning up; it is slaves' work. My slaves grow hungry and tired of rowing in pursuit of what everybody perceives as phantoms. Even I am beginning to

Blood and Fire

question the veracity of this quest. I was not allowed to take my band of warriors and instead was forced to fill this band with Svears and Northmen. One race thinks they are better than me and the other takes sick delight in devouring their awful mushrooms and tearing their enemies apart by hand. They do not value me as their warlord. I, in turn, do not share a blood bond with them. Odin preserve us!

We were greeted in this desolate land by wayward, wandering villagers. I was surprised they were left alive due to the state of their farms and village until…until we got closer. They appeared dead: bludgeoned, stabbed, hacked and, it seems, bitten. As they saw us, they came in our direction. I was confused at first, thinking they wanted help. Agnar would have become a meal for these demons if not for swift and decisive action. We thrust and chopped at them but they never stopped until we removed their heads. They were strange foes. Gnashing their teeth as though they were trying to bite us, they too had been bitten, by human teeth. Neither I nor my men have seen anything like this. Even the Northmen, savage as they are, were disgusted at first. What kind of man eats another man? And is <u>this</u> what is caused? The young girl's head at my feet has been dead for days; that is a fact. Yet it tried to bite my hand when I turned it over. These things are foul and must be destroyed.

"What are we to do, lord?" Agnar asks. It is a hammer blow to my thoughts.

I take a moment to gather myself and turn to meet his gaze. "Round up the woolen cattle and inspect them carefully for wounds. Those with wounds must have their heads split and their bodies burnt. Those without are to be killed and taken to the slaves for preparation. Tonight we will dine."

Agnar smiles broadly. It will be the first fresh meat in as long as they have been on this voyage. His smile disappears and his face grows grim. "And tomorrow?"

"To the sea again, Agnar."

His shoulders fall a little as he walks back towards the other men. I am sure they will curse me for the lack of adventure, for the lack of mead, for the lack of blood, even after they dine of these massive creatures roaming this hilly land. I am growing weary of this.

***

The sea is rough today; the men are silent. I have ordered the slaves to draw in the oars, eat and sleep. We will reach the final stop on this voyage by nightfall: an even greener land with grey skies always sending rain. A place the thunder god favors.

It is always solemn in the hours before a battle. The men contemplate their fates; it is an honor to die in battle but it is always dire when one faces death. I suppose the nature of our enemy is also adding to their solemnity. These men are fierce in battle but it is always difficult when the nature of one's enemy is unclear.

For now, they sleep. Their bellies are full of meat and their thirsts even sated with a little wine pulled from a stone church. Enough wine to keep them happy but not enough to sicken them. They must be strong and clearheaded. They will need it this night.

Blood and Fire

***

"My lord! My lord!"

It is Finn of the East who awakens me. He is a tiny man by all accounts but very savage and precise in battle: an asset to any band of warriors. I shake the sleep from my eyes and pull myself to my feet. "What is it?"

"Look to where the sun sets!" He points out at the horizon but they are much closer than that.

At last! It is a drakkar with pointed dragon head at its prow and a tattered black sail. It is the largest I have ever seen. Seagulls and crows litter the sky around the ship like some strange crown of scavengers. We are close to land.

"Finn! Put a fire into the slaves. Get them to the oars immediately and take chase!" He leaps from his haunches and runs quickly below deck.

The men stir from rest; grunting as they carefully rise to their feet. Many begin to shout as they look out at the dark ship in the distance. Swords and axes are unsheathed and held in the sky as shouts of derision escape their eager mouths. Normally I would admonish them for such savage behavior but true battle has been a long time in waiting. Slaying wounded walking catatonic villagers is hardly substitution for battle.

"Ragnar! Hrodi!" Two lean and tall archers turn to await my orders. "Bows, arrows and torches!" My order is met with a load roar of approval by all and swift action on behalf of the archers. I feel like a warlord again.

The pace of the ship quickens as the slaves take to the

oars. We are sailing against the waves so the ride is rough but the ocean spray does nothing to cool the bloodlust that has taken hold of my men. It is jarring to the knees to come crashing down over such huge waves. The crest of each wave propels us up into the air and the weightlessness on descent disturbs not the warrior's mind. The lapstrake assembly of the hull creaks incessantly but it will hold long enough. The ride home will be a calm one.

The dark ship is taking to ground. The sky above it is grey and growing darker still. The storm god shall have his entertainment this very night. The sky thunders and rain begins to fall in sheets. The men have calmed; they are saving their energy for battle. The Svears hold their short swords tightly to their foreheads and whisper prayers. The Easterners wring their hands in anticipation. Even the Northmen have calmed, they have lain their arms down but only to greedily devour their blackened mushrooms; it disgusts me but their savagery will be useful in this battle. My brethren, the Danes, sharpen their swords and field axes. I grip the handle of my Chieftain sword, earned from years of victorious battle, and say a short prayer to Odin.

We are moments from being within arrow's range of their grounded drakkar. The anticipation of battle builds in my heart with each beat. I am certain my men feel it even stronger than I do. I have learned over my years to save energy for vicious bursts on the battlefield. A warlord must have a clear head, especially in the moments before a battle.

The tattered sails of the dark ship cut a ragged silhouette in the grey sky. They beckon us, warn us. The air is charged with the anticipation of battle. Rain falls forcefully in our faces, urging

Blood and Fire

us back. The closer to land we get, the smaller the waves are and our ship cuts right through them. We are traveling faster than before. The Northmen sit in meditation waiting for their awful mushrooms to take effect but it is time to bring fire to my men's hearts and bloodlust to their minds. One look at Finn sends him to his feet to rouse the men from whatever prayer or activity they may have been involved in. Smartly enough, he leaves the Northmen alone; bothering them at a time like this is a mistake one only makes once. I move to the bow of the ship to prepare my orders.

Within moments, the dark ship has taken ground and we are approaching rapidly. As we near the ship, I can see the individual passengers shamble off; scavenger birds following them as they slowly move off of the beach onto more solid ground.

I turn to face my men. While we lack the bond of kin, all men are brothers in warfare. They stand resolute as the ship cuts through the smaller waves. Most smile or grit their teeth waiting for battle. The Northmen's skin pales and begins to sweat. In mere moments, they will be the most ferocious warriors this world has seen; now they look as though they have eaten old eggs.

"Archers!" Six men stand forward from the crowd with bow and arrow prepared. Three slaves emerge from the very back of the crowd of warriors with torches. They light the fuel-drenched, cloth-wrapped tips of the arrows and step aside to let the archers step to the bow of the ship. Bows drawn, they aim for the sky. "Only one ship leaves this beach today!"

Desmond Reddick

The flaming arrows tear into the grey sky and arc downward toward the dark drakkar. All but one strike the ship; the black sail bursts into flame almost immediately while the rest of the ship slowly burns. Black smoke rises from the sail of the ship rapidly. The…things…turn to look first at their ship and then at us. They line up on the beach preparing for our assault.

It all begins to dawn on me. I know why this group of men was chosen and why I was chosen to lead them. They are not my warriors. I am a fierce warlord but by no means am I the fiercest or most accomplished. No warrior-true expects to return from battle. But all nations want their warriors victorious. We are not meant to come back.

I turn to look at the warriors at my back. They stand waiting for my words. I comply: "We are doomed. I am doomed. It is my duty not only to lead you into death but to make sure that no fate worse than death befalls you like those things out there." Silence still.

"Those things are not men. They once were but have been denied the honor of death: warriors unfit for Valhalla or even Hel!" A few shouts of approval ring out.

"I have been chosen to lead you because my death will not greatly affect my nation. You have been chosen from separate tribes and villages even within your own land. Because you are not brethren to any other man among you, you should have no hesitation ending the suffering of the man next to you. And that is what you must do. If one of those things out there bites you, you will end up like them: a fate worse than dying beardless. Gladly take the head of your comrade to spare him this awful

Blood and Fire

fate." Nods of acceptance sweep through the crowd of warriors.

"Fight hard. Be unrelenting and merciless. Watch each other's backs but watch your own more carefully. Only then may you go home with your head intact." The shore rushes towards the ship and our enemy becomes clearer in our sights. "Whether you live or die on this day, I will see you all in VALHALLA!"

The men raise their weapons and give one whooping grunt in unison; now, they are saving their energy. The shore comes at an alarming speed and the archers let loose another volley of flaming arrows, this time at the tree line off the beach. The rain is new so the trees catch without much delay. There is nowhere for them to run.

As the ship nears the shore, the first wave of men, the Northmen, stand at the ship's bow whooping their dark mushrooms into effect. I have witnessed this action cause mighty armies to shudder but the creatures are solid as stone waiting for our assault. The rest of the men, myself included, grasp any part of the ship we can in preparation for impact. As the ship runs aground, the Northmen leap through the air and bring swords and axes crashing down upon the heads of our enemies. These Northmen are savage and I would not trust them to stand behind me in battle, but their fighting capabilities are awesome to behold. Limbs fly readily before the rest of us are even able to touch the ground.

These things were not only just men, they were my people. Their garb and weapons are all too familiar. Their braids and complexion tell me they are Danes...or, they <u>were</u> Danes. Their bodies back from the dead due to some dark force, no doubt. They move slower than us but they are resilient if we are able to plunge our swords through their chain mail or a weak spot in their helmets. Their armor tells me they used to be very successful in pillaging when they were men, or maybe afterwards. Our travels in pursuit of these demons tell me they still pillage thanks to the terrible carnage they leave in their wake. But it is us who must be successful this day.

Battle is a living thing regardless of the dead creatures we face. It swells and throbs like a heart and bleeds like one too. There is no better way to cleave the neck of an opponent than being amongst rain and fire. The gods are smiling on us this day. The gods and the ravens, both will feast regardless of the victors.

My division of Danes and Finn, the Easterner, has driven our first mass of enemies backwards into the inferno of the forest. But they still lumber out, flames pouring out of their armor, ready to continue battle. The longer they burn the easier they are to destroy. The smell of burnt rotten flesh and the sound of popping tendons is oddly comforting. They drop their weapons when they can no longer physically hold them and run towards us in a last effort to sink their foul teeth into our flesh. They are tenacious but their hot flesh is even easier to cut through.

In a maelstrom of blood and fire my men are at home, seething as one violent mass yet individually making their marks. Swords and axes are swung with lightning speed as the thunder booms above us. The sky opens up and rain falls even harder, like innards from a slit belly. Thankfully, it is not enough to quell the fires already raging throughout the beach, and in our chests.

This is glory in the highest sense. We do this not only for

Blood and Fire

our land and people, but for all who draw breath. These things are a disease in the guise of man, a growth waiting to be lanced. We are winning this day, but the more of these monsters we cut down, the more, it seems, appear. One cannot swing their sword without hitting one of them. For them to be this numerous there must be another ship on the beach around the island. We knew we would be outnumbered due to the size of the ship we were chasing but this may be more than we can handle.

Birger, a fierce Dane swings his axe freely but before I can warn him a stringy bearded corpse stabs him through the belly and sinks its rotten teeth into his exposed neck. It pulls the flesh off his neck in a quick backward jerk and blood rushes out like a hot spring. Ever savage, Birger swings his axe behind him and almost completely severs the head of the desiccated monster. As it falls to the sandy ground and lurches, Birger walks towards me in the heat of battle clutching the massive hole in his neck. The battle rages on without him and around him. An errant sword clips his shoulder but he barely falters. I dispatch the creature who keeps snapping its teeth at me with a quick hack at its neck and give my undivided attention to a comrade who seeks death.

He begins to lumber as his face goes paler and paler. His hand, still pressing hard against his neck, tries to stem the constant flow of blood but the crevices between his fingers are making that very difficult. Stopping one body length in front of me, he silently removes his hand from his neck and leans back exposing his throat. The blood running quickly down his chest ensures he will not be on his feet long. I nod to him and whisper a short prayer underneath my breath. He does not cry out but the look in his eyes tells me he can no longer bare the pain. I swing the sword as fast as I can to make it as quick a death as possible. This is not the most honorable of deaths but the gods must make allowances. After all, there is less honor in turning into one of those things.

I have never had to dispatch one of my own men while he stood on his feet. And doing so allowed more of those damned things to creep in. I swing my sword wildly to try and widen the gap between myself and these monsters. I have no room to take delight in killing these things. There are too many.

All around me, the Danes are falling to the multitude of creatures. We ventured too far into the throng and let them surround us. We tried to put their backs against the fire but ended up being put against it ourselves. They are not the worthiest of foes I have faced but the sheer numbers are making it impossible. We <u>are</u> going to die on this day.

I fight now with my sword and a burning branch but it is getting increasingly difficult to hold them back. Agnar and Finn, back to back close to the burning ship, are being swarmed as well. Agnar looks over at me and I can see his teeth bared from where I stand. He swings his axe with such might he takes one of the creature's heads and embeds its blade into the skullcap of another. But as he steps on the thing's head to remove the axe, Finn is overcome and he is pushed backwards into Agnar. They disappear amongst the crowd of dead men devouring their flesh.

Even the raging Northmen falter in their savagery. I had thought their berserker mentality would be ideal but the swarming mass of dead begs to differ. They fight even with their bare hands to the very end but they will not last long.

My sword is heavy in my hand and my shoulder aches with each exhausted swing. However, I have managed to get out of the trap against the burning woods. I feared I would be pushed into the fire, a trap I myself devised. Backing towards the ship, I hope to gain higher ground to easier fend off these monsters. But I have to pass the wretched drakkar first.

As I turn around, I get the first close look at their wretched ship. Somehow, the fires have stopped with seemingly little damage to the ship itself. But its wood is grayed with rot and cracked with age. It looks as though it has been pulled up from underneath the sea. With very little sail left but tatters, the ship must push itself across the seas on sheer force of evil.

There is a sharp pain in my ankle as I hit the wet sand below. I look back to see Agnar: his fingernails digging in with a desperate clutch. I smile for an instant before I notice his teeth still bared as they were before and a huge hole in his chest. It appears putting my men out of their misery is the order of the day.

I plunge the tip of my decorated sword up through the tender flesh under his bearded chin. It is an easier thing to do, thrust rather than swing. The sword stops at what I can only guess is the inside of his skull and his body goes limp. His hand lets go of my ankle when I pull back but I still fumble to my feet at the base of the rotted drakkar.

I feel the thing biting into my shoulder blade only a moment before I lose the feeling in my arm. My sword hits the ground. I try to break free but more of them are on me. The smoke from the burning forest drapes itself across the beach towards me. Perhaps the gods are mercifully trying to obscure my vision to the horrors I am to befall. Or perhaps the gods themselves do not want to see.

Again the smoke stings my eyes amidst the popping wood and burning flesh. There is no honor in this.

***

... until I know for sure that we are doomed. In the distance behind the hellish ship, two smaller ships flank it.

I call out for Father but he is already behind me. His face tells me all I need to know. I run to the fields with my mother while Father and other men in the village gather tools to protect the farmstead. Even I know it is all futile. These men are savage fighters with insatiable lusts for anything of value. This is what our church tells us.

Mother and I huddle and whisper prayers to our Lord. She is frantic in her scripture, so frantic I allow my curiosity to get the best of me. I peer over the grassy hill at the edge of the field and what I see disembarking the ship is far worse than I could have ever imagined.

The End

Make Way for Utopia

by Scott M. Sandridge

"Make way for Utopia!"

The sound of the whip crack echoed down the street, accompanied by a man's scream.

"Make way!"

Jordan cast his gaze on the procession the moment it became visible atop the hill. As it descended the hill, he tightened his grip on his grandfather's hand, checking to make sure they both were standing far enough away.

"Almost here." His grandfather directed a vacant stare across the street, his head tilted to align his right ear toward the procession. "I'll be glad when this damn thing is done, so we can get back home."

Jordan shushed him then quickly looked around. "We don't know who might be listening."

"Bah!" His grandfather dismissed the warning with a hand wave. "No Guardians around us. I'd smell 'em if there were."

Jordan chewed on his lower lip. "Still...."

"You're too young to remember," said his grandfather, shaking his head. "It wasn't always like this. Our people were free. We had buildings filled with books." He let out a sigh. "We had towers and palaces, buildings made of stone, statues of gold." He lowered his head. "Now gone. All gone. Everything—gone."

Jordan shook his head. "Just stories, Grandfather." His gaze went toward the howdah in the procession's center, being carried by two servants per side. Like always, the veils obscured any good look of the occupant within. "That's all they are."

"Just stories?" Grandfather's voice rose. "Just stories!" He balled a fist and spit on the sunbaked clay street. "I was there!"

Jordan tugged on Grandfather's sleeve. "Silence! Do you want to die?"

But his Grandfather jerked his arm out of Jordan's grip and stomped out onto the street. "I was there!" He pointed a finger at the howdah. "I know what you did!"

"Silence, cretin!" one of the guards growled. The guard directed his whip at the old man's hand. The man's scream rang louder than the whip-crack.

"Grandfather!" Jordan rushed toward the only family he had left.

"I know who you are!" Grandfather bled profusely from the cut across his hand. A second strike tore open his right cheek. He flinched, covered bloody cheek with a bloody hand. "There is no ruling a dead world! No matter how hard you—!"

His voice was cut off by a gauntleted fist to the jaw.

"No!" Jordan beat his fists against the guard's massive armored chest, tears streaming from his eyes. "Stop hurting him!"

"Worthless worm!" The guard drew a blade.

"Enough!" The sultry commanding voice, so accustomed to obedience, made even Jordan cease. The head of the feminine shadow behind the veil cocked to one side. "You are fortunate that you are the age you are, young one—and your grandfather, also, is fortunate. Anyone else would have already died for such an outburst."

Jordan felt his heart skip a beat during the shadow's brief pause. She waved a hand in dismissal. "If they find living in paradise to be so disagreeable, then perhaps life in the Wastes will be more to their liking. Take them outside the city walls. If they try to enter again, kill them."

"No! Please!" Jordan fell to his knees. "Grandfather is too old! He will not last long in the Wastes!"

"That is not my problem, child." The silhouette of her head turned toward the guards. "Take them away!"

Terror nearly made Jordan's heart stop. Outside Utopia City awaited nothing but death, for the walled, self-sustaining city was all that remained of life on this world.

***

"All this used to be a paradise." Grandfather wheezed through dry, cracked lips. He laid still, his eyes unfocused. "Trees everywhere."

"Don't talk, Grandfather." Jordan squeezed his sweat out of the soaked cloth, letting the drops fall on his grandfather's lips.

"Save your strength." He looked around at the sunbaked pockets of dirt amidst a sea of salt. "There has to be water somewhere."

"Not for many miles, if that." Grandfather shut his eyes. "There used to be a sea where we are now. I remember the sails. I was but a child. The world was so beautiful. But then <u>she</u> came. Destroyed everything."

Tears would have soaked Jordan's face were he not so dehydrated. It had already been two and a half days since they had been banished from Utopia City—two and a half days since their last drink of cool water. "Stay with me, Grandfather."

Grandfather's lips cracked open when he smiled. "It is too late for me. Leave me, child. Survive. For me."

"I'm not leaving you! We live or die together! You're the only family I have left!"

"Live. Live to avenge me. And your parents. Live to avenge us all. Live—" Grandfather let out one final exhale.

"Grandfather?" Jordan whispered through a dry throat. The world spun around him, and his own eyesight dimmed. He blinked. "Wake up." He nudged his grandfather, but there was no response. "Please."

Grandfather's last words echoed in his head. *Live. Live to avenge me. And your parents. Live to avenge us all. Live—*

"But—I'm just a boy...."

***

Jordan had no recollection of the first three days after Grandfather had died. It was as if a deep dark void had sucked his memories away.

Make Way for Utopia

The other days and nights were a blur—hot days, cold nights; burn then freeze, burn then freeze. And always, always, the dry ache of cracked and bleeding lips, sun-burnt flaking skin, and the torment that came only from a body that had begun to devour itself. He had long since stopped sweating. His urine had stopped trickling yesterday (or was it today?). All he had left to drink was his own blood, and he would not live for much longer while drinking that!

And all he found during those days were cloudless skies and the yellow-white of the salt flats. A curved horizon was broken only by a sparse collection of rocky plateaus.

And bones.

Always the bones.

Animal bones, human bones, and bones of…other things—most were shattered, as if some massive blast wave had blown their bodies apart.

According to Grandfather (oh how he missed him!) this had all once been a vast ocean. And yet he could see the bones of what had to have been land animals—large ones, too. How far had the blast thrown their bodies?

He looked at the hollowed out arm bone that he had used to collect his bodily moisture—even the stains had evaporated. *If I don't find water soon, none of these questions will even matter.*

He kept walking.

As he passed by a large humanoid skull (one of the "ogres" he had heard about in Grandfather's tales?), he fingered the crude bone blade that was tucked in the small salt-crusted rope tied around his waist. He had fashioned and sharpened the blade with a piece of flint he had found and cloth strips from his tunic.

I'm going to die. Will all this salt dry out and preserve my body like the mummies in the city necropolis? Or will I decay? Or perhaps my bones will be picked clean by rats, rats that know where the water is, water that I'll never reach before I die?

"Stop talking like that, Silly!"

Jordan stopped in his tracks, spun around. The voice had come from every direction as it echoed off the walls of the canyon he found himself in. In his condition, he had never even noticed that he had entered a canyon. Nor had he seen anything resembling it along the curvature of the horizon. *How did I walk in here without knowing?*

"Because you do not know!" A child-like giggle followed the melodic feminine voice as it bounced off the canyon walls. "You did not walk here, Silly! We brought you!"

"How do you know my thoughts?" Jordan's hoarse dry voice rasped, scarcely echoing it was so low. He winced and rubbed his raw throat.

The voice answered with yet another giggle. "You so silly, Silly!

"There's a cave to your left. Unless you plan to lie down and die right now, which would be very silly of you indeed, you might want to come in. Food and water awaits our new guest, naturally."

Jordan was running toward the cave mouth the instant he heard "water." As he entered the cave he wondered how he could move so fast considering his condition. But then, survival can make one do things they never thought they would, as he had already learned....

But what had he learned? What had happened during the first three days after Grandfather had died? What was his mind blocking out?

Inside the cave mouth, Jordan found himself within a small cavern. A yellowish glowing orb revealed a tunnel at the other end.

"This way." The orb pulsated with each echoing syllable. "Follow my pet."

Jordan blinked. "Pet? But, it's just a ball of light."

Again the giggle. The orb pulsated rapidly from it and even changed shape to an octagon, triangle, and a hexagon, before returning to its original roundness. "Silly!"

Jordan followed the orb down the tunnel. He could hear the echoing tap tap tap of water droplets ahead, and it made his dry, swollen tongue feel even drier. The tunnel opened up into a cavern only slightly larger than the one he had left. In the center, a pillar connected the ceiling and floor. Droplets of water trickled down the left side to form a small pool at the floor.

Jordan rushed toward the life-sustaining liquid.

"Careful," said a melodic voice to his right. It was the same voice that had come from the orb, only it sounded less filtered. "Only drink a few drops for now to wet your lips. Then drink a little handful at a time. Don't drink too much too fast!" Again the giggle. "You also might want to wash off your hands, first."

Jordan washed his hands then wet his lips. Then he drank a small handful to ease his aching tongue. He turned his head toward the direction of the voice. His breath left his lungs, and he even momentarily forgot about his hunger and thirst.

The column was comprised of two large stalactites and two stalagmites of equal girth, all fused together. Hollowed out within the column was what resembled a carved seat, and in that seat was the most beautiful creature Jordan had ever set eyes upon. Limber limbs on a petite frame, soft skin so pale as to almost seem silver, long wild hair as orange-red as lava, long slender ears that tapered to a fine point, and violet eyes that seemed to pierce directly into his soul—Grandfather had once told him about such creatures, but at the moment Jordan could not recall what they were called. Tiny multi-colored lights, like fireflies, circled about her, and some nestled in her hair. Her cherry-red lips curled upward at the corners, revealing mirthful amusement. She giggled. "What's wrong, Silly? You've never seen a Faerie before?"

Jordan opened his mouth then closed it. As a shiver travelled up and down his spine, the words in his head, by the time they travelled to his mouth, came out as "Uh…um…ah…."

The Faerie reached her hand out toward the orb, and it was then that Jordan realized that she had six fingers. The brightness of the orb dimmed until Jordan could see what had been creating the light. It was a tiny bluish-purple dragon, barely the size of the Faerie's finger.

"This is my pet, Rosebud." She straightened her arm out toward Jordan, the dragon perched on her hand. "Say hello, Rosebud!"

The tiny dragon belched purple sparks, its eyelids

drooped as if drowsy—or annoyed.

This can't be possible!

The Faerie cocked her head to one side, the delicate-seeming features of her childlike face conformed into a look of passive curiosity. "What can't be possible?"

"Y-you read my mind?"

Well, it's not like you weren't throwing your thoughts out for me to hear. Her words almost seemed like his own thoughts in his own head, but not quite. If she hadn't already demonstrated the ability to read his thoughts, he might have dismissed it as him just imagining her voice in his head.

Jordan took a couple more drinks from the pool. "So, uh, my name's Jordan. What's yours?"

The Faerie shrugged. "That depends. Are you asking for my true name, my given name, or the name I prefer?"

"What's a true name?"

A brief spark of red enveloped the violet in her eyes. "None of your business, that's what!"

Despite the melody and pitch of her voice, Jordan still felt a tendril of fear go down his spine. "Uh, sorry. What, uh, name would you like me to call you?"

The Faerie scratched her chin as if in deep thought. After looking up at the ceiling, she grinned, bit her lip, and then snapped her fingers. "Your Gracious Highness, Princess Peanut!"

"Uh…okay…."

The Faerie laughed so hard she fell out of her seat. "You're so silly!" After her fit of laughter resided, she said, "Just call me Violet."

Jordan scratched his head then smiled. "Pleased to meet you, Violet." He looked around the chamber. "But, ah, where's the food?"

Violet crossed her arms and pretended to be annoyed. "Boys! All they ever think about is food!" She giggled then beckoned him to follow her.

Violet passed her hand over a patch of glowing moss on the back of the "throne pillar" (Jordan figured it was good enough a name as any for it), and a grating sound echoed through the cavern. A hidden door opened in the floor next to them, revealing a set of roughly hewn steps. Rosebud's scales began to glow again, and Violet led Jordan down the steps. "Careful. They can be slippery."

The stairs wound downward for what felt like half an hour. On occasion the monotony of the descent got broken by Violet stopping then stepping over a tripwire and then gesturing at Jordan to do the same. A couple times she stepped carefully in a specific pattern and directed Jordan on which part of each step was safe. "After all," she told him, giggling, "you wouldn't want to end up burnt."

Jordan had heard stories from his Grandfather about vast caves and secret tunnels, but he had never believed such tales until now. Considering how easy it would be to hide in such places—not to mention defend them—he began to understand why the telling of such stories had been illegal. That, and—he began to realize—it insured the continuation of the now obvious lie that no life remained outside of Utopia City.

"But why does she lie?" He whispered more to himself

than to anyone else.

"You mean Mor—oh, wait, 'Utopia'?" Violet spoke that last word as if the word, itself, had tasted bitter. "How else can you control people?" She shrugged her slender shoulders. "Besides, it's not a complete lie, only half the truth. Pockets of life still exist on this world, but it's so scarce now that Mother Nature will probably have to start over from scratch. Whoever is left on this world is doomed—including the slaves of that city."

Jordan let out a depressed sigh. "How long do we have?"

Violet shrugged again. "Decades, years, weeks—maybe even until tomorrow. It all depends on when Mother makes her decision on how to end it.

"She can be quite the fickle dame," she added with a giggle. Violet pointed at a door near the bottom of the steps. "Stay put until I tell you to follow. The door has a mind of its own, and I have to explain to it why you're here." She then looked at Jordan, one side of her lips curved up into a half grin as one violet brow rose upward. "The last thing I need is your unshielded thoughts distracting it."

Jordan blushed.

Mere seconds later, the door opened on its own, bathing the stairwell in yellow-white light. "Okay, c'mon!"

Jordan followed and found himself inside a place that was no longer a cave.

Stone walls lined a vast round room, and sunlight shone through large circular windows. Statues of silver and gold lined each side of the hall. The floor gleamed like polished marble. In the center rested a large round table with thirteen gilded chairs.

And on the table, food.

Jordan rushed to the table and began devouring at random. Roast chicken, ham and gravy, strawberries, and stringed beans. Apricots and watermelons. Pudding, milk, and toasted bread smothered in melted cheese. Jordan ate until his stomach felt full.

He then sat down in one of the chairs, let out a large belch. His cheeks blushed. "Uh, sorry."

Violet, who had been watching him eat the entire time, giggled. "Such a silly, silly boy!"

Rosebud flew to one of the statues then perched on the top of a round shield.

Jordan looked around. "Where am I?"

"You," came a deep male voice behind him, "are in the great hall of Camelot, the castle that had once housed King Arthur and the Knights of the Round Table.

"And you, my dear boy, are sitting in the King's seat."

Jordan stood up then turned around. A gray-haired, bearded man stood by the chair. He was dressed in dark gray robes that contained embroidered symbols—Jordan could not recognize any of the symbols—that glowed like silvery moonlight. Upon the man's head rested a silver circlet that held a glowing silver orb just above and between his bushy brows. He clutched with his left hand a gnarled oak staff, its plainness a stark contrast to the man's attire.

Jordan stepped back, nearly tripped. He felt the warmth of his cheeks blushing yet again. "I-I-I'm sorry."

The man waved his hand in a dismissive gesture. "Don't

be. It's been too long since that seat has been occupied." The man looked down at the chair with his dark hawkish eyes, a solemn and sad stillness to his face. "Far too long."

The man then looked back up at Jordan. "But permit me to introduce myself." He gave a slight nod. "My old name no longer matters, so I will not give it. But those who know me know me as The Merlyn." He shrugged as a slight smile crept onto his lips. "Often they just called me Merlyn then followed it with The Magician, The Mad, The Devil, or That Damned Fool."

Violet giggled. "I just call him Grumpy."

Jordan gave a brief smile then winked. "He doesn't look like a dwarf to me."

Violet and Merlyn both looked at him with blank expressions. Violet asked, "What's that supposed to mean?"

"I, ah, just an old story Grandfather used to tell me."

"Not all stories are true, dear boy."

Violet shrugged. "At least not in this world."

Jordan looked around. It was then that he noticed there were fourteen statues in all, thirteen armored men and one woman who stood next to the tallest of the thirteen. At the opposite end from the door he had entered from stood another door, flanked by the male and female statues. Jordan looked at it and pointed. "What's in there?"

"Hope," answered Merlyn. He added with a shrug, "At least that's what I'm hoping." He raised a finger up as if he was beginning a lecture. "You see——."

A loud painful shriek came from the Door behind Jordan, and then the door blew off its hinges, shattering into several pieces of fiery wreckage. Through the wreckage stepped a woman. She walked as if she had been the special guest to a party. Her striking beauty caused Jordan's breath to escape his lungs. Her jet black hair, each strand in perfect place, hung in a long pony tail to her waist. She walked with a lithe supple grace, the curve of her hips swaying like a pendulum. On her head she wore a circlet much like Merlyn's, except her globe radiated a bright gold. Ice blue eyes that seemed to glow on their own accord looked upon Jordan, and her full lips turned upward at the corners. "Hello, child. We meet again."

Merlyn gripped his staff with both hands. Despite the fierceness that now shone in his eyes, his voice remained still and calm. "Hello, Morgana. Or should I say, Utopia?"

Morgana frowned at Merlyn. "You should've stayed asleep, old man."

"Worldwide destruction is hard to sleep through, wife."

Jordan felt his head swim. "Wait. What? How?"

Morgana looked at Jordan and sneered. "Not even true stories are completely true.

"As it is," she said while giving a mock bow, "I must thank you for leading me to my old adversary. If not for you, I might never have found him," she then glared daggers at Violet, "or our precious child."

Violet's eyes teared up. "You're not my mother! Not anymore."

Morgana snorted. "Giving birth to you had clearly been a mistake, anyhow."

Jordan's legs felt numb. "But...how is that possible?"

Make Way for Utopia

Violet walked over and placed a hand in Jordan's. "Some humans carry Fey blood, often when a human mates with a Faerie and has a child. If two with Fey blood mate, the magic of their blood prevents the offspring from being human. Only those with Fey blood can use magic."

"Yes," added Morgana, "like the boy."

Jordan blinked. His throat felt dry.

"Come now, child. Don't tell me you never noticed how your grandfather never talked about his wife. That's because he never had one." Morgana smiled. "Why would he when he could have me?" She then frowned. "Alas, the heir I had hoped for proved a disappointment. And you," she looked straight at Jordan's blue eyes, "proved even more so." She then shrugged. "But at least I found one good use for you."

"An heir for what, Morgana?" Merlyn asked. "There is nothing left of this world to rule."

Morgana cocked her head to one side and looked past them and at the intact door. "There's always the next one."

"This can't be!" Jordan wrenched his hand away from Violet's then placed his hands against his throbbing temples. "I can't use magic! I've never used magic! How can I—"

"Oh, the poor dear," Morgana cooed mockingly. "He blocked it out of his memory." She then clucked her tongue and shook her head. "And neither of you had the courtesy to tell him what he did."

"Morgana." Merlyn's voice remained calm, but it held a warning tone.

Morgana's gaze once again met Jordan's. She whispered,

"Remember."

"Morgana! Stop!"

But it was too late.

Blocked memories rushed through Jordan's mind like water from a burst dam.

***

He wept over Grandfather's corpse, pleading for him to wake up, knowing he never would. He wanted so much for Grandfather to be alive. And then....

A sensation overwhelmed him, like fire and ice all in one running through his nerves, both painful and pleasurable all at the same time. Ancient words entered his mind; words he instinctively knew had existed since the creation of the world, words that had been part of the creation. He could not translate them, but he knew their purpose.

They would bring back his grandfather.

He spoke the words.

Grandfather's body twitched. And then the eyes opened. But the clear soulful sparkle in his eyes was gone, replaced by something soulless, malevolent.

The thing that had been his grandfather rose to a sitting position, turned his head toward Jordan, and then smiled. The thing grabbed Jordan's arm in a viselike grip.

"Come here, boy!" The thing's voice sounded nothing like Grandfather's. It was hollow, void. "I need food, and your meat will more than do for now."

Make Way for Utopia

A struggle commenced. The creature was far stronger, far faster. Jordan was certain that he would die.

Then more ancient words came to his lips, and when he spoke them Grandfather's body erupted in flames. The creature screamed from Grandfather's mouth, flailed Grandfather's arms, rolled around in Grandfather's body, shouted curses that Grandfather would never have spoken. And then, stillness.

The shock was too much to bear, so Jordan's mind snapped. He ran off in a random direction, not caring where he went, no longer concerned about what would happen to him. Fits of laughter erupted from him uncontrollably. Tears poured from his eyes. And then everything became a dim dreamlike haze for three days.

***

When Jordan's mind returned to the present, he heard Merlyn's sympathetic voice, "If there is one thing that's impossible in this world, it is that you cannot bring back the dead. You can only make the corpse a vessel for…something else.

"You did not know. It is not your fault."

Morgana laughed. The laughter sounded like the cackling of a raving madwoman. She clapped her hands. "Bravo! Bravo! Perhaps you're not as useless as I had thought."

"Morgana, enough!" Merlyn struck his staff against the floor. Cracks of thunder echoed through the room.

Morgana merely sneered. "Or what?" She looked up toward one of the windows where sunlight poured through. "I hold the True Name of the Sun. Your power is nothing compared to mine." She let out a chuckle. "As the state of this world so clearly shows."

"You are drunk on power, and it has made you mad."

Morgana rolled her eyes. "Yes, and your point is?"

"I had hoped it would never come to this." Merlyn let out a sigh. "But I will not allow you to destroy our final hope. You must be stopped."

Morgana snarled. "You should've stayed asleep, old man." She then looked at Jordan and smiled. "But I think he should at least be given a choice, no? Or does free will no longer matter to you, Merlyn?"

Merlyn's shoulders sagged as he let out a longer, more resigned sigh than the last one. "You are right. The choice must be his."

Morgan held her hand out to Jordan. "Come with me, Grandson. You will no longer want for anything if you choose me. And I can teach you how to use your power even better than this old fool. Together we can conquer all the worlds. Or," her look softened, and her voice sounded sincere, "if you wish, we can rebuild this world. Make it a true paradise!"

It sounded tempting. No more struggle. No more running. Ultimate power and a chance to renew all that had been destroyed. And all he had to do was take her hand. . . .

A hand stained in the blood of millions, including Grandfather's, and my mother's, and my father's!

Jordan took a conscious step back. "Any world renewed by your hand would never be a paradise!"

She snarled at Jordan. "I'll deal with you and my 'daughter' after I'm finished with him."

Merlyn looked toward Violet. "Take him through the door. I will hold her off."

Violet's gaze drifted from one parent to the other. "But—"

"Go!"

Violet grabbed Jordan's hand. At first his feet refused to move. But then Violet's eyes stared into his. "We've got to go."

Jordan nodded, and the two took off as Rosebud flew past them to beat them to the door. Behind them, Jordan heard what sounded like violent explosions as lightning arced over them. The heat of flame singed the hair on the back of his neck, and yet he shivered and could see his breath. A spear of ice struck one of the statues, instantly freezing and shattering it.

Above all the noise, he could hear Morgana's laughter and Merlyn's screams.

When they reached the door, Rosebud hissed out an incomprehensible set of sounds that almost sounded like syllables. The door opened and the three went through. As soon as they were through, the door shut instantly behind them.

Jordan found himself in a room much smaller than the previous. Only lit torches held in sconces provided any light. In the center of the room rose a pedestal. Upon it was a sword. He already had a good idea which sword it was.

Violet picked the sword up off the pedestal then tossed it to Jordan. "Here! This should protect you."

He looked at the blade in awe as it reflected the torch light as if it were a mirror. There was no denting or chipping, or any of the signs of wear and tear a sword so ancient should have. It looked as new as if it had been forged yesterday.

A timeless blade for a timeless legacy.

Jordan tore his gaze from the sword. "What about you?"

Rosebud landed on Violet's shoulder as she let out a giggle. "I'm a lot tougher than I look. Fey are practically immortal." She then frowned as she looked to the floor. "I fear Father's time may be over, though."

The door blew off its hinges. In stepped Morgana, her body wreathed in flame. "His death is not the only one you have to fear, you unruly child!" Her eyes went to Excalibur. "Give me that sword, boy, or I'll roast you from within like you did to your grandfather!"

Jordan gripped the sword in both hands, feeling awkward and clumsy as he did so. "Violet, stay behind me!"

What am I doing? I've never held a sword in my life!

Morgana laughed. "Put that sword down before you hurt yourself!"

Jordan felt a presence within the sword, soothing him. It was then he knew that all he had to do was let go and just let the sword do what it was created for. He spread his legs, kept his feet planted firmly, and readied himself.

Morgana held up a hand and began to utter the ancient words.

Wait for it. Wait....

Rosebud took to the air and bolted straight at Morgana. Tiny bolts of lightning erupted from his tiny mouth, aiming for Morgana's face. She raised one hand to shield her face and tried to swat away the little nuisance. But as she did so her spell discharged, causing the ceiling to collapse around her.

Jordan charged, screaming. He leaped past falling debris then thrust the blade, piercing Morgana's heart. She stumbled backward into the doorway as the arch collapsed, crushing her.

Jordan rolled out of the way of the falling debris. He choked from a cloud of dust, unable to see. He felt a soft hand grab his. "This way!"

Jordan followed.

Through the dust haze, he saw with watery eyes that the pedestal was now turned over. Violet stood next to him with Rosebud once again on her shoulder. At the floor where the pedestal had once rested was a small opening and a set of stairs.

Violet led him down into a dimly lit chamber. The ground shook beneath them, and what little light that had crept from up above was snuffed out as debris tumbled down the steps.

Jordan coughed, barely able to breathe from all the dust.

Once the dust settled, he looked around. In the small chamber they found themselves in was a large iron pot filled with what appeared to be water, but with a bluish glow. Violet looked up from where they had come, frowning. "There's no going back now." She then looked at the pot. "That is where we have to go."

Jordan laughed. "Into a pot?"

Violet giggled. "It's not a pot, Silly! It's a wyrm-hole." Upon seeing his forehead wrinkle in confusion, she added, "A gateway."

"To where?"

Violet held out her hand. "To another world."

"And where exactly is this other world? And what awaits us there?"

Violet shrugged her shoulders.

Jordan took her hand.

"Just look into the water and let your mind drift off."

Jordan did so. At first there was nothing, but then the glow spread around him, surrounding him in a nimbus of warmth. Before he knew it he felt as if his body was hurtling down into bottomless depths at a speed his mind could not comprehend, speeding toward a bright white light.

And then darkness.

***

Jordan awoke to find himself lying on fresh green grass. Around him were trees, more trees than he had ever seen in the gardens of Utopia City. Next to him sat Violet. Above him on a branch rested Rosebud. "Where are we?"

"Safe."

Violet stood then helped him up. "You passed out during the trip." She giggled. "I guess human bodies just aren't built for that sort of thing.

"Come." She led him through the forest. "There's something I want you to see."

Jordan followed with Excalibur still gripped in one hand.

The forest opened out onto a vast green field under a bright yellow sun. In the distance something shimmered, almost like silver or crystal. As they got closer Jordan realized that what he was looking at was a vast lake. "I've...I've never seen so much water before...."

Violet laughed loudly as she ran then dove into the water. "This is magnificent!"

Jordan dropped Excalibur and joined her.

Hours later they sat on the shore together, watching Rosebud dive-bomb for fish. Jordan picked up Excalibur and stared at it in deep thought. "There is power in this sword—the power of True Names. Such power should never end up in the wrong hands."

Violet nodded solemnly. "And even then only for a short time."

"That was how Morgana learned the True Name of the Sun, wasn't it?"

Violet nodded. "She found Excalibur while Father still slept. I managed to steal it from her after he awoke. She didn't have time to learn all the True Names within it, but she managed to learn one of the most destructive ones. That is why people like her, and Father," she looked at Jordan with sadness in her eyes, "and you must never be allowed to keep it. It was created by Fey, and the Fey alone were entrusted to keep it during the times it wasn't needed."

Jordan stared into Violet's eyes—the most beautiful eyes he had ever seen, on the face of the most beautiful person he had ever known.

He handed Excalibur to her. "Will I ever see you again?"

Violet grinned. "From time to time." She pointed toward the center of the lake. "On the first day of every Spring, there is where you'll find me. There is where I'll wait for you.

"And one day," she added, looking into his eyes, "you might just bring a friend along. Every world has its Morgana, just as every world needs its King Arthur."

Jordan smirked. "And its Merlyn."

The End

The Twenty Year Plan

by Jay Wilburn

"Colt, you are the youngest to ever be chosen. There has only been one other expedition twenty years before and it did not return. This is the second."

Colt answered, "Yes, sir, I am aware."

"You are only sixteen," he continued. "Like me, you were born in Seclusion and we do not know the wide world. We do not know the time before."

"Yes, sir," Colt answered, "but Mary and Elizabeth do. They were of age before. They will know."

"The truth is that none of us knows, Colt," he corrected. "The plan is every twenty years. We, as a people, survived the plague years and we have been spared from attack by man and monster for many years because we followed the strict codes put forth by the founders. We risk Seclusion every twenty years as they set forth in the law and it is a grave risk to us all."

"I understand, sir. I do not take this lightly."

The leader breathed deeply and folded his hands behind

his head. He rubbed at his temples between his forearms and glanced over at the fire pits inside the larger chamber of the night caves. The people were being obedient to the law. The blackout drape was over the outer tunnels. The fires were below the stones of the pit walls. There was silence in the outer chambers.

He could hear the music faintly drifting up from the back of the caves. There were strings softly, but no drums. He recognized the melody as one his mother had whispered to him softly, when he and his brother were children. It was a tune from before the fall of the wide world.

"You must not," he continued. "You absolutely must not."

"Why would you think I would, sir?"

The leader dropped his arms and leaned over the table between them. "You volunteered, Colt."

"That would seem to be a virtue."

"Likely so, son. I don't...doubt it...necessarily."

He paused and ran his fingers across the rough-hewed surface of the boards. No hammering or rough sanding was used to build the tabletop.

"Speak plainly, Mr. Johnson. I am not a boy with soft feelings."

"You and I are both young, Colt." the leader countered. "I was born months after the arrival and establishment of our village. I am not forty and I am the leader of these people. Even at the eve of the second twenty, many of them were born before the fall and I am responsible for them all. You, Colt, have traveled the farthest of anyone since the founding of Seclusion."

One of the maids offered to refill the leader's cup. He

lifted it and moved it to the other side of the table away from her pitcher instead of sliding it across the table. She held the pitcher out to Colt. He looked up silently and nodded. She lifted his cup and tilted it so the water flowed over inside without pouring. She set it back down gently and walked away.

"The farthest of anyone still living," the leader added.

"So you are young to lead and I am young to far hunt," Colt agreed. "We serve both positions well."

"I accept your endorsement, Colt, but there is more. My brother was one of the three men that set out on the first twentieth year. They did not return. We mourned their loss, but we also feared their failure. We knew that coming back from a wide world infested with monsters would lead them to us."

Colt offered. "Perhaps your brother was a hero. He did not return because of that very reason."

"It does not matter, Colt," Mr. Johnson looked down so that his face was washed in shadow from the walls of the glowing pits. "They may have found other men in the wide world that did not allow them to return, humans with monstrous souls. Men are capable of terrible things. The risk being that torture could force confession. We waited vigilantly for the possibility that one from the expedition might have had his tongue forced to map a path back to families waiting here."

"But they did not come," Colt said. "Whatever the fate of the first twenties, they did not lead man or creature back to Seclusion."

"They had families here that they would protect at all costs," Johnson said.

Colt looked down at his water. There was silence between them.

"I understand the calling of being a twenty," Colt said.

"I'm concerned," Johnson said.

Colt looked back across the table. "Is my lack of blood relatives a concern for you in this regard, sir?"

"Is that why you volunteered, Colt?"

"It is not," Colt said. "Is it why I was selected?"

Johnson said, "Certainly not, son. Even the possibility of the loss of you to our community pains my heart…even as you sit before me."

Colt spread his hands, "Then, I don't understand your concern beyond the basic care you would have also for Mary and Elizabeth, who do not sit before you now. I am as able as anyone could be for the wide world. I understand the law. I understand more than those who never walk beyond the boundaries of Seclusion or the ledge gardens or the livestock fences. I know the cost if I were to encounter one of the monsters or men in the deep forest or the far mountains in a far hunt. I have passed that test every time, sir."

Mr. Johnson said, "Colt, you are as able, but you are the only twenty that was never in the wide world before. Also, you have never in your life encountered a monster or a man from the wide world. You've not truly been tested."

There was silence. Colt folded his hands again.

"I will continue to extend to you respect, sir, even though you are completely wrong," Colt said. "I am tested every time. I know the law. If I am injured while in the deep forest or lost in the far mountains, there will be no one to come for me. I am tested at least twice a fort night through all seasons and in most weather. I have maintained discipline for the sake of all Seclusion as if the entire community were my blood family. I have returned most times with successful game and all times uninjured."

Mr. Johnson smiled and then covered his face with both hands. He lowered his face back into the shadow and dropped his hands. "I accept your respect and your correction, Colt."

He raised his face back into the flickering light. "That is why you were chosen. I want more than anything for you to come back. As your leader, you are my son…and my brother. I do not want to lose another. I do not want to wait until the next twenty to find out what is in the wide world. I do not want to live in fear for all those years between now and then again."

"What if the wide world proves to be worthy of greater fear than we imagined, sir?"

Johnson looked across at Colt's eyes. His face was turned out of the light.

He answered, "I'll take the fear from knowledge over the shallow comfort of ignorance…but not at the cost of Seclusion."

"I think we understand each other."

Colt stood. He bent up at the knees so as not to push back the chair legs nor to disturb the table.

"We are not done," Johnson said.

Colt lowered back into the chair slowly.

Johnson placed a brass cylinder on the table between them. Colt had never seen one intact. He had seen what brass remained in the village and he had heard in detail what it had been. He was unaware any still remained in this form nor understood why they would.

"Do you recognize it?"

"Yes."

"Do you understand what they do?"

"They make noise," Colt answered.

"They do far more than that," Johnson explained. "They take life as assuredly as the finest arrow or the sharpest blade."

"Why do you still have one?" Colt asked.

"Because the wide world might still have them."

"You would use this were the monsters or men to find us? The law is clear even in that worst case, sir."

"My answer is not complete," Johnson said. "I have it to show you that it is possible the wide world might still have it. They are loud, but by the time you hear it, it might be too late."

"I take your meaning, sir."

"My father gave it to my brother shortly after I was born. He kept it even after they were broken for their metal and powder. My brother gave it to me when he became a twenty. That is the real reason I have kept it. You may touch it. Its false magic is null in this lonely state."

Colt shook his head. Johnson removed it from the table with two fingers.

"I want to hear the law of the twenty from your own lips, Colt."

Colt brought his hands to his chin still clasped together and looked down. "The world may be purged of life or returned primal. Even in that state, we wait a fort night to be sure we are without plague and then we return or we die in the wide world if we show symptoms."

Colt licked his lips. "We may find the world infested in two possible ways...."

Colt trailed off as he looked into the light and saw the eyes of the other villagers staring from the fire pits. Mr. Johnson looked too. The others turned their eyes away and went into whispered conversations. Two men with thick beards turned their bodies toward the fire pit and away from Colt's conversation with the leader. Colt looked at their grey hair as it captured the fire light at the edges.

"Continue," Johnson said.

Colt recited the law of the twenty as he had been told.

Johnson steepled his hands as Colt finished. "You are to be successful and return as you have done every time you have left Seclusion. We call them the deep forest and the far mountains, but the truth is they are all very close and the wide world is very far. There are many ways the law prevents you from returning. I want you to prevent those obstacles from occurring with all the discipline you have employed as a far hunter."

"Yes, sir."

"You must sleep. The slightest mistake could end us all."

Colt lifted his cup and took a deep drink.

There was a crash near the pits. Water soaked into the stone floor around the shattered pieces of the pitcher. There was an inhale of air through the cave, but no gasps. The maid covered her mouth with both hands and walked deeper into the cave crying without sound. No one moved to disturb the shards.

The two grey men turned and met eyes with Johnson. He nodded. They stood and walked through the blackout drape.

Colt set his cup down on the table and took his fingers away from it slowly.

***

They walked between the huts built into and around the broad trees. Sunlight filtered through the leaves and the vine netting above the structures.

One couple was rebinding thatch on one of the roofs. The older girl was gathering the dried grasses on the ground below her parents. A younger girl was putting things in her mouth from the grass.

The mother lowered a piece of metal to the ground from under the patch on the roof. It landed near the girls against the wall. It was a remnant from a larger sheet that must have been removed from the roof some decades ago. It was dark and was twisted from being bound under the thatch.

The smaller girl saw Elizabeth walking on Colt's right. The little girl tried to run toward her. The older girl put her hand over the little girl's mouth and pulled her back. The parents looked down from the roof.

Colt wasn't used to seeing metal out in the open in the village. It had been removed from every surface where it might reflect light. When he was little, he remembered seeing swords made from it. His father had practiced with the designs he crafted in the firelight in the very back of the night caves while Colt had sat and watched. The weapons had since been reformed into gardening tools.

Twenty Year Plan

Elizabeth waved and the little girl waved back. The parents looked, but then went back to rebinding the roof of the day hut.

Elizabeth turned away and bumped Colt's bow as she adjusted the sewn, leather pack on her back. Colt reached back over his head and slid the top of the unstrung bow further down behind his shoulder.

He decided that metal would not make a good sword or plow. He recalled Johnson's magic cylinder and looked away from the scrap at the hut.

Colt reached over with his other hand on the other side of his pack and felt the heads of the arrows. He ran his fingers blindly over the stone points, the sharp edges, and the pits in the worked flint. There were twenty. He hoped that was enough. It was all he had left. Most were stained with some common form of blood from squirrels, fowl, deer, or other large game.

He felt the finer surfaces of two of the arrows. He could not tell by looking at them, but he could feel the difference. The others were carved by him. These were all he had left from a better craftsman.

Mary hooked her thumbs through the straps on her pack on Colt's other side. She pulled to lift it off her shoulders.

Colt looked at her and then down at their shoes. He wore the same boots he had hunted in for years. Their shoes were lower around their ankles. The material and laces were from before and were older than Colt by a considerable stretch. The soles and stitching had been replaced.

He looked at his own hunting boots and then back at their exposed ankles.

Mary looked at the quiver on Colt's back and then whispered, "Is something wrong?"

He was shaking his head before she was done asking the question. Each of the women looked back at Seclusion once as they left the boundary between the frames of the screens.

Colt stepped through first and they followed. Their packs jostling the poles and rustled the loose ends of the woven leaves.

They continued single file as they weaved down the stone in the first embankment.

***

Colt sat with his pack between his knees in the cove at the base of the first mountain. Night was falling and they had smothered their fire in dust. Colt pulled his cloak around him.

"How much of it do you think will be left?" Mary asked.

"Hopefully, very little," Elizabeth answered.

She sat on her pack and pulled her hood up over the braid of grey, streaked hair. Mary dropped her chin to her folded arms.

Mary said, "What do you think happened to the first twenty?"

"Maybe they kept talking and got themselves discovered," Colt suggested.

Mary looked at Colt without raising her face from her arms. "I have been following the damn law for longer than you have been alive. I'm tired of the heavy silence, Colt."

Colt licked his teeth inside his closed mouth.

He parted his lips and asked, "Are we going to end every

conversation on this trip with comments about each other's age?"

Mary lifted her head and looked at Colt.

Elizabeth answered, "No, we're not. We can be quiet, but we need to discuss what may be waiting for us."

"How much do you remember from before?" Mary asked.

"Enough...too much," Elizabeth said.

"You mean from the wide world?" Colt asked.

"We just called it the world then," Mary said.

"How old were you before?" Colt asked.

Elizabeth hummed before she answered, "I was seventeen when my parents took to the woods with Johnson's father. I guess we were your age."

Mary said, "I'm two years younger."

Elizabeth smiled. "Don't get haughty, Mary. We are both old maids now."

Mary asked, "Is that why you volunteered?"

Elizabeth looked down and answered, "I don't think he's still out here, if that's what you're asking."

"I wasn't," Mary said. "Twenty years is a long time. I just meant the old maid part."

Colt looked at Elizabeth. He squinted to try to see her face in the dark.

Elizabeth said, "My children are grown and have children of their own. If it wasn't me, it might have been one of them. I don't want my grandchildren to grow up without a father like my daughters did."

"You did well," Mary said. "He was a hero."

"We don't know what he was or what he faced out here,"

Elizabeth said.

Colt said, "What did...."

They both looked at Colt. He paused and cleared his throat.

He began again. "What do you expect we'll find?"

Mary said, "We've gone through the possibilities. We could find emptiness, we could find monsters, we could find men, we may find that —"

"No," Colt interrupted, "I'm not talking about the contingencies. I mean, what was there? Once we get past the base of the mountains, what was there before? What lay east that might still be standing? What were the...villages like?"

"That's hard to answer when Seclusion is all you know in terms of men," Elizabeth said.

"I'm not stupid," Colt said. "I can imagine what I'm told. I can understand what is explained to me."

"We don't think you are stupid," Elizabeth said. "We just lack the ability to explain well."

"Then explain poorly," Colt said.

"There were houses...cottages and cities...very large cities...monoliths," Mary said.

"The houses probably have not lasted forty years," Elizabeth said.

"Unless there are men rethatching the roofs," Colt said.

"These roofs weren't thatched," Mary said. "They had solid shingles."

"Like slate?" Colt asked.

"No," Elizabeth said, "the shingles were tar over...paper?"

Twenty Year Plan

Colt stared a moment. "There is no chance they are still standing."

"The cities were far," Mary said. "Surely we won't go that far."

Elizabeth shrugged and dropped her forehead to her knees.

"What are the monsters like?" Colt asked.

"Has no one described them to you?" Mary asked.

"Poorly," Colt answered. "We are going into the wide world taken by the plague and the monsters it created. I need to know what we may face...plainly."

Mary inhaled, but failed to speak. Elizabeth didn't look up from her knees until the crash in the forest behind and below her outside the mouth of the cove. She stumbled as she bolted from her pack. She nearly staggered into the buried coals of the fire.

Mary whispered, "What...."

Colt dropped his cloak off his shoulders and waved his fist back at her in the air. He lifted his bow from the ground and strung it over the notch of the top nock. As he strung the stave and the string went taut, the top limb of the bow above the grip creaked. There was another crash in the trees below the slope of the cove's mouth. There was a low growl and then abrupt silence. It was too brief for Colt to place it.

Mary breathed. "Is that an animal? Can you tell?"

Colt felt through the quiver and pulled one of the finer heads left him by the late craftsman. He rubbed the head of the arrow like a talisman as he watched the empty space and waited.

Mary whispered. "What is it, Colt?"

"Damn it, woman," Colt said. He let the arrow slide through his fingers to the sinew and then set the notch into the string without drawing it. "If you have no respect for the law, be silent for your skin."

Something was digging at the ground below the cove. It was close. Colt drew back the string and aimed at the empty space above the noise. The growl built again, but it was deep. It groaned or whistled through lungs and a throat Colt couldn't picture. The ground under his toes and knee vibrated from the digging.

Elizabeth whispered. "I'm sorry, Garrett."

Colt gritted his teeth. The digging stopped. The groan stopped. It was not abrupt this time. It choked off with a few squeaks and the sound of breath over fluid. Colt's hands shook with the tension suspended in the string as they had not done since he first learned to draw the string by the guidance of the craftsman.

The breathing continued shallow, harsh, and wet. The trees crashed below them and they could see the foliage high on the trunks waver and then whip with the force of it. Colt tried to focus on the space he was targeting at the head of the cove instead of the thickness of the trunks that were being moved.

"It's moving down the slope," Mary said.

"And you're still talking," Colt whispered.

"We have to go back," Elizabeth said. "This was a mistake."

"We can't go back," Colt said.

"They are too close to the village," Mary said. "How could

they be this close? Didn't you hunt this far, Colt?"

"This far, but not this direction," Colt answered.

He stood and relaxed the bow, but kept the arrow in place. He took three steps forward and stopped. He looked up at the dark gap of sky through the trees on the rock facings above them. If no one knew they were here, this was a good position to hide. If you were being hunted by something that could move trees, it could be a death trap.

"We have to go back," Elizabeth insisted.

Colt snapped his eyes back to the mouth away from the sky. He approached the opening of the mouth.

"We can't go back," Colt said. "We are the twenty."

He stuck his head out into the exposed mountainside and peered over at the dirt below them.

"What are you doing, child?" Elizabeth huffed.

"I have to see the marks to know what stalks us," Colt answered. "And I am nobody's child just as you two are nobody's wives any longer."

The gouges into the hillside were deep. He would have to feel the grooves in the mud to be sure, but the claw marks appeared to be inches deep. There was no trail down the slope. Colt looked up again expecting the monster to drop on his neck like a myth from the sky. Empty darkness hung above him. The darkness might be concealing the tracks or broken clues in the brush, but Colt knew trails and he saw nothing that supported a beast weighty enough to shake ancient tree trunks in its path. It could have been a bear, but he suspected not.

Colt drew back into the cove.

"We need to consider going back," Mary whispered.

"We cannot." Colt said. "We are the twenty and we will not feed your grandchildren to that beast."

"We should consider moving from this place," Elizabeth said. "It may have marked the spot for a return attack."

"Wandering in the darkness is no plan either," Colt said.

"Could it be a natural animal?" Mary asked.

"It could," Colt said.

"Do you think it is?" Elizabeth asked.

"I think we need to end our conversation for the night," Colt said.

***

They all rose with the faintest light of morning and ate in silence. Colt suspected that they had all slept as little the night before as they had eaten that morning. Not sleeping and not eating would be a real problem very quickly.

They moved out of the cove. Mary and Elizabeth looked around the trees as they gripped the straps of their packs. Colt knelt and looked closely at the torn Earth. He looked around the slope and the trees.

After finding nothing, they continued down the slope and through the remaining passes until they reached a river in the forests along flat ground. They called the area Colt had hunted the deep woods. He wasn't sure what to call this forest as they pressed into the wide world.

They stopped at the river to eat from their supplies. Colt

would have to hunt eventually, but he did not want to leave the women to go into the strange wood alone.

"How could they be so close?" Mary said.

Colt looked back through the trees after she spoke.

"We don't know what that was?" Elizabeth said.

"Is that how they sound?" Colt asked.

Both women looked at him as they ate.

"The monsters...after the plague...Is that how they sounded? Like that unseen beast last night?"

"I've never heard anything like that," Elizabeth said.

"I had old pipes in my house that used to sound like that, but nothing living," Mary added.

Both women looked at each other and then back to their food.

"You have to tell me what they are," Colt insisted. "I can't fight them, if they are unknown to me."

Elizabeth swallowed and wiped her mouth. "They...it is...it was like a sort of possession."

"Like demons?"

"No," Mary said, "like a parasite."

"Like a tick or a leech?"

"Smaller," Elizabeth answered, "we were young and we survived because our families moved fast before the world collapsed. The doctors didn't know what exactly was happening. The plague and the monsters may have been two different events."

Mary said, "Whatever that was...unless it was a bear or a mountain lion...that was not around when we fled to Seclusion."

Colt was shaking his head as Mary was speaking.

***

They found a spot to cross the river and continued east as they had been instructed. Colt was looking for better shelter as afternoon began to pass over them. There were not huts or villages in evidence that he saw.

"It couldn't have been a monster," Mary said. "That close to the village we would have been discovered long ago."

"Are you convincing yourself or telling me because you think I hold the opinion that it was?" Colt asked.

Mary said, "I think we should go back."

"Your courage fails you?" he asked.

Elizabeth said, "We would get back just in time to stay in that same canyon where it found us the —"

The ground shifted under them. They stopped and looked down. Colt reached for his bow and the ground collapsed. Their feet plunged below the surface and they sunk into the brittle ground with a deafening crackle. Colt ceased falling at waist deep. Both women sunk to the underside of their flat arms above their chests.

Mary screamed and then clapped her hand over her mouth. The sound echoed out through the trees.

In the odd silence that followed, Colt shifted feeling the hard, loose material shift around his legs. Something sharp bit at his legs. He halted again. He reached down and picked up a long, blackened shard of what was holding them. He turned it over in his hands.

"What's happening?" Mary hissed.

"A femur," Colt said.

Twenty Year Plan

"What?" Elizabeth asked.

"Bone," Colt said, "these are bones…human, I think."

Mary whined in the back of her throat and then choked it off in a gurgle. The sound made Colt shiver. She struggled against the pile of darkened bone, loose soil, and thick leaves.

Elizabeth said, "Calm down, Mary. Don't struggle. It might still be in the bones. Don't cut yourself."

Mary froze and the sound of the shifting debris stopped again.

"What does that mean?" Colt asked. "What may still be in the bone? Plague? The parasites?"

"I don't know," Elizabeth shifted slowly. "These bones are from people that died from something. Don't cut yourself on them."

"I can't stay in here," Mary groaned.

"Move slowly," Colt said.

Mary clawed at the dark mulch of leaves revealing more bones without extracting herself.

Colt drew out one leg and planted the knee on top of the pile to draw out his other leg. He felt bits of soil and chunks of broken bone inside his boots. The skull under his knee crumbled and sliced through the material of his pants.

Elizabeth struggled to find purchase, but felt jagged pieces deep in the grave pressing into her clothes and the skin underneath. She began pushing the bones away from her chest to dig herself out. She slid down a few more inches. A small gasp escaped her. Something had her ankle. She felt it move. She opened her mouth to cry out, but she slipped down another inch and her voice failed her. She couldn't catch her breath.

Colt lifted his knee slowly to see if he had broken the skin.

"Everyone be still a moment," a man said as he rode out into view of the exposed grave. He wore leather armor with rows of dark knobs across the material under a metal mesh cover over his shoulders. The horse was brown and draped in a mottled green and brown cloth that reminded Colt of a view through the forest.

Colt was more taken aback by the animal. The horse neighed and snorted. The noise startled him beyond the voice of the stranger. Colt couldn't see the horse's neck, but the noise from the animal frightened him and told him its throat had not been cut by the husbandry to render it silent like the work animals back in Seclusion.

Two men stepped out on both sides of the horseman with bows drawn back and aimed into the pit. Their bows were fixed on Colt, but their eyes were looking over Mary and Elizabeth. Colt heard movement behind him in the brush on the other side of the pit.

He reached over his back for his own bow.

"Hold. Still your reach, dirt farmer," the horsemen bellowed.

The archers looked on Colt now. Their bows were dark and included materials he did not recognize. The staves at the tops and bottoms were mounted with wheels that turned as the strings were drawn. He did not understand the function. He suspected neither these bows nor their armored archers were used for hunting.

One of the archers said, "We can let fly before you begin to string and set that wood stick and fishing line of yours."

Colt dropped his hands.

"We appreciate you uncovering this death pit for the sake of our horses," the man said from the saddle. "Remain where you are in those ancient, cursed bones in the event we need to leave you there once we have spoken. Take the toys from the boy, please."

Colt reached as he felt his pack, bow, and quiver being pulled from his back.

"No, Colt," Mary whispered.

He bit his lip and dropped his hands again.

The horseman continued. "This is the governorship of Lord Smith. You do not wear the colors of his serfs nor do you bear the seal of travel. I am led to assume that you are here both illegally and to ill intent."

"We are not," Colt said.

A young boy came around the pit with Colt's pack and his weapons.

The horsemen took the unstrung bow. He bent it harshly. The wood groaned and protested, but did not break. "That is good quality craftsmanship. Did you fashion this, dirt farmer?"

"No," Colt said, "My father was the craftsman."

Elizabeth whispered. "Colt, don't...."

The horseman looked at Elizabeth and drew his sword. He lifted the bow and sliced through the wood above the handgrip.

"No," Colt yelled.

"Pull the drowning wench from the pool of bones," the horseman ordered.

He took the quiver of arrows and swiped his sword smoothly through one side of the leather and into the arrows inside.

"No," Colt growled again. His vision blurred.

The archers relaxed their draw and advanced on Elizabeth.

The horseman shouted. "Dirt farmers do not give orders to us or each other on this land and you do not have the privilege to carry your own —"

The violence was so swift that Colt missed it completely in his blurry-eyed sorrow and rage. He wiped his face on his sleeve in confusion. Both Mary and Elizabeth were screaming and so were the men around and behind them. The women were not being careful any longer as they scrambled free on the bones in the pit. The horse was rearing and spinning in place, but the rider was absent. The warrior bows were cast on the ground as well.

Colt struggled up and crawled forward across the pit embedding shavings of blackened bone into his palms as he set them in the points of ribs and the edges of empty joints.

Colt saw one of the archers jerked out of sight into the thick of thorns. The size of the monster was clear in the shadow as it thrashed about painting the leaves above in blood, but the shape of the beast was concealed in the foliage.

The head of a man bounded across the pit and came to rest with lines from the former internal connections stringing behind. It lay in the wet leaves at the edge of the collapse between where Colt knelt and where Elizabeth was climbing out coated in mud and broken bone.

The horse reared again as the head stopped and it ran wildly into the trees. The forest filled with the pierce of a growl that Mary had described as water through pipes. Colt could not imagine living with plumbing, if that was the sound it made.

"We must run," Elizabeth screamed.

Colt fished his hands through the broken shafts of the arrows. He pulled out two of the heads that were separated from most of their bolt.

"Help me," Mary screamed.

Colt pocketed the heads and turned to take hold of Mary's hands. The creature was peering out of the brush level with Colt's eyes and he froze as prey was prone to do.

The eyes did not match. Though he could not see its snout nor its other features. Its back was hulking and asymmetrical. The beast appeared hairless and fleshy pink. The folds of skin over its body were bulging and swollen.

One of the men screamed and stumbled through the forest to the left. The beast whipped its head to the side on a misshapen neck and bolted through after the sound deep in the shadows. Its body impacted the trunks as it crashed through shaking the branches high above them.

Colt saw a flash of claws and then predator and prey dropped out of view with a gurgling cry.

Colt pulled Mary out of the pit with one harsh motion. She groaned, but did not protest.

"Run," Elizabeth yelled.

Colt watched in the forest where the man who had run had been taken. He heard the other beasts feeding around the edges of the clearing as well. The horse made another terrible neigh somewhere in the forest and then its cry was cut silent. Colt shivered at the noise of the muted animal.

He was not sure running was a good idea, but his legs were pumping on adrenaline and fear before he was aware they were moving. He and the other twenties careened blindly through the forest.

***

The current across the river was heavy, but they waded as they were swept sideways into the smooth boulders.

"Just keep moving," Elizabeth said. "The water will cover our scent, yes?"

"With most beasts," Colt called over the water.

"We have to warn them," Mary yelled.

Her voice echoed off the rocks over the rage of the river.

Colt felt something against his leg and tried to look below the froth of the water around the rocks. He reached down, but felt nothing. He continued to look as they waded on gripping the slippery curves of the stone.

"Who do you wish to warn, Mary?" Elizabeth called as she began to rise up on a lip of stone under the water.

Elizabeth slipped and went under the foam. Colt reached forward, but could not find her. He climbed up the lip of stone slipping too. His hand found something soft and he pulled. Elizabeth came up coughing and thrashing. Mary held Colt's belt as she pulled herself onto the rise.

Twenty Year Plan

Mary said, "The monsters were at the base of the mountain. Seclusion needs to know. Our families need to prepare. Those… things must know the village is there. Hiding is not an option any longer. We have to go back."

Colt held Elizabeth as they felt sticky mud under their feet again approaching the bank.

"We can't go back," Colt said. "We are the twenty. We owe the ones that went before us."

"And the ones we left behind," Elizabeth said as she pulled herself up the slope by the roots.

Mary said, "They have to know."

The growl tore across the expanse of the river behind them. Cole turned to reach down for Mary. As she grabbed his hand with both of hers, he saw it jump. The bulging warts of flesh rippled pink in the air over the hairless body as it landed on the first boulder near the center of the current. Its black claws screeched on the dry top of the granite as it scrambled to gain position. Its neck was protruded on one side in a tumorous growth. The beast's eyes were not even as they peered across the water. The largest eye rested on Colt first and the smaller one followed. The thin lips peeled back under the wrinkled snout revealing wet, black fangs that were narrow, long, and curved like its claws.

The fangs parted and its white tongue laced out between two of the teeth. Colt kept waiting for the tongue to spread out flat, but it remained rounded like a pale snake twisting in the air. The creature bellowed out another growl as it reached one naked paw forward to the next boulder.

More growls issued from the trees behind the monster.

Mary scrambled up the bank and passed Colt. Colt held the monster's eyes a moment longer.

Colt whispered. "We have to keep going. It will either follow us away from our families or follow us back to them. We have to keep going."

*****

They came upon the structure in the darkness of the forest. The monsters were dogging their trail and flanking them. They kept adjusting their direction to avoid the growls, but the creatures continued to track their headlong retreat.

Colt looked into the narrow gap between the sheets of collapsed roof. The shingles on the outside were intact, but covered in moss on one slope and lichen on the other. He swept away webs as he looked in on the dry ground and tilted beams scattered in the dark space.

"It appears the roof was all that survived," Colt said.

"This is no shelter," Mary said. "This will not protect us from the beasts."

"I can't keep running," Elizabeth said.

Colt said, "There are no good options, Mary. That leaves poor options or no option."

Elizabeth said, "If we keep going, we will collapse in the darkness and lay exhausted in the open."

"That is the no option," Colt said.

They climbed through the gap and retreated into the

dark. The growls continued through much of the night. Colt rested during Elizabeth's watch. He ran his fingers over the flat of the arrow heads in his pocket.

***

Colt was shaken awake. He struggled under the tight grasp.

"Colt, they are outside circling around us," Elizabeth hissed.

Colt sat up. His stomach cramped in hunger despite the desperate fear. They had left all their supplies behind with his broken bow and the broken bodies.

Light filtered through the gap where Mary crouched on the ground looking outside. Colt looked at the underside of the roof. The remaining beams holding it aloft were blistered black with charred lips of damaged wood.

Colt looked around the burned framework. "I wouldn't think burned wood could survive four decades."

"Who cares, Colt?" Mary said.

He put his hand down and scattered bone as he stood. They were blackened like the remains in the pit.

"Did they burn the infected?" Colt asked.

"Sometimes," Elizabeth answered as they looked around the floor.

"The ones that went mad with the plague and those that fell dead," Mary answered.

The bones trailed back into a banking pile against the back edge of the collapsed structure.

"This is a den," Colt said.

He moved forward as he saw one of the malignant beasts lumber by the opening. Another circled in out of the trees. The creatures growled and hissed at each other. Colt ventured closer to the opening beyond Mary. There were two along the tree line and three crouched with their twisted hindquarters just feet from the opening. They growled at each other in overlapping whistling roars that carried through the forest.

"What is this?" Elizabeth asked.

Colt looked down and saw deep gouges dug into the dirt in front of the opening.

He said, "I think they are fighting over who eats first."

The beast in the center facing away from the gap stood on its hind legs raising its claws above its head. The two in the trees stood and walked forward snapping and baring their claws. The other two sprang forward and the monsters ripped into one another with claws and fangs quickly wet with blood.

"We need to run," Elizabeth said.

"They will track us," Colt said as he watched the monsters macerate each other.

"They're tracking us now," Mary whispered.

"This is our only window," Elizabeth said.

Colt rubbed the arrow heads in his pocket. "Let's go."

They slipped out and walked around the roof. Colt sent the women first. One of the standing monsters turned and looked down at Colt. There were deep, red gashes through the flesh above its snout. Two cuts ran below its enlarged, right eye. Two lines were cut above it.

It peeled back its lips over thin, bloody fangs and roared at Colt.

It turned back and joined the others in the belly of the still living monster they had pinned to the ground.

Colt ran.

***

They were not eating enough. They were not sleeping enough. For the last four mornings, they awoke to find gouges dug into the dirt outside the cave or ruins. On one more occasion, the pack of monsters had engaged another lone creature that had tried to stalk Colt and the women.

"Why don't they just kill us?" Mary asked as they ran.

"They're playing with us," Elizabeth choked.

"We have to lose them," Mary said.

Colt heard the explosive noise at the same moment that it bit into his shoulder. He pitched forward into the leaves. His blood splattered out in a trail in front of him. Elizabeth and Mary knelt beside him. He sucked in air as they turned him over.

"You have to keep running," Colt said as blood soaked into his shirt.

"It went all the way through," Elizabeth said.

"We need to bind it," Mary said.

The men mounted the hill above them looking down on their prey. Some had swords of poorer quality than what his father had crafted when he was a child. Two had bows. One carried a long, metal wand that was smoking from the end.

"You need to run," Colt said through gritted teeth as the women shed layers of their own clothing and began twisting them into long strips.

One of the men sneered and began trudging down the hill waving his sword making it slice through the air with each audible slash.

"It's poor quality," Colt whispered as he watched the man descend alone.

Elizabeth wrapped the bandage tightly over the wound making Colt gasp.

She said, "A poor option is better than no option."

Colt opened his mouth. He wasn't sure if he intended to yell at them to run or to explain about what he was talking.

The pack of monsters speared into the backs of the men on the hill. They tried to scatter, but black claws tore through their throats and chests as the men tried to flee. The monsters stood on their hind legs taking down every victim as they turned. They were not eating.

The swordsman turned to see the carnage and then ran toward the twenties. He was no longer waving his sword as he pumped his fists. He wasn't smiling. One of the monsters bounded down the hill after him as the other two cut down the remaining hunters.

"You need to run," Colt shouted.

"Get up, boy," Elizabeth shouted.

"I'm bleeding," Colt yelled, "It will follow me. Just go."

"Get up, Colt. Get up," Mary screamed.

The man dropped his sword as he called, "Help me.

Twenty Year Plan

Please."

The claws erupted from his chest in four, black spines. He was still alive as he was hurled sideways in the air. His body slammed into the broad trunk of a tree several feet above the ground. He struck with bone crushing force and then fell limp to the forest floor in an unnatural heap.

The beast stared at them through the infected gashes around its right eye. It stood on its hind legs bent at odd angles and heaved for breath through its bared fangs. Its misshapen chest and hunched back expanded and contracted with each hale.

It reached down to the ground and swiped its claws through the dirt scarring the earth by its hind paws. The hilt guard of the crude sword was snagged by the claws and lifted into the air. It skidded to a stop against the bottoms of Colt's boots.

The creature extended its bent neck and leaned toward the ground as it roared at them. Elizabeth pulled Colt to his feet and they ran.

***

His wound was not healing well. They could not find herbs they recognized. There were lines of red infection extending out on both sides of his shoulder. It bled and leaked puss if he worked the arm too much.

They continued through the forest.

"Why though?" Mary asked.

"I can make no sense of it," Elizabeth said. "Unless they

are using us for bait to draw out their food."

Colt said, "We've come at least eighty miles or more into the wide world from where we first encountered this pack. They seem to have territory based on the encounters we've had with other packs we've passed, but the trio following us has fought other of their kind to…keep claim on us it seems."

"They are the same three…we are sure?" Mary asked.

"I'm sure," Colt answered.

"It's a hundred miles," Elizabeth said.

"How do you know?" Colt asked.

They emerged from the woods on an eroded slope. Large slabs of rock formed a bridge of massive boulders and stepping stones across the vast water to an island shrouded in fog. There were twisted spires of metal protruding between slabs caked with rust. Colt looked along the crumbling face of the forested cliff in both directions and then back along the giant, stepping stones.

"What is this?" he asked as he adjusted the sword in his belt.

Mary looked across at Elizabeth. "This can't be. We couldn't have come this far."

There was a roar in the forest behind them and the monsters came crashing forward shaking the trees in their path.

"We have no other course," Colt said as he moved forward.

"Another poor option," Elizabeth sighed.

They ran carefully over and between the exposed stone above the water. The monsters roared behind them and tumbled down the slope through the collapsing dirt.

Twenty Year Plan

"Faster," Colt shouted.

They reached the island barely ahead of the monsters clawing their way along the bridge. The twenties ran through the fog on the island as more piles of stone towered above them on each side.

"What is this place?" Colt asked as they ran.

"Where are the buildings?" Mary asked. "Did they all collapse?"

"They dropped heavy fire on it when the plague swept over," Elizabeth said. "I remember hearing about it as our family fled."

Colt stopped. He looked up at massive ruins that extended into the sky beyond his sight in the mist. More twisted, rusted metal hung out of countless floors. He opened his mouth to speak, but then he saw one jump across the gap from one massive building to an opening on the other a few floors down. A deep growl echoed through the fog from above and then two more hurtled between the buildings high in the air.

Colt drew his sword.

Something lumbered across the cluttered street in front of them. Louder growls bellowed out from the direction of the bridge.

Colt moved sideways. "Come on."

They ran along the avenue weaving between piles of stone. The roars built and Colt continued to see motion in the air above them and to the side. They came out in the open by the water again along a metal railing that extended in both directions.

As they turned, three of the pink monsters walked out on

all fours with black claws clicking against the cracked pavement below them.

Colt slid the hand below his bad shoulder into his pocket. His shoulder burned with pain around the wound, but he kept sliding his fingers over the arrow heads in his pocket.

Mary turned away and leaned on the rail. "I can't see the statue."

"We're on the wrong side," Elizabeth answered.

The monster in the middle rose on its hind legs as it reached them. The other beasts paced along on both sides. It focused on Elizabeth with its large eye between the gashes. It stood in front of her and raised two claws to the side of her cheek. She closed her eyes and whimpered.

Colt stepped forward and raised the crude sword with his good arm. The other two monsters stood with claws extended at their sides. The creature with the scarred face turned and looked at Colt with its disproportional eyes. It looked down silently at the sword and back at Colt's face.

Colt stood a moment and let the sword dangle at his side again.

There were growls behind them and the three monsters turned toward the new noise still standing on their hind legs. The space between the streets began to fill with more of the horrid, pink creatures. More climbed over the top of the rubble looking down on the ones by the rail. Their white, ropey tongues snaked out of their dark fangs.

The pack of three stepped forward with claws and fangs bared standing between the humans and the approaching army of monsters from the fallen city.

Colt raised his sword behind the pack that had stalked them across the land.

The air filled with roars that echoed across the water behind them. Then, Colt heard it.

The monster in the middle of the pack standing in front of them ended his growl with garbled, but identifiable syllables, "El-iz-a-beth!"

Colt looked over at her. She covered her mouth in shock.

"What was that?" Colt whispered.

Mary whispered. "This can't be how this ends."

Elizabeth extended her hand and reached slowly toward the back of the monster in the center of the small pack.

"Garrett?"

The other creatures from the ruins advanced on the twenties.

The End

Nightmares and Dragonscapes

by Mandi M. Lynch

You can hear the whooo-whoooo of wings flapping long before you can even see them. Your position on the edge of the forest has blocked the view, so you turn to look. Dragons. More of them. Cursing, you spin around, towards the trees, hoping to hide in the forest, but before you can, you feel a searing heat as the dragons unleash their fiery breath on the grove of trees.

The tops of the trees go up in flames, and you are so startled that you slip and fall. Now where? To your left is Edouard's Hill, and you run for it, dodging the altar and sprinting up the path towards the scared caves. Normally, a mere mortal like you wouldn't be allowed in, but now that The Order had abandoned the city of Shy, it didn't matter anymore. All that mattered was survival.

Without a thought, you dive into the cave, making the appropriate gestures as more of a reflex than a matter of choice, and tuck yourself behind some stalagmites. In the pocket of your apron is a packet of hard biscuits, dried meats, and your water flask. Hopefully, your provisions will last longer than the dragons do....

Eleni woke with a start, springing into a sitting position, and struggled to catch her breath. The sweat poured from her body, making her uncomfortable, and she was glad she had shrugged off her tunic before lying down. She choked back sobs of frustration; every night since the dragons, she had woken with the same nightmare. Wasn't it already bad enough that she had lived it? Did she really have to re-examine those events every night?

At the mouth of the cave, the first tendrils of light were reaching in. Dawn. She had slept longer this night than any of the seventeen nights since the attack. She sighed and pulled on the soot-covered tunic that hung nearby, rolled her bedding and tucked it away, and gathered her pouches before settling in the opening to watch the sun wake the world. Her mother was the medicine woman, before all this, and Eleni had taken it upon herself to salvage what she could and continue on the traditions.

Behind her, she could hear Yonah and Petr stirring as well. The village of Shy had once counted almost four hundred people, now there were just three. The thought of all who were lost slid down her face in the form of one large, salty tear.

***

"Come, Eleni," Petr called, "there's no point in dragging this out now that it's just the three of us."

"Yes, Eleni, he's right." Yonah splashed water at her bare feet as she stood on the shore.

"But–"

"No 'but,' Eleni. This isn't the time for such concern. Get in."

She had always been guarded around members of the opposite sex, choosing to wait until the men had bathed before getting in the river. But they were right, now wasn't the time, and with only three of them, it was more important to just get on with necessities and move on. "Just...close your eyes until I'm in the water, okay?"

The men made a great show of turning their backs. "Should I tell her that I watched her sleep last night?" Petr asked.

"You're kidding, right? Leave the poor girl be. She's barely a woman!"

"I can hear you, you know." Eleni was neck-deep in the water by then, and had splashed her way into the center of the river. "And, really, Petr, did you?"

"Well, I mean, you were in your bedroll already."

"Remind me to stay in my tunic, too."

"Oh, come on, Eleni. Lighten up."

"Kind of hard to do when the world has just ended, don't you think?"

Yonah went to her side and put an arm around her shoulders. "The world hasn't ended, it's just shrunk a bit. But there's a reason that we're still here, and we need to relax and make the best of everything."

"I guess. It's just hard. Look at everything we've lost."

"Look at everything we have," Petr said. "I mean, I know it's not a lot, but we have each other, we have quite a few possessions still, and by the time this is all over, who knows what else. Come on. We'll be in Cart-Hedge by sun down, and then you'll see."

"I can't see. I don't know what's what anymore. Am I a woman? The aging ceremony was supposed to take place tomorrow. Without it, what am I? Why would the Order leave with aging ceremonies looming? And the joinings that never happened." She gasped. "What will happen to the babies? Alix and Nikola never had their wakening! How do they move across if they're still asleep?!"

"Calm down! You performed the Moving with every bit of dignity and compassion your mother ever would have used. The gods will understand what has happened, and they will take Alix and Nikola, just as they will the others." Yonah gave her a little squeeze. "We have done the best we could with what we were given; nobody asks for any more than that."

"You're right." She relaxed in the warm water, more than happy to rest her aching body and wipe off the layers of soot and grime. "What do you think we did wrong?"

"Excuse me?" Petr stared at her. "What we did wrong?"

"Well, we had to do something, right? Last moon, The Order left us, and then this moon, the dragons came. There was no moon ritual, no sacrifice of herbs, no sacred words chanted at the moon. And then the dragons came, and wiped us out. We were lucky. We weren't the fastest or the smartest, just the luckiest."

Nightmares and Dragonscapes

"I'd like to think that we're not the stupidest, Eleni."

"I didn't say that, Yonah."

"Come on, let's relax. It's a beautiful day, and if you don't look in the direction of the charred forest, it's like none of that even happened, right?"

Both Yonah and Eleni spun to face Petr directly. "You're kidding, right?"

"Look, there's a reason we survived. No, we weren't the smartest or the fastest—Eleni's right about that. But we are the ones who survived. And when we get to Cart-Hedge tonight, we'll find an inn and then we'll tell the whole town what happened. Okay?"

"Right. Let's go. The water's making me all pruney." Eleni got out of the river, fully aware that Petr was watching her every move, and slipped into a tunic quickly. "Are you guys coming, or am I going at this alone?"

Wordlessly, they followed suit, and the men grabbed the packs, allowing Eleni to lead the way. Under normal circumstances, the walk to Cart-Hedge took most of a day, allowing for regular water breaks and a decent lunch somewhere along the way. These were everything but normal circumstances, and as the trio trudged on, it became apparent that the fiery path of destruction left by the dragons went further than they thought. The path normally meandered through the woods, but with no woods left, the direct route proved fast and they were at the outpost gates in just a couple short hours.

"Shit."

One of the four gateposts remained, singed black and

cracked in half, but stood in protest to the devastation. In the center of the outpost, a large rock stood, a carved greeting in seven languages. "Marghrie Mie," Eleni said to it out of habit. She wondered when she would stop these mechanical pleasantries and see the situation as it was. If the outpost was burned, too, another seventy residents and hundreds of transients and travelers were gone. She turned to her friends. "We will have to reach City Proper tomorrow. Down the path to the river is a cavern that they stored goods in. Search the outpost and take any remains you find down there. Any goods that weren't scorched beyond use, we'll take with us."

"You're going to do another Moving?" Petr asked.

"I can't not."

"Didn't we say—"

"You can say what you want to, Petr, but I am saying this. The dragons came and tried to wipe us out, but they didn't succeed. We are here, we are breathing. If you won't help, then you shouldn't have bothered with survival in the first place!"

"Whoa, Eleni!" Yonah said, coming over to them. He, too, cast a quick greeting at the rock. "Don't say anything you will regret with the sun, Eleni. Petr, let her have her peace of mind. Go to the cave, empty it if you have to, and catch us some fish for a meal. At least we have something to eat, yes? I will check for remains, although the dragons have made easy work of that for me, and Eleni can prepare her ritual."

You walk through the woods, on a meandering path that is all too familiar. You've been here a million times in your young life, and you can walk this with your eyes closed. An owl hoots, sending chills down your spine. Owls? During the day? You dodge a low hanging branch and the path starts to widen.

A commotion sounds in the woods, and dozens of creatures come charging at you. A deer almost tramples you, and you crunch yourself under a tree, the rough bark scratching at your back, and move through the forest this way until you reach the clearing. Now you know what the commotion was about. A whoosh of fire explodes in the opening, and the white fountain that your grandfather once helped build is immediately reduced into blackened remains. A second burst starts and as you raise your arms to shield your face, you realize you're not alone. "MOTHER!"

It's too late. You're alone in the world. Around you, the trees catch on fire, and you join the animals' stampede and run for your life. . . .

Eleni woke with a start. She was breathing hard and drenched with sweat. In the air, she could still smell the char of the outpost around her. They had tried to find a secluded spot, but there weren't any, other than the cave, and she wasn't about to sleep there—nor would she let the guys talk her into it.

They were grumbling when they lay down with her, but they stopped when the stars came out. There was just something soothing about looking to the south and seeing the dual moons rise; most people liked the brighter, peach-colored one, but Eleni always liked the old moon, with its blue cast. It was larger and more peaceful.

On this night, they counted shooting stars and drifted

to sleep. But the nightmares persisted, and that was what woke Eleni from her slumber. It was her, in turn, whose restless pacing woke up the men.

Despite Petr's impatience, and Yonah's attempt to calm him, Eleni did her ritual flawlessly, and the group had lunch before they continued down the path to City Proper. The charred remains of the once great forest led their way, and the blackened stumps stretched on for miles.

Just before the city limits was a large bend in the river and an outcropping of rocks. Around the outcropping were lush, green plants—the first they had seen on their entire trip. "Guys, are you seeing what I'm seeing? I mean, there's grass and, and… it's so lush!! Plants…plants everywhere! Does this mean that the city's safe?!"

"I wouldn't get too excited, Eleni. I mean, with everything that happened so far on this trip, I'm not sure that I would expect something amazing. I see the plants also, I'm just not going to get that excited about what's up ahead. For now we need to get food while you get some rest." Yonah looked at his friend and placed a comforting hand on her arm. "Look, I want to be excited, I want to jump up and down and scream and dance and…. What if we're wrong, if the next thing after that bend is more charred remains…? If the next thing that we see is nothing, then what? What happens when we get our hopes up that a miracle has happened and we realize that all the left is devastation? These people were our friends, our families, neighbors, lovers, strangers yes, too, but even then, these people in these cities are our entire lives. We came in and we went together, and the only thing that separates their fate from ours is dumb luck."

"Well, Yonah, you got that right." Petr looked at the two and actually applauded politely as he approached them. "Here we are in the middle of nothing and she is off praying to gods that don't exist anymore, and you're off.... What are you doing Yonah? You're not taking sides, you're dancing between us as if you need to. It's the end of the world! Don't you get that? Our city is gone. Our family is gone. And everything that was ever known, everything we've ever done, every herb and every chance.... For what? For death and destruction! The three of us are somehow the ones that have been chosen by dumb luck. Not chance, not by half-dog gods in the sky, to carry on, somehow someway make this work. Hope, dreams, wishes.... Too late for those."

Eleni's chin wavered as if she were about to cry, and she fought back the tears that were welling up in her eyes. If all this was stupid and nothing good could ever come of it, then what exactly were they doing? "Do you try to be a bastard, Petr? Is that what this is about, being the bully that you've always been? Did you maybe think that you might be wrong? That maybe there is a higher deeper meaning to all of this...something much bigger than you could ever hope to be? Of course not! You're too wrapped up in yourself. You've always been too wrapped up in yourself." Her voice rose with every note, and by the time she was done she was almost standing on her tiptoes shouting.

"Both of you stop it!" Yonah forced his way between the two and pushed them apart. "What is wrong with you guys? We may be the only three people left! Just...just Yonah and Petr and

Eleni. Nobody else. Maybe that sounds like nothing. Maybe it is nothing. But maybe it's more than nothing, and if that's the case, if it's more than nothing, if it really, and truly is something, then we need to stop bickering, and we need to act like it wasn't just dumb luck that put us here. Can we at least agree to get along until we reach the city? We will know then what world we are looking at. We'll know then if it's the three of us, or 33 of us or the entire population of the city plus the three of us. If we don't stop this now, there was no point of crawling out of the cave."Yonah struggled to keep his composure, but what he really wanted to do with punch Petr square the jaw. In all his years of living with Petr as neighbors, it had always been Petr against the world. The problem now was there was no world to be against. "You are either for the world, or you shouldn't be a part of it."

Petr looked at the two, disgusted, and decided that further discussion wasn't worth the effort. He walked away, leaving Eleni and Yonah to stare at each other in awkward silence. Both of them wanted to say something but neither one really knew what to say. After all, this wasn't one of those moments that you spent your whole life preparing for. It wasn't a walk through the woods on your way to your first ritual, or a discussion on what part of what flower was poisonous. There was no sit down with grandma and grandpa, listening to stories about how the world ended three generations back, complete with details on what their parents had done to survive. What they needed most was a roadmap, and the mapmaker with this, is absent on the day that it was most important.

Eleni walked toward the outcropping, deciding that it

was the best option for their situation. As a child, in the rare occasions that they made the journey to the city, they always stopped at this outcropping. It always seemed to follow like a good place to take a break as the rocks afforded them some level of protection from predators of any sort. She knew these rocks as well as she knew the back of her hand, and she used the opportunity to forage for what little food they could find. If the city was still there, this was an exercise in gathering, but if the city wasn't there then it may very well be their only choice for food, and she wasn't about to blow it.

Eleni had barely managed to fill her pack when she came across a sickly looking nest of eggs. In all her travels with her mother, she had seen plenty of eggs, but none looked quite like this. They didn't belong to any of the exotic birds that she knew so well. They were much too small for that. Most bird eggs were blue or pink, phoenix eggs were bright fiery red, and, of course, dragon eggs were green.... These were brownish, beautifully shaped, but bumpy. Another confusing feature, since all the eggs she knew of were nice and smooth, save for one family of dragon eggs, which boasted beautiful, smooth scales in various shades of green. They weren't turtle eggs, and there weren't any other creatures that laid eggs in these parts. Eleni was at a total loss.

Still, Eleni had never heard her mother warn her that an egg was unsafe to eat if it was fresh, so she took great care to put these in her pack. When they got to the city, they would have the eggs, berries, and perhaps the fresh fish or two. It would be a far cry from the jerky that they had been sharing on the trip.

With Petr sulking and Yonah angry, she took the

opportunity to get comfortable on the rocks; the rest of their journey would be far enough without having to do it in the twilight. *One more night, then we could finish the trip.* She could hear the boys settle around her as she drifted off into sleep.

You walk down the path through the woods. They're familiar to you, the woods of your childhood. As you head down the packed dirt trail, you look around you. The trees are silent—too silent—but you continue anyway. In the middle of the woods is a clearing, and you can see it quite a distance before you reach it. Your mother is in the center, standing in front of a stone circle—the fire pit is the ritual pit, and you know she's working on something. The plants spread out in front of her are somehow familiar—yarrow and ivy, sage and twigs from the sacred tree. But you hadn't ever seen them mixed that way.

"Come, my child," she says to you and beckons. You're confused, but you go to her anyway. She's your mother, and you've already promised to be at her side and learn your trade. You're not an apprentice, something more. . . . "I'm glad you're here."

You want to speak but you can't. Instead, you nod and stand by her side, staring into the pit as the flint is thrust into your hands. The words tumble off your lips, and you don't even realize that you're saying them. The translation is lost to you, lost to time, but you get the point. You're asking something bigger than yourself to grant you the pleasure of the fire. The flints knock together and a spark takes the leaves, the fire fighting to come to life.

"Good," your mother coos. "I need to tell you something. It's important."

Before she can finish, the fire cracks and leaps out of the pit and

Nightmares and Dragonscapes

ignites the grasses around them. "Mother——"

"Shh, child."Your mother continues as if she can't even see the flames."Listen to me."

You're scared. Terrified, really, and you just can't relax, even with your mother's soothing arm on your shoulder. The flames are getting higher, dancing away from the safety of the clearing and heading towards the woods at an alarming speed. But you listen, because you're rooted in place in fear and you hope that listening to her will at least distract you.

"You, my child, you are the key."

"They key to what?"

"To everything."

Eleni sat up, drenched in sweat. She was tired of this, the nightmares, the sweat when she woke up. It was more than enough. But this one…there was something about it that made her think twice. The other nightmares had been familiar, but they hadn't spoken to her in quite this way. Was she really the key to everything? What was left for her?

The world had always been constant, but now it was a scary place. She longed for her family, her friends, even the community, though she had often fought to find her place in it. Yonah and Petr were all she had left, and she wasn't sure they would have been the ones she chose. Eleni thought back to the old stories, when they talked about making new worlds from the ashes of old. She had always thought they were fake; could a handful of people really restore all life?

As quietly as she could, Eleni slipped away and found herself at the river's edge before she knew it. She wasn't a fish, hadn't quite been drawn to the water and to swimming the way so many people she knew were. *Had been,* she mentally corrected. *They're all gone now.* Her shoulders slumped, but she sat down and dipped her toes in the cool liquid. With everything that had changed, the river was the only constant. The fish still swam, and the underwater plants were no doubt still green.

Back in her childhood, she remembered the awe over a school of flying fish. It was her sixth birthday, and she had watched for hours before returning to the village and telling everyone about the fish that had danced for her. Now, the water was smooth save for a few white bubbles of current around the rocks and shores.

A twig broke behind her, and Eleni turned to see Yonah making his way to where she was sitting. "Did I wake you?"

"Yes. No." He took a seat next to her. "I mean, even when I'm sleeping, I'm not. I listen for you, and I listen for...." His voice trailed off. They both knew what the rest of the sentence was. He was listening for the dragons to return.

"I listen, too. For everything. Is it wrong of me to hold out hope that somebody will suddenly jump out from behind a rock and scream 'Here I am, they didn't get me after all!' and then bring fifty other people out with them?"

"No. One of my brothers was out hunting when everything happened. Whenever we get quiet, I think of Kris and wonder if he found a place to hide. I could see him again, you know? He wasn't along this road, he was out in the wild, in another direction...." Now his words ran together excitedly.

"Yonah—"

Nightmares and Dragonscapes

"If you're going to tell me I'm wrong, stop. We all need something to hold on to."

"I wasn't going to tell you that you were wrong, Yonah. I wish I could have something like that on my mind."

"What do you mean?"

She took a deep breath and held it for a minute before slowly pushing the air out between her lips. "I've been having nightmares."

Yonah wasn't surprised. "And you wake up every night because of them."

"Yes. I think they're trying to tell me something, but I wake up too soon. This time, I had a conversation with my Mother. She said that I was the key to everything."

Yonah was silent for so long that Eleni thought the conversation was over. She felt defeated, and started to stand up when he grabbed her arm and held her in place. "Look, Eleni. You are our bridge between what was before and what now is. If things were left to Petr, where would we be? Blindly forging ahead until we walked off a cliff. But here you are." Eleni sank back to her seat and stared at him. "You're our link, our reminder that between life and death is humanity. You will keep us grounded, and because of that, we'll soar."

A smile creased her mouth at the last line. She remembered Yonah's grandfather saying some form of that throughout her childhood. A link to the past that she could hold for the future. "I feel like...."

"...like you don't know which way's up?"

"Yes."

"Me, too. I...I need to promise you something, Eleni. I will keep the peace between you and Petr as long as we can. And if I can't, I will follow you. I'm frightened, terrified...what's worse than terrified?"

"Petrified?"

He giggled and relaxed a little bit. "I'm scared. But I know that I'm as safe as I can be next to you." Yonah took a deep breath. "I smell food; Petr must be up."

They walked back towards the outcropping and spotted Petr across the dirt road with a small fire going. "I decided to get cleaned up, and caught a couple fish while I was at it." He looked better for his effort, and seemed a little calmer, too. "Look, I was a jackass yesterday."

"Yep." Eleni took the seat next to him.

"Come on, El. I'm being honest here. Look—with everything going on...." He flashed a look to Yonah, who said nothing, and then continued. "I'm trying to apologize, okay? Sorry I was an ass, lookie, here's breakfast."

"Thanks for the fish," Eleni said. She cast Yonah a look and he finally took a seat next to his friends.

Petr pointed to a charred and hollowed out branch. "Found some sea greens washed up on shore, good enough to eat if I can cook them like that. Only ever saw Da wrap them in leaves and smoke them, and, well, not exactly surrounded by leaves, you know?"

"I'm sure it will be fine." Eleni pulled a knife out of her pack and passed it to Petr so he could portion the fish. "After this, we'll be on our way to the city. What do you think we'll find?"

"It's a ten minute walk past the bend, and then.... I didn't see anything. Doesn't mean there's not still somebody there, but it also doesn't mean the towers are standing."

"Yonah, when did you do that?"

"Before I went and found Eleni. I figured if she was sneaking away from us, she wanted a few minutes to herself." He shrugged like it was nothing. "I hope I'm wrong."

"Yeah, well." Petr took a huge bite of fish and cursed as he burned the roof of his mouth. His companions both laughed until he turned red, and then he, too, joined in their laughter. It was the first laughter of any of them for a few days, and it felt good to laugh, even better than it felt to eat animal again.

They took their time eating, and the meal ended on a lighter note than it began, the trio taking up the time between bites with old stories of when they were little kids. Even the sea greens turned out better than they had planned, although a bit more bitter than they were used to, since he hadn't had herbs to put in with them. By the time they cleaned up, nobody was dreading the walk.

It was barely an hour and a half before they got to City Proper, and mere seconds to take in the devastation. The three stopped just outside what would have been the gate and stared at the scene before them. The towers were made of stone, but in the destruction had fallen over, leaving a pile of rubble in the center and a good coating of dust over the char of everything else.

"Marghrie Mie," Eleni whispered, walking past the post-holes that now marked the entrance instead of posts. Even the ash that should have filled them was missing. Yonah and Petr followed behind and they spun around, taking in everything and nothing at the same time. "I...."

Yonah put a hand on her shoulder and kept it there while she screamed.

"IT'S NOT RIGHT! YOU CAN'T HAVE EVERYTHING, WHATEVER YOU ARE! BRING EVERYONE BACK!" She sunk to the ground, landing on her knees and hunched forward, and sobbed for several minutes before she could calm down. When she did, tears streaked her face, and she stood up without even dusting herself off. "Both of you check the rock piles. See if anyone is left. Bring me any bodies you may find."

This time, Petr didn't object and he and Yonah set off in different directions to scan the rubble for survivors. They managed to only find provisions, two ribs, a femur, and the charred stump of somebody's left arm, which Petr almost didn't want to touch, but which he carried to Eleni at Yonah's insistence.

She had made her way to what was left of the life monument and instructed Yonah and Petr on how to dig the hole for the remaining parts. She carefully did her ritual, now almost second-nature, as the boys walked away to see what was salvageable for their own needs.

After the Moving, she also did a Healing, asking whatever gods remained to save them. It was evening before she found the boys in the half shelter of a scorched hut, several strangers with them.

"Is everything okay?" Yonah slid over so she could sit in

the shade next to them.

"Yeah. It's done, whatever good it will do." She eyed the strangers for a minute, gaze resting on their clothes. "I'm Eleni. You must be from the other side of the river."

"We are," the tall man said. "I'm Wain, these are Grett, Nomi, and Rue, and the young one is Jezel." He pointed to each of them as he spoke. "We found Jezel on the trip here," he explained as if he had asked her not to come but she followed anyway.

"Hi, everyone. And hello, Jezel," Eleni said in a soft voice, trying to coax the little girl out of the corner. Jezel's eyes widened at the greeting, and she sat there, transfixed and scared. "I'm not going to hurt you, sweetheart." It was a long, silent minute, but the girl finally believed her and crossed the room to her, crawling in her lap as soon as she could. The girl couldn't have been more than three. "So, did anybody see anything?"

"I saw the most," Grett replied, "which is to say, not very much. Rogue dragons by the dozen. They screeched and swooped in and bathed the world in fire. But something was wrong with them. They were a sickly brown color. I've never seen a dragon that color."

"She described it to me and all I can think is a story that my Da told me when I was very little," Rue added. "He said that many lives before him, the dragons had started to lay eggs that color. His Da's Da was responsible for checking the nests whenever eggs were laid and smashing any that were brown and had any texture other than smooth or scaled. The lands over the mountains didn't do that, and their dragons turned on them, wiping them out, but our village and the lands across the river, were safe because of what he had done."

Eleni's mind raced back to the eggs that were in her pack. The story of the lands across the river didn't mesh with what she had been told as a child. "I thought the lands over the mountains were lost to other things," she said.

"Like what?"

"The great fire that was started because of the harsh winter, for starters. My mother was a healer, and she knew the stories from the other healers. Except that the lands over the mountains had given up on those things, and when the fire broke out, they were too splintered to save themselves as a whole. A few weary travelers made their way here, but they died soon after."

"Well, I don't believe you," Grett said, "and if I ever find another egg, I will smash it to bits. We saw the result of the dragon's sickness—corpses lined part of our journey. They're gone now, they can't hurt us again. And if I have the power in me to stop that from happening again, then I will."

Eleni went quiet, her thoughts turning to the eggs in her bag. So they <u>were</u> dragon eggs. She knew from her mother that the dragons' scales were the color of their eggs, and now Eleni wondered if the eggs were really the culprit for the rogue dragons, or if they were a mutation in the color of their bodies. When she was young, she had seen the same mutation happen in a bird's nest, and her mother had explained to her then that it was the way things sometimes worked. Now her mind reeled. Could something else have really turned the dragons? Were these eggs really the last of the animals that walked the grounds? She made a mental note to protect them with everything, and casually slid her pack behind her, where she used her body to keep them warm.

"Eleni!"

She snapped out of her thoughts and back to reality. In the short time she was thinking about the eggs, the others in the room had started arguing, and Jezel was curled tighter against Eleni's body.

"Eleni, make them stop!"

"That's enough, guys, okay?!" Eleni didn't even know what they were arguing about, but she knew that it was no way to solve their problems. Her plea was lost over the shouting and the scraping sounds made by Grett and Petr jumping up from their spots to have at each other. "GUYS! Yonah, get Petr, will you?"

Before Yonah had a chance to respond, Grett shoved Petr hard. His body landed in the small fire the group had made, and his head bounced off the rock-hard floor, pooling blood from his head in the same motion. Flames licked across his skin, and Petr made no attempt to even moan.

Yonah screamed and tried to stand up, but found he was rooted to the spot.

"Yonah," Eleni whispered. "Let's go."

"But Petr!"

"It's too late. Come. Let's get out of here." She nudged him again and he rose to his feet, taking Jezel out of Eleni's arms so she could stand. The young woman carefully shouldered her pack and they slipped out of the ruins while their companions sat in horror.

"Do you remember the old stories of the protected valley?"

"Sort of, why?"

"I know where it is."

"But those were just stories!" Yonah stared at her in shock. "I mean, nobody's been there."

"The healers have. I have. With Mother. Come on. I know how to get there and they don't. It's the only place we'll be safe."

"But Petr—"

"We can come back for his body. I'll do a ritual. But for now, we need to save ourselves."

The little girl whimpered in Yonah's arms, and that shook him back to reality. "You're right. Lead the way."

"Be quiet and follow."

They made their way out the back of the city, sneaking behind a pile of rock before they were spotted. From there, it was a short walk to Cliff's Edge, and Eleni led them around another statue and to a hidden path. "It's narrow," she whispered. "Watch yourself." She was careful on the way down, worried that Yonah would lose his footing and drop Jezel, but they made it to the bottom safely.

Ancient, gnarled trees greeted them, and she expertly made her way through, as if on a path that Yonah couldn't see from his spot just two steps behind her. Once through the trees, he stopped and gasped. Stretching before them, as far as they could see was a lush, green valley, untouched by the dragons.

Nightmares and Dragonscapes

Several birds twittered about, dancing from tree branch to tree branch, and a family of turtles meandered through the open space. "Am I really seeing this?"

"Better than home," she replied. She walked forward, a little more sure of herself with every step. Just a few yards in front of them, what looked like a fissure opened up into another cave, and two old women walked out of the entrance.

"Eleni? Where is your mo—"The crone stopped as soon as she saw Eleni's traveling partner.

"Hello, Crone Maga. We've come to seek shelter. I have a terrible story for you that I don't want to bear the burden of."

Maga hadn't taken her eyes off Yonah yet. "But he can't be here."

"He has to be. I know the rule, but I need to break it."

"Maga, let her speak her peace at least. We can turn her away in the morning if we must, but for now, the light is almost gone. Surely there must be some importance to her message if she braved the mountain in the darkness."

"Hello, Crone Dell," Eleni responded. "Thank you for your words of confidence. The turtles, have they nested yet?"

Dell nodded her head in the direction of more rocks. "You can just see mother turtle's head if you look right. The eggs won't hatch for a while."

Eleni pulled herself away and made her way to the turtle, cooing as she did. Mother turtle stood up, stepped in front of her nest and stuck her neck out at Eleni. The girl continued to coo, pulled the eggs out of her pack slowly, and reached around the turtle to add them to the nest. "You are the key to the future as well, mother turtle. For that I thank you."

She turned back to the other people, and was relieved to see that Yonah and Jezel had been welcomed down into the crones' home. She followed after them, stopping only to fill the water pail from the pond.

"You three may bed down for the night, but in the morning...."

"I will tell all, Crone Maga. I promise."

The woman nodded, pursed her lips, and left them alone. The sparse bedding was only enough for them if they curled up tightly, and so they did, a new family woven tightly in a world that was otherwise unraveled. It wasn't long before Eleni drifted off to sleep.

You've somehow made it to the river's edge, safe from the burning trees and falling fireballs, and you realize that a boat is waiting for you. Your mother is on it, and she looks impatient, as if you should have met her there hours ago.

"Hurry, my child. For I have much to tell you and very little time."

You board the boat without saying anything, deciding against mumbling an apology, and push the boat from the shore. Your mother is an expert with the oars, and she guides you safely around the chaos around you both.

"Listen carefully. What you see now is not what will be tomorrow. You are the key to everything, the one who will restore what is to what has been."

"But, Mother...." You start to interrupt. You have specific

questions, you want real answers, not vague statements, but the look on her face makes you stop.

"Stay true to your heart, never waver from it. Steer away from anything that isn't a clear choice. And remember—"Your mother pauses now, so long that you're worried she won't finish talking. "Remember, the right choice is not always the easiest, but if you stay with your heart, you'll know."

You don't know what she's talking about, but you nod anyway. "I found the eggs...."Your voice trails off.

"I know," she says, looking in your eyes. "And?"

And. Of course your mother would want your answer instead of giving one of her own. "I don't know what they are, but I gave them to Mother Turtle. Whatever creature, it deserves life, too."

Your mother's taken the boat to a sandy beach, and she nods to you. You take the cue and stand up, carefully exiting the boat into the unfamiliar alcove.

"Goodbye, my child."

"Wait! Aren't you coming with me?"

"You don't need me anymore." She pushes away and you watch as she continues down the river. You notice the waterfall, and want to shout a warning, but your mouth stays shut. Somehow you know better. As the boat pitches over the edge, your mother rises up, shrinking in front of your very view, until she has morphed into the smallest bird you have ever seen and flies away.

The End

The Stone-Sword

by Magda Knight

I've seen thirty summers and I still remember how the long golden days used to be. Now there's only never-ending winter. Perhaps that means I won't get older, having just the one season against which to track my age, but I feel in my stiffening bones that I am. I'm long past maiden and heading inevitably from mother to crone. I'm aging one snowflake at a time.

I hear a noise above the sound of the forge and look up from my swages to see a man both handsome and ruined of face, his greasy long hair waterfalling into a wolf-cloak, his legs ending in boots that have seen a lot of walking and snowshoes that have seen more slipping and sliding than he'd care to admit.

An adventurer, then, or mercenary. You can always tell. It's the eyes that do it. I make a quick gesture to Alvin, who's standing by patiently as ever with the tongs, and my sweet younger brother quickly raises his hood and retreats to the shadows at the back of the forge before he's clearly seen.

"Where's the blacksmith?" asks the man before me, looking me up and down, sleepy and expectant as a fireside cat.

Those adventurers. All the same.

"Right here. You're speaking to her," I say shortly. He appraises the muscular arms that bunch against my linen shirt, the leather apron shielding me from sparks. He frowns as he lingers on my full bust, on my hair cut soldier-short to stop it catching fire from a loose spark, on my stone-hard face.

"You don't find many women in the profession," he notes. He clearly does not think much to what he sees, but his lilting tones veer between pragmatism and seduction. I'm no woman any man would want to tup, and yet...he's an adventurer. He can't help himself.

I stand up to my full height, taller and broader than any man, and creak the stiffness out of my back. I let him get a full view of my height and girth. I'll not have him insult me in my own forge.

"Well, here I am, stranger. Rules were meant to be broken. There's always me."

The adventurer cranes up to get a clear view of my face, his mouth open, and quickly shuts it again when he notes the hard flint in my eyes. Yes, it's obvious that giant-blood runs in my veins. But I will not have it spoken of. Not by a friend, and most certainly not by a stranger. Not when we still had summers, and especially not now.

He comes to a decision. "I need a brooch for my beloved. I have coin. A design in silver, I think...or maybe tin."

I snort. She can't be much of a beloved if it's a tawdry tin brooch he seeks.

"You'll need a silversmith then, won't you? Someone

who works with the white metals. I only work with black. Iron and steel, that's what I do. You want a sword, you come to me. You want a brooch, you need to go elsewhere."

The adventurer is about to retort but thinks better of it. I see he is deciding what kind of exit to make. Will he be courteous or turn on his heel? In the end he opts for good manners and a silver tongue.

"Then I thank you for your time, sweet sister," he says, and shuffles off into the evening, no-doubt heading for the nearest inn, or some new beloved's bed, or some private camp in the mountains, the ever-falling snow already beginning to cover up his tracks. I wait till he is gone.

"You can come out now, Alvin."

My brother comes out of the shadows, back to the heat of the forge. He has our mother's giant blood too, but though he is taller than a man he is shorter than me. His face is handsome where mine echoes the mountain crags they at least partly came from, but he is not an adventurer. Not anymore. He is a sweet, sweet boy who wouldn't harm a hair on a baby's head.

He picks up the tongs and helps me hold the metal in place as I begin to work the iron once more, banging it with tender fury to let the carbon in and turn it into steel. Alvin has a far lighter touch than me, and has a feel for minerals I can never hope to equal. It is his inheritance. His skill is so great that he should be feted and showered with coin, forging swords that bards will sing of long after their owners have crumbled into dust. He should not be set aside to skulk in shadows and hold a pair of tongs like some acne-ridden apprentice.

But I will not let him take on the beating and the shaping ever again; not after what he did. I cannot risk it. The boy is blessed, of that there is no question, but his talented hands are cursed.

"You've missed a bit," grins Alvin. It always pleases me when he does that. He carries a burden greater than any of us. To see him smile is to see him lighter.

"Look. Just there." He points to a small spot on the steel sword which is slowly beginning to take shape. He's right, of course. He's always right. I direct my hammer to the place in question, and feel the metal begin to sing beneath my touch.

Then I hear a sound behind me, and as Alvin scurries off I wheel round heavily.

"I told you, I do no <u>tin</u>," I start to say, but the words die on my lips.

Standing before me is a pair of boots.

I should have heard the giant approach minutes ago. The only reason I didn't was because the sound of the forge masks all save whatever happens near enough that I can reach out an arm and touch it. With a feeling of disquiet I lay down my tools and head to the door of the forge and look up.

And up, and up.

Oh, he's tall, this one. Not the tallest I've seen—they've sent a messenger, not their oldest and strongest. But tall enough to do me harm, and to let the entire village know by his very presence that I, a humble blacksmith, entertain guests like these. His arrival at my forge could mean Alvin's execution if I am not careful.

The Stone-Sword

With a brisk tread I step outside.

"I am Bemia, daughter of a man you'll not know named Edmund and of the giantess Thalaskia Snow-Song," I say, and bow deeply, making myself even shorter to this giant than I was before. "And she was daughter of Bemorth Who Lives In Clouds. How may I help you?"

Rudely, the giant does not give me his name. Or perhaps, since he is a messenger, merely a mouthpiece for one who has something to say, his name doesn't matter. He is tall enough that he could peep over a castle's battlements if he wanted to, but ever since the winter came, most of our castles are little more but heaps of blocks pulled down by vengeful hands. It's all gone to rack and ruin, all of it...ever since the sword and the stone. Lords and kings have no place now. Only the ice giants rule.

"You have been sent for," he booms, the snow shaking on tree branches. "You and your brother."

Mention of Alvin makes me blanche and I hurriedly nod in his direction, but his wit is as quick as his hands and he has already grabbed the packs of belongings we have prepared in advance should this day ever come.

"As you wish," I say, already trying to think who will mind the forge when I am gone. "Where, sir? And when? And who is it that we must meet?"

"You must drag your sorry selves to Beinn Nibheis, the Mountain with its Head in the Clouds," booms the unknown giant. "It is some way to the North, in the Grampians. You will be there in three-day's time, and you will not dally. And when you get there you will fall at the feet of Jotnar, the king of Britain, and hear what he has to say."

The giant's voice carries so well across the air that everyone in this village and the next will have heard the news, and I fear what will happen to Alvin and myself if we stay and risk the king's wrath. But then, I'm even more concerned about what will happen to us when we leave, and what will befall us when we arrive at the palace of the ice giants' king. Nothing good can come from such a visit, I'm sure.

"We'll be there," I say. "Of course we will. In three days. Blessings on you and your kin...."

My pretty pleasantries fall on stone ears as the giant turns his back on my humble forge and wanders off down the mountain path, leaving a new trail of smashed trees and terrorized birds flocking up into the grey sky as he goes.

When the villagers are certain he is gone they creep out of the huts and stare at me, their faces a mix of mistrust and concern. Mostly mistrust. The giant has left nothing but destruction in his wake. The roof to the communal food salting cellar is a broken mass of splinters, and we'd only just built it the week before.

I sigh. "You heard him. I'll be heading off for a few days," I announce in a carrying voice to all those watching. "Mark my words, I'll be back. If anyone touches my tools there'll be a reckoning."

I head back into the forge and put what portables I can into a storage room, its heavy wooden door secured by bars and padlocks of my own making. Unless the villagers are of a mind to burn the door down, it will hold.

The Stone-Sword

"Good riddance!" yells a villager. "We always knew you were one of them, you filth...."

"I pity your poor lost father," says my neighbour, spite on his face. "How he found the guts to put his pizzle in the gaping crevasse of your mother's womanhood, I'll never know."

"It's the mother I pity," laughs his wife. "The chances are she never even felt a thing."

"Come, Alvin." I turn to my brother, the only one who means anything in my eyes, and ignore the villagers. They are what they are. Life is what it is.

Without another word, Alvin and I shoulder our packs and head off down the mountain path, following the footprints of the giant. We will be able to track these for days in our bid to reach Beinn Nibheis. The giant's prints are deep enough that the snow will not blanket them in a hurry.

Even so, it's clear to me that the giant's tracks will be covered better than Alvin and I have managed to conceal ours.

***

We make good time across the mountains and the desolate iced plains that used to be fields, and within two days we are in the mountains again, at the foothills of the Grampians where the new kings of Britain hold their court.

Alvin makes a mournful face. "I can't go any further, Bemia. Honestly, I can't. I'm starving." He points at his rumbling belly. "Can't we make a stop at the next village? The Scotsmen are all mountain folk, after all; they won't blink an eyelid on seeing folk as tall as us. And we have the coin."

I consider his words. We've been following the messenger's tracks for days now, taking cover when small folk approach, secreting ourselves in narrow gulfs or on hill tops above their line of sight, covering ourselves as best we can in our yellow-pale winter wolf cloaks. Alvin's tall and strong, and I'm stronger, but if a large group really wanted to take us and had the weapons to do it, they could. Folk don't take kindly to half-breeds now that the ice is here. We remind them too much of what they've lost.

"Oh, go on, then. I see lights in the distance, just over there. We'll stop with people for the night, if we must." I heave a sigh to show that this is a work of great charity and to make it very clear to Alvin that I'm giving in only because he's in dire need of comfort, more than I.

He snorts with laughter. He knows I want a belly full of stewed wolf and a dry floor to sleep on just as much as he does.

Another hour's walking reveals the bright lights in the distance to be not so much a village as a collection of hovels nestling in a crook of the fork of a wide flat river. There is a bridge across, but it looks slender and rickety and I'm not sure it'll take our weight, so we ford the river instead. Holding the packs and fur cloaks high above our heads we end up getting chill and wet right up to our collar bones.

"They'd better have something to eat after all this," moans Alvin.

"We'll hunt if they don't," I reply, feeling equally displeased about having to ford the river. "We'll buy if they do."

The Stone-Sword

One of the hovels has the sounds of laughter and people coming from it, and in front of it stands a hastily-painted sign hanging from a post and swinging in the cold breeze.

"The Sword in the Stone," says the sign.

"Looks like an inn to me," says Alvin with some relief.

"It sounds like a hotbed of insurrection to me," I say, nodding at the sign. "The Sword in the Stone, it says. Sounds like we'll be spending the night with folk who openly hate the new kings of Britain, and yearn for the summers we had before."

Alvin has the grace to look sheepish, and I wish I'd had the sense to hold my tongue.

I knock as gently as I can and, stooping in the low doorway, I enter.

Our arrival is greeted with dead silence, but I have time to look around. Several tree stumps are arranged around the hearth as seats, some of them still empty. Everyone is supping from bowls with mugs of water beside them. I sniff the air: no, not water. Something fermented and sweet. Mead. I'd almost forgotten the taste of it.

"We're travelers," I say. "On our way to Beinn Nibheis, to an audience with Jotnar. Have you a couple of spare seats and perhaps a bowl of stew to spare? We have both the coin and the need."

I let the mountain folk take in my girth, my height, my open hands held out in a sign of peace.

"Oh, go on then, half-breed," says one of the men amiably. "You can join us in our feast, if you like." He has a head as fat as a bull, and grimy black curls spring to form a mass of beard and hair. With a gesture to two free stumps he bids us sit as a bowl is brought to us, and an old woman with only a single tooth left in her head bites down on the coin we offer in return before slipping it into her pocket.

"What brings you to the Land of the Free, plain-dweller?"

"Not so much a plain-dweller," I retort. "We're mountain folk too. Different mountains, perhaps, but we know where the clouds are better than we'd ever know the location of a meadow-flower or the sea. As to why we're here, we were summoned for no reason by Jotnar. You can imagine why we have a desire to rest easy tonight!"

The hovel fills with knowing laughter. "Well, you'd best have a cup of mead then, if you can afford it," says the man with the curling black hair. "You have need of it, from the sounds of it. What's your name, big woman? My name's Gelis."

"Bemia," I say with relief at our kind welcome. "And this is Alvin, here."

Another coin is brought out and bitten, and then cups of mead nestle in our hands. It is an age since I have tasted it, for the ground is bare now of grain. Its heady honey sweetness goes straight to my head, and after a trial sip or two I regretfully put it back down.

"A song!" claps Gelis. "A song for our guests!"

A man with fierce red hair brings out a fluted bladder-sack and puts it to his lips, creating an unearthly wail, then sets it down.

The Stone-Sword

I tell you now a tale
Of a boy who robbed us all of hope
He plucked from a cursed stone
A sword not meant for mortal hands;
It was a giant's destiny
And the fool lad took it on himself to set the damn blade free.
Oh cursed, foolish lad!
Who asked you to prove your might
And bid us all suffer in winter's blight?
Oh cursed, foolish lad!
Wherever you may be
We curse your name, you fool, you dope,
You bastard child, you simpleton,
You pox-ridden canker-minded whore's son,
For sealing the fate of the Land of the Free.

The song is tuneful enough but the words cause Alvin and I to look at each other with ill-disguised horror.

I clear my throat. "My. That <u>is</u> a pretty song. Is that how the blight actually happened, then? A boy pulled a giant's sword from a stone?"

"Why, yes," says Gelis, perplexed. "Under cover of night. The sword was there, then the next morning it was gone and Jotnar, damn him, had turned the whole world into an ice garden."

"How do you know it was a boy who did it?" I'm careful to look Gelis straight in the eyes as I sip my mead, and avoid all contact with Alvin.

He stares at me as if I've gone mad. "A boy's linen shirt was found at the base of the rock, untorn but soiled with sweat. A large shirt it was, big enough to tie to the mast of a boat and call it a sail, but it was still the collarless shirt of a boy. I can only think he must have taken it off as he laboured to pull free the sword. I thought everyone knew that. And now we're frozen in a tyranny of endless ice, under Jotnar's will. One day I'll find out who that boy was, and if I ever get my hands on him I'll wring his bloody neck."

"Mmm," I say, but no more. I take a sudden interest in my cup of mead.

Gelis relents in his fury. "Aye, well, this is hardly cheery talk with which to entertain our guests. We'll speak no more of it. To freedom!" He roars and downs his cup in one and everyone else in the hovel follows suit. Not wishing to give offence I politely sip at mine, though the cup is barely bigger than a thimble in my huge hands, and out of the corner of my eye I see Alvin doing the same.

"It seems brave of you," I say, "to speak ill of Jotnar when you live beneath his very feet."

Gelis' face darkens. "What of it? What's the worst he can do? Kill us all? I'd rather die with a sword in my hand and the truth on my lips than a beggarly death, falling asleep in the snow with a nagging ache in my empty belly."

"Aye," says one of his men. "Gelis has it right. I feel the same."

The old woman with the one tooth croons and nods at me, and then Gelis has an ill thought.

The Stone-Sword

"Are you spies, to even suggest speaking well of Jotnar?" he asks slowly. "Or can you really be such cowards, big as you are? Whose side are you on, half-breed? The people? Or the giants?"

I share a glance with Alvin.

"I'm on the side of summer, of course," I say eventually. "And on my family's side. But life is what it is. Summer may not come again, and my parents are long-dead, giant or no. Alvin is all the summer in the world to me, now."

The chill silence is broken by nods and "ayes" and wistful glances at the fire. It seems I have said the right thing.

"I hear what you say, big woman," says Gelis. "Aye, what is left but family, when all is said and done? Kings and seasons come and go, even if we do not see the change in our lifetimes, and even a lover may blow away like a leaf in the wind when all is said and done. We'll support each other till the bitter end, whenever that may be, my brothers and I." He nods at his brothers, for such they are, around the fire.

"Sleep, now," commands Gelis. "Or sleep when you wish, but I am tired, and will take myself to bed. A good night to you, travelers. You can rest in this hut, if you like. We all have beds elsewhere."

"Good night," I reply, and it seems that Gelis is the leader here, for when he gets up to leave all his brothers and the old woman with the one tooth follow suit, and Alvin and I are left to enjoy their hospitality all alone.

It should have been a fine night, warm and dry and paid for with coin, but it goes ill.

I awake from a dry warm sleep notched with bad dreams

to the sound of screams and Alvin is no longer beside me. Stumbling out of the hovel, cracking my head on the doorway in my half-sleep, I see Alvin being dragged away by Gelis and his men towards the river.

With a giant roar from my mother's lungs I stride towards Alvin faster than the men can run and pull first one man then another off his back.

Bellowing at Gelis, I hold one man up by his flame-red hair.

"Is this how you treat guests?"

Gelis spits on the hard white ground. "Put him down and hold your peace. You cannot fool me, big woman. Who else but a half-breed would wear a boy's shirt big enough to fashion into a boat's sail? It was a young half-giant who took that sword. And look at you and your whelp brother now, coming to Jotnar's domain on his command, without even knowing why. It doesn't take a cunning man to know it was this <u>fool</u> <u>brother</u> of yours who took the sword and ended all our summers in one go. And Jotnar knows it, and now so do we all." With this he takes a swipe at Alvin with his shovel, and Alvin barely feels the blow, but I can tell from his face that it hurts his heart more than it does his skin.

"It's not my fault," says Alvin softly. "I'd undo it if I could."

Alvin only spoke the words inside him, the words I never allow him to say aloud, but Gelis rushes at him with an aim to kill him for it.

I have no sword on my person. I bear no iron of any kind. But I have the arms of a half-giant, and they are seamed and hard from years of toiling in a forge pit. So I knock down first one man and another, and their slender bones crack and they do not get up again, and I do not have to look at their fallen bodies to know they never will.

And I kill them all, even Gelis, and though tears spring to my eyes at the ill of it all they freeze almost immediately, and my face is set and stone.

"Get up," I say to Alvin, who is cowering by the river's edge. "You'd never hurt a fly. It's not your fault that this happened. You weren't to know. Get up."

And he does, sniffling, and I tenderly wrap his winter cloak around him.

There's nothing left for us in these hovels, on these foothills, so we build a cairn of stones over the fallen bodies of Gelis and his men and when the morning light comes, what there is of it, we travel onwards to the lair of Jotnar, the giants' king.

***

His kingdom has no need of gates. It is blocked by a cliff so high that only a giant could think to climb it, with ice-giants standing guard on either side.

"We're here to see Jotnar," I scream above the tearing wind. "He bid us come."

These giants here are among the tallest I've ever seen: they are the king's guard, strong and tall and sworn to protect him.

One of them raises his boot and makes to bring it down

on our heads, but the other stays him.

"Climb onto my shoulders," says the second giant, his breath a gust of fierce wind, and squats down. With some effort Alvin and I clamber up until we are sitting on the giant's shoulders and holding onto his hair. When we are safe, he rises up and we scrabble onto the cliff edge until we are on a level with Jotnar's home.

We see Jotnar seated before us. He is so big his throne is a mountain, and he is a mountain himself, bearded and terrible, wearing armour that could never have been wrought by human hands, for no forge could be made of such size and heat. The armour must have been fashioned in the belly of a fire-mountain itself, far to the south.

"So this is the boy that dragged out Fjothnar's sword?" His voice sunders the air, and his voice rings in my ears so badly that I am surprised it does not conjure storms.

"That sword was not meant for you, boy. Only a giant can pull it out, and only one giant among many. How did you reshape fate?"

I nudge Alvin. Whatever he says, it must be true, and it must be listened to.

"I'm…good with rock," says Alvin in a near-whisper. His quiet words carry well in mountain air, but he makes himself speak up. "I tried and tried. First one way, then another. It was not strength that made me force the sword from the stone. It was an understanding of metal, of what it wants and how it is."

"And now we have no new king," booms the great giant, Jotnar. "For you cannot be a king, boy, for you are only half a giant, and half a giant is worse than none at all. I have no heir. No legacy. No giant withdrew Fjothnar's sword, the sword of heirs, and now our age will pass, for there is no-one to lead us when I pass. And small folk wonder why we beat the clouds in our fury, and why we throw a winter upon you, so that your lines and lineage will fade along with ours. Is it not clear why we must do these things? You've broken my kind's future, and so you must fare as ill as we."

"You could build a new sword," I say hastily. "The first sword vanished when Alvin pulled it out. Magic. Not his fault. But you can build another."

"We cannot," says Jotnar in a groan that shakes the guts of the land. "Our hands are too large. It is a small sword, with a giant's weight. Our smiths will never make another sword of its kind."

I take Alvin's arm and slowly tuck him behind me, wanting to keep him out of view.

"Why bring us here, then?" I ask, loud as I dare. "If you sit and do nothing, and will not help yourselves, what is it to us? What can we do?"

"You can feel pain," says the new and terrible king of Britain. "The boy will be stretched out on rocks and spread with honey for the ants to feast on while he lives, and his bones will be given to all the tribes of England, one bone to each tribe, and they will do what they choose with them, my only decree being that the bones are kept apart, never to join. And the boy will never have a cairn."

"No!" cries Alvin. The king judged his punishment well.

It is a fate worse then death, to have no ground to sleep in, no roof of stones.

A terrible feeling rises in me and I turn round, but I am too late. My hands grasp air as Alvin falls backwards, arms stretched out, and I see him looking up to where the sun used to be with no mattress to lie on but empty air.

As he pushes himself off the cliff I am too late, and the king's guards standing below are too late, and Alvin falls to his death without a sound.

I am undone. All my summers are undone.

"I have small hands," I say in a voice as weary and final as old age. "I work the dark metals. I will build your sword for you. I will spend my years making you a sword so fine that when it is thrust into rock no man can pull it out, nor giant either…none save one. If I do this, will you bury my brother as he is meant, in one place in the ground?"

"If you can do this we will bury your brother as he is meant," booms Jotnar. "And we will restore summer to the people of Britain, and we will keep the long winter for ourselves once more. But it is an idle promise, half-breed. You cannot do this."

***

And so I stand, naked and chained, in a cave cut into a high cliff. Even if my manacles were unpicked and the cave lay flat on a green meadow, I still would not choose to walk away.

Together but unburied still, my brother's bones lie piled

The Stone-Sword

in a heap in the corner of the cave. White and clean, picked away by carrion, they have lain there for some time. Years, perhaps; in this long winter, it is hard to tell. I would see Alvin have his cairn before I die, for he is a good boy and would harm no-one. It is not his fault.

And with my skin now a pockmarked mass of melted fatty flesh from the sparks that strike, I hold in place my bellows, my tongs, my swages, all alone, with none to help me.

And as I say a prayer to nameless gods I start to fashion yet another sword, hoping it will not join its iron brothers and sisters in failure. I have not Alvin's skill, his hands, his heart. It is size that I was gifted from my mother, not grace.

As metal clangs rudely against metal the winter winds blast into the cave, carrying with them snowflakes, so soft and cold, as inevitable as old age.

Perhaps this new sword will be the one to slide into a giant's stone and remain there.

Perhaps.

But I fear it will not.

The End

In the Hills Beyond Twilight

by William Ransom

Darkness lay heavy across the hills, cold and still and silent. Hetta remembered, as they walked, the soft purple glow of their village. The sky there was full of light, enough to read by, enough to farm. Here the only light was the thin red glow they kept along the horizon, and the sharp curtain of stars like broken glass above.

Hetta was the middle brother. Jer, the oldest, the hunter, the killer, took the lead. He carried his spear, always watching— as if there was any danger here from which he could protect them. Hetta came next, leading the horse, keeping her calm. She trusted him. Last came Col, the youngest. He walked with paper in his hands, trying his best to make maps of their journey.

"We'll be able to use them," he said when Jer asked why he was bothering. "To find our way back."

It made Hetta feel old, to be around someone so young.

None of them had ever been this deep into night before, not even Jer. They had no destination. They simply travelled south, keeping that red line on the horizon to make sure they weren't straying deeper.

***

The fire was brighter than the stars. They kept it banked low, but it still made Hetta nervous. It made him feel watched.

They had cleared a wide circle of earth to keep from igniting the powdery remains of the dead scrub that had once covered the hills, and Col was asleep in his blanket, rolled tight against the chill. The horse was snoring.

Jer was paging through Col's maps. "These are good," he grunted.

Hetta sighed. "He's always been smart."

"Smart. Huh." Jer looked at him. "He thinks we're going back."

"Because we told him we were."

Jer frowned, and looked back at the pages. "He might not have come otherwise. He would have wanted to stay and make amends. They would have hung him."

None of them had shaved since they left the village, and they were all becoming haggard—even Col, young as he was. In the firelight Jer's face looked hollow and pale. Hetta's stomach growled. Jer had been able to hunt some small game at first, but once the light was gone, there hadn't been anything but the supplies they'd brought with them.

"What are we doing?" Hetta asked him.

"Finding a new home."

In the Hills Beyond Twilight

"Where? How much longer? We can't keep going forever. The food will run out. Or eventually we'll be found."

"We won't be found," Jer said sharply. "There are only three of us."

"And a horse."

"Three and a horse, fine. The village didn't start talking about an exodus until there were two dozen families. We're fine."

"That was in twilight. This is night."

"And there are only three of us. We're fine."

Hetta looked out at the darkness, listened to the occasional faint hiss of wind. He could see his breath smoking in the cold. He didn't feel like they were fine. He felt jittery and strange, like there was a thought he couldn't quite grasp. He missed the light. Real light, not this fire that was marking them out in the dark like a shout.

"We couldn't have run towards day?" he said.

"Too big a risk of coming across another village."

"If we're not looking for a village, then what are we doing? Where are we going? We need to decide!"

For all that he claimed they were beneath notice, Jer eyed the night around them very closely and gestured for Hetta to lower his voice. "We can't just join the first village we come to," he said. "What do you think they'll do if three strangers come walking out of the night? Give it a little more time. We'll find the right place. When we turn back towards day, if we can find a place in twilight then we can settle there. Start our own village."

"There's no way that we can turn this into a real exodus."

"Col already thinks that's what it is."

"Col's smart, but he's an idiot," Hetta said. He wrapped his blanket around his shoulders and lay down within reach of the fire. Even with his eyes closed, he could see its glow. He tried to go to sleep. He tried not to feel watched.

***

He dreamed that distant cries woke him, and that he woke alone; and that the Beast hunted him through the darkness of the night. He dreamed of a shadow twice the height of a man stalking around their camp. He dreamed of a door.

But when Hetta woke his brothers were there, Col loading their bags onto the horse, Jer standing tall to peer out at the night as if he could see their path. The fire had burned down to embers so faint that Hetta could only see them because of the darkness.

They were all quiet as they set out; even Col was withdrawn. Their footsteps and the horse's hooves were the only sounds. When they crested a hill a soft wind breathed almost silently across them, so gentle it barely touched them. Nothing like the great storms that could sweep across the villages in twilight. The air was cold against Hetta's face, sharp in his throat. He tried to watch the stars like Jer, to gauge their progress, but the stars stared blindly back at him.

It was after their middle meal, jerky chewed hard as they walked, that they came upon the road. Following a gulley between two hills, they stumbled across a litter of large, regular stones, each the size of a man. At first, none of them could make sense of it; then Col exclaimed, "It's a road!" and showed them where it ran away in each direction. The spot where they stood had been washed out by some ancient torrent, but ahead of them—at the very edge of their vision in the starlight—they could see the spot where it became whole.

"Do we follow it?" Hetta asked, knowing before he said it how Col would react. Their younger brother's grin was visible even in the dark.

"We have to! Have you ever seen a road this wide before? Or this well-made? Look at how solid it still is!" Col had climbed up the bank onto the road itself, where the paving stones were laid so tightly that he couldn't fit a finger between them.

Jer climbed up beside Col, kicked at the stones to test them. "Solid," he said. "And it follows our course. We could make good time."

Good time to where, Hetta wanted to ask, but didn't. He felt a sour unease, looking at the road, so wide that all three of them could lay across it with their arms spread and still have space between them. It was old—anything built in the night had to precede the darkness, when the sun still moved across the sky. Older than the oldest living memory.

But Jer and Col were watching him, waiting for him. He couldn't argue with Jer without Col finding out that they were fleeing, not on an exodus; and this was the first time since they'd woken up that Col seemed himself, excited and eager. So he led the horse up the embankment onto the road, where it shied briefly at the clop of its hooves on the stones. He stroked its nose and made soothing noises to calm it, wishing that he felt as confident as he made himself sound.

They made good time on the road on their journey to nowhere. Without having to navigate up and down hills in the darkness, they didn't have to worry about their footing. Hetta checked the dayward horizon often, eyeing the faint red glow, making sure that the road wasn't pulling them into the night.

They hadn't been on the road for long when they reached a fork—it continued running straight through the hills ahead of them, but a branch broke away and ran deeper into night. Hetta eyed it as they approached, his unease renewed by the change. They were almost to the split when he saw where the new branch led.

There was a city nestled in the dark hills, barely visible in the gloom. The remains of a wall rose up, crumbled in several places to show a sprawl of buildings on the other side. The road ran down to an open gate, a hole in the wall full of darkness, and vanished. Everything past the wall and the first row of buildings was hidden in the night. There was no way to tell how big the city was.

Hetta felt clenched so tight by fear that he was almost shuddering, but when he looked at Col, he saw his younger brother's eyes wide with amazement. Jer leaned on his spear, watching the city with no expression.

Col started walking towards the gate where the road passed through the crumbling wall. Hetta grabbed his shoulder and yanked him back. "What are you doing?" he hissed.

"We can explore it," Col said, confused. "Look for

supplies. We could even camp there. There's no telling what we could find—"

"No," Hetta and Jer said at the same time.

Hetta used his grip on Col's shoulder to push him along the road, away from the city. "We can't go in there. There's no telling what's there. We have to keep moving."

"But...." Col's face slowly fell. Hetta felt relief mixed with guilt; but the relief was much stronger, and he didn't stop pushing. It was as if he could feel the city crouching there, watching them. A thousand empty buildings in the chill dark.

They walked until Jer could see no trace of the crossroad behind them, and then on Hetta's insistence they went further, though they were already tired and hungry. Col walked on his own, but in a sullen silence. He didn't try to make a map, or even look for landmarks. He walked with his head down, staring at the paving stones.

When they finally stopped Hetta could still feel the city somewhere in the dark behind them, but it wasn't looming over them any longer. He knew that if there was light enough to see, if they were back in twilight, it would almost certainly still be clearly visible; but without being able to see it he could at least pretend it wasn't there.

Jer went into the hills with his spear to try finding fresh game. Hetta gathered what kindling he could from the ancient scrub that lined the road and started the fire. This deep into night the plants were all long dead, most of them reduced to little more than dust, but some of the larger ones still had enough brittle wood left to burn. The light made him as nervous as always, but the heat felt good as he crouched over it. Col sat and stared at the ground, still not speaking.

When Jer returned he was empty handed, but Hetta hadn't expected any different. He'd already gotten some of their dwindling rations out of the horse's saddlebags. The three of them ate in silence, while Hetta tried to think of something to say. Night pressed in close around the edges of the fire. He felt that sense again of a thought that he couldn't quite complete, and turned to look behind him, down the road towards the city.

"How much longer do we have?" Col asked.

Hetta turned to him with something close to relief, even though he'd been dreading the question. "Not much further," he said.

"Are you sure?" Col asked, staring at him. "Where are we going?"

"Someplace where we can be safe," Jer said. "We need to find a spot for the new village."

Col's eyes slid towards him, and then back to Hetta. "I'm not an idiot," he said flatly. "And I don't sleep as heavily as you two think. And you talk louder than you realize."

Hetta realized his mouth was hanging open. He shut it, but couldn't think of anything to say.

"What are we <u>doing</u>? Where are we going? At first I thought we were just trying to go on exodus to prove to everybody that we could. That's why I was keeping maps. I thought we'd give up and go home. But we're not going home, are we?" He was angrier than Hetta had ever seen him. "Why are we out here?"

"I killed two of the village elders," Jer said. "Malat and Ebenus."

In the Hills Beyond Twilight

Col turned to look at him. Jer stared back, unblinking.

"I found out that they were planning on sending us away. The three of us, a few other people. Sending us out on exodus. So I went to them and I told them they couldn't. The village was too small to need an exodus. There were too few of us to send. You're too young. But they wouldn't listen to me, they told me we had to go, and I...." Jer's voice caught for a second. "And after, I got you and Hetta and we left. Hetta knew, he saw the bodies, but I didn't want to tell you. I didn't want you to know."

"It wasn't supposed to be like this," Hetta said. Something uncontrollable tried to bubble up in his throat, either a laugh or a sob. He felt like the night was watching them. "We were just trying to...."

"To <u>what</u>?" Col asked, when he didn't go on. "You killed them so that we wouldn't have to go on exodus? For that?"

"They were sending us out to die," Jer said. "Elder Malat saw the way his daughter was looking at me. He wanted me gone—they wanted all of us gone. You two don't remember the last exodus, you're too young, but I do. Four families went out. More than two dozen people. We never heard from them again, they never came back for their possessions or for more people. Exodus is a death sentence. They were trying to kill us."

Col leaned forward, the firelight catching in his eyes and the growing hollows in his cheeks. Speaking slowly and clearly, he said, "So to save us from an exodus, you brought us out on an exodus with only <u>three people</u>?"

The laugh finally belched its way out of Hetta's throat, and he buried his face in his hands. It was really more of a sob. He looked up at the four of them sitting around the fire, the night at their backs, and said, "We're going to be okay. We just—"

Four?

He turned left. There was a figure sitting there, and in one brief moment, Hetta got a perfectly clear look at it in the light of the fire. It was a man, but with a patchwork face, a face made of a hundred other faces, a thousand. Every time he tried to focus on some detail, it was different. It wasn't like looking at a real person; it was like looking at a shadow cast upon a wall. Countless mouths grinned through one mouth. Eyes deeper and darker than the night stared at him.

The Beast had found them.

There was only that one moment, before everything exploded into motion. One frozen moment, but Hetta felt as if it would never end. Staring into those eyes, he felt something come undone inside him, some vital latch that held him together.

Then Jer was lunging, spear in his hand, leaping across the fire. The Beast was already rising, moving so that Jer landed in its grip. Its arms circled him. The hands that had stopped the world clutched him tight. The shadow of its image was changing, and blood was flying off of Jer like rain in a storm, but Hetta didn't see. He was running, sprinting down the road as fast as he could. Running into the night, leaving the fire behind. Running. Somewhere behind him Col shrieked, his voice climbing and climbing, but Hetta never looked back.

There was a thunderous drumming behind him and Hetta choked on his fear, tried to force more speed out of his legs. It caught him and passed him—the horse, eyes rolling wild and white, galloping past him and then gone.

Hetta stumbled, found his footing, stumbled again, ran, ran. Was that Col's scream, still? It didn't matter. He fled down the road, sure that at any moment he would hear the Beast's footsteps coming for him. The road split ahead of him, forked to the side into the hills—

He'd run the wrong way. The city lay there, waiting for him.

He slowed and stopped at the crossroad. There was nothing back the way they'd come, nothing but seemingly endless travel with no supplies. But if he could hide—if he could go to ground and let the Beast pass by, then he could try to follow the road further, to something like safety. A new village, or even just someplace in the comforting twilight.

There was no trace of Col's scream behind him. The Beast had finished with them. It would be coming for him.

Hetta forced himself away from the crossroad, towards the city. Towards the wall growing slowly clearer in the starlight, great fallen sections like bites taken out of it. Towards the gate that gaped dark and empty ahead of him. He almost froze there, but then he heard something from far behind like running feet, and he darted through.

It was darker inside the city walls. Starlight glimmered faintly on the cobblestones but every building seemed to rise out of a pool of shadow. Doors and shutters hung open or missing. Windows were open holes. Hetta stumbled forward, turning at every echo of his footsteps, but he was the only moving thing. The city was cold and empty.

He didn't want to go far from the gate. Once the Beast had left, he needed to be able to find his way back out. He took one turn right down a side street, and then one to the left to be safe. He walked down the middle of the street, not willing to draw close to the buildings until he had to.

Finally he stopped, and stood, and listened. The night was perfectly still and perfectly silent. Arms outstretched, watching his steps from the corners of his eyes, Hetta crept to the closest doorway. The door had been shattered, smashed inward with such force that the hinges had been pulled from the frame. He had to steel himself for a moment, remind himself that there was nothing there—there could be nothing there. The only thing in the night was the Beast, and it was somewhere outside the city, looking for him.

He crept through the doorway into a pitch-black room. He took a step along the wall and then sank to the floor, arms wrapped around himself against the cold and to stop his shivering. He would wait. He wasn't sure how long, but he would wait. He would know when it was safe.

***

Hetta woke, certain that he'd heard a voice.

He lay motionless, lost, listening. The flight, finding his hiding place, all of it was a jumble in his mind. There was no sound—through the doorway, the starlit darkness was silent. Still he felt as if he had been woken by a voice, that stopped just before he opened his eyes.

In the Hills Beyond Twilight

He didn't even remember falling asleep, but here he was, lying curled in a tight ball in a corner. He eased himself out, groaning as he stretched his legs and then freezing at the sound. Small echoes faded away.

He leaned against the wall for balance as he stood. Every muscle was tight and sore. He stood there for a moment, gathering his wits, trying not to remember the scene around the campfire too clearly. How long had he been asleep?

The doorway was visible in front of him, starlight faint and silver against the blackness inside the building. Hetta moved slowly towards it, every step of his boots sounding like a cacophony, and eased outside, looking carefully up and down the street.

There was nothing. No sound, no movement. The uneasy sense of discomfort he'd felt at the campfire was gone. Now he was just cold and thirsty and alone.

His brothers were dead. He wouldn't let himself think about it. He could mourn them later, in the light.

The street was cobbled, scattered with chips of stone, but if he moved slow and careful enough his feet made almost no sound. He headed towards the main street, turned left and walked a block and then turned right. Buildings hid the stars around him, the tallest buildings he'd ever seen; looking at them more calmly now, he saw that half of them were in ruins. Something that might have been a shop gaped open to the street, its entire front wall missing. A black shape lay across his path; when he got closer, he saw that it was an anvil, with a huge dent smashed into its side.

He must be almost to the gate. He looked up, peered ahead for a long moment. The night seemed to grow colder as he realized that the gate was nowhere in sight.

Hetta turned slowly, staring carefully at the street, at the buildings, trying to recognize them from his flight in. He'd retraced his steps. He'd turned right off of the main road and then left to find his hiding place. Hadn't he? Or had it been....

Moving slowly, not letting himself run, refusing panic, he turned and made his way back. Left off the main street again, go a block and turn right. This was the street where he'd hidden.

Wasn't it?

His breath was short and fast as he turned and walked back again. There—a much smaller street tucked between two broken obelisks. Was that it, and he'd missed it? He followed it with growing, horrible certainty that it was not before it opened back into the main street. He stood there for a long, long moment, fighting to get himself under control, before he began to creep along towards the gate again. Two blocks later, he finally admitted to himself that in the darkness, lit only by stars, surrounded by ruined buildings and empty doors, he wasn't sure that this was the main street at all.

He crouched down in the road, panting, pressing his hands against his face so hard that lights crackled behind his eyelids. A single sob escaped him like a cough. Lightheaded, he sagged forward until his forehead was pressed against the smooth, worn stones of the street.

Hetta stayed there on his knees, trembling, until his dizziness faded and he caught his breath. The cold ground felt almost soothing against his skin. When he finally had himself under control, he stood. This might not be the street through which he had entered the city, but it was broad and straight. If he followed it, he would eventually reach the wall. If he followed the wall, he would find the gate. Even built in the time before the Beast, before the endless night, the city couldn't be so large that he would never find his way out.

Under the watchful stars Hetta walked, down the great street through the empty city. He passed through a section of several blocks which had burned almost to the ground, so long ago that the ruins didn't even smell of char. He passed a pit filled with what might have been bones. An ornate chair, mounted on poles and draped with a canopy of rotten silk, lay on its side in the middle of the street. The delicate golden spirals engraved in its wood gleamed faintly in the starlight.

As carefully as he moved, some faint echo of his footsteps still escaped, whispering back at him from the darkness. At first he flinched at it, then accepted it, and then stopped noticing it, until he realized that the echoes of his steps were louder than the steps themselves.

He froze. The steps continued. Somewhere, something was walking. And getting closer.

Hetta leaped for the shadows, out of the starlight that suddenly seemed to reveal him as clearly as a fire. He jumped through the nearest open door and almost plunged down a flight of stairs, invisible in the black. He went down far enough that he could barely see over the top, through the doorway and into the street. He was breathing too loudly, and he clamped his hands over his mouth.

The steps drew closer. Solid and clear—something walking without stealth. Closer. Hetta sucked in a breath and held it tight, and at that moment a dark figure passed in front of the doorway. It never paused. The steps began to recede.

Weakness washed over Hetta, so deeply that he thought for a moment he might faint. Twice he had escaped the Beast. He would wait here for a little longer, and then he would continue—

"And the wizard grew jealous!" shouted a hoarse voice from outside, in the street.

Hetta's head snapped up, his eyes wide. That was Col's voice.

"For in those days the Hundred Knights were known by their deeds, through all the land! And they were the king's strength, and his pride!"

A trick. It had to be a trick. But the voice was drawing away. Hetta crawled to the top of the stairs, eased his head out into the night. There was no one in sight, no motion, only the echoes of Col's voice fading from down the street.

Hetta licked his dry lips. Could the Beast speak? In any story he'd ever heard, had it taken a man's voice? He couldn't remember.

The city was silent. Slow, slow, Hetta crept outside. He waited until his legs began to ache and he had to stand.

He needed to keep moving. He had to get out of the city, get out of the hills, get out of the night. He began to follow the street again, listening for footsteps.

"I have seen!" came Col's voice, from what sounded like

blocks away. "I have seen! I have <u>been shown</u>!" It was his voice, without a doubt. Rough, as if it had been overused, but Col's. He sounded…happy? Excited?

"And so the king became proud! He looked upon the Hundred Knights and said, 'Their works are my works! Their fame is my fame! Their love is my love!'"

Every time Col shouted, Hetta stopped and waited for the echoes to roll away before he moved again. His brother was somewhere ahead of him. Could he catch up to him? Make him stop shouting, bring him along? He thought of the way he had abandoned Col on the road, and felt something that with time and safety could grow into shame but right now was simply an empty twinge. If Col kept shouting, the Beast would hear. Hetta had no doubt of that. And Col was ahead of him. But he couldn't turn around; he'd already followed the street so far.…

"So the jealous wizard told the proud king, 'Their works and their fame and their love is nothing! For you think that the strength of men in this world makes you great, but there is a world behind the world, and you have no understanding of its power!'"

The street opened into a huge, empty square. Hetta paused, hesitant, and then began to make his way across it in a low crouch. He had to go in a straight line. He had to find the same street on the other side, or he'd end up wandering in a new direction.

Something loomed up out of the dark ahead of him. Hetta staggered back, his feet slipping on the stones as he tried to run, before he saw what it was—a huge fountain, cracked and broken. It rose far above his head in a maze of bowls and spouts, all dry as bone. Delicate figures danced around empty pools where water had once flowed. Up close, Hetta saw that every one of their faces had been chipped away.

"And the proud king and the jealous wizard made their wager!" Col's voice seemed to be coming from the edge of the square now, somewhere off to the side. Hetta crouched beneath the ruined fountain, peering into the darkness, but there was only the cobbled stone of the square fading away into the night.

"The Hundred Knights, against the wizard's works! Strength against power, fame against awe!"

Col laughed, high and careless and full of delight, the same laugh that Hetta had heard all his life. But it was loud. So loud. Echoes bounced back and forth in the square, as if there was a crowd all laughing, sounding less sane with every moment. Col's laugh climbed higher, cracked once, and it no longer sounded anything like his normal joy. It sounded more like his scream in the road.

Before he could reconsider, Hetta left the fountain and hurried as quickly and quietly as he could across the square. In the direction he'd been going, searching for the street he'd been following. He would never be able to find Col in the darkness. Even if he did, the Beast would find them soon after. He had to get out.

"And so! And so! The wizard spoke, and reached out of the world!"

There—the edge of the square, the street. Hetta made himself slow down, made himself stay silent. He tried not to listen to Col, expected at any moment for his words to turn into a scream.

"The wizard *opened a door!*"

Were those footsteps? Hetta stopped, scrambled for a doorway. It was impossible to tell if there was any other noise under Col's shouting.

"And through the door came the shadow in the darkness! The hunger! The stranger, the outsider, the calamity! The Beast!"

Its name seemed to shudder in the air.

Hetta waited, sure that naming it would summon it. He huddled inside the doorway, hands clenched into tight fists, teeth grinding against each other. He couldn't think; his mind chased itself in circles, trapped in an echo of its name. The Beast. The Beast.

Slowly, the echoes in the street faded away. Silence fell.

He crept back into the street and went as fast as he dared, pausing to listen with held breath every few seconds before moving on. His cloudy breath caught the starlight faintly, faintly. He ached for light, for warmth, for wind and water and to be home.

"I have seen," Col said, his words climbing into a jagged cackle. He was falling further behind now, growing distant. How much further could the street run? How big could the city be?

"The wizard and the Hundred Knights were equals, for neither could stop the Beast. So ended the wizard's wager with the king. And the Beast reached into the sky, and stopped the sun in its passing, and made the world grow still! And it pulled down the moons and ate them, one by one! And it hunted in the night that never ends!"

Col was almost out of earshot, now. Hetta felt no shame and no regret. He felt nothing but a clawing need to run, to flee. He had to see the thin red line of distant twilight across the horizon.

The street opened ahead of him. He thought at first that it was another square, and had a horrible moment to wonder if he'd been going in a circle. Then he saw the wall, stretching to either side, broken in places but still high above his head; and he realized that he had reached the gate.

"Every city," came Col's voice faint and fading from behind. Hetta began to run. His feet slapped loud against the street, but he didn't care, and couldn't have stopped himself if he did. "Every castle! Every town! The Beast came to all of them! Until finally men huddled tight together and cast each other out when their villages grew too large, to save themselves and hide from the Beast's hunger. But the Beast sees. The Beast watches. No one is beneath the Beast's notice, and the Beast spares no one! The Beast sees every village, every family, every life! The Beast merely waits!"

Hetta burst through the gate, out of the city, into the open night. He almost shouted for joy. He was out, he was free. He would reach the crossroad. He would strike through the hills, back into twilight, find a village, find a home—

But there was no red line of light along the horizon.

The stars fell in their razor curtain straight to the black hills. The night was unbroken. There was no light, no hint of distant heat. Only the empty road and the empty dark and the empty hills, covered with the dust of a vanished world. He was on the wrong side of the city.

Hetta sobbed, but before his steps could slow, he heard it coming behind him.

He looked back over his shoulder. A shadow twice the height of a man was bearing down on him, eyes like the stars watching him hungrily.

Hetta ran. He ran, though he knew it was hopeless. The Beast drew closer, closer, letting him stay just ahead, toying with him. He laughed and sobbed and ran. He would run forever, until he reached frozen midnight.

The Beast was beside him, looking as it had at their campfire. It grinned at him with its countless patchwork mouths, and reached out to take him by the arm.

***

Col had climbed the side of a tower, and now he perched on a shattered ledge. He rested his chin on his drawn-up knees, looking out into the night. He couldn't see Hetta or the Beast, but he knew where it was. Knew what it was doing to Hetta. The Beast had shown him everything.

"I have seen!" he called again to the city, let the echoes die one by one away.

He sat there for a long time. The Beast finished with Hetta and moved on, to some village or some exodus or some other ruined city. There were plenty to choose from.

Eventually Col stood, his toes almost touching the

edge. He walked to the other side of the tower, fearless above the drop. From this height, the red line of twilight painting the dayward horizon seemed brighter, although it could have been his imagination.

He would go there, Col decided. Perhaps he would spread the knowledge the Beast had given him. He would cross the hills, pass through twilight and evening, greeting all the people as they waited for the Beast to come, telling everyone he met what he had been shown. In his mind it was all perfectly clear, mountains to cross and seas to swim, into the day's hot embrace.

He would keep walking, until he reached bright and burning noon, and burned away.

The End

Blade Of Fire

by Steven S. Long

"Keldar, you can't do this. It's too dangerous, and you know it!" Vina said, putting her hand on his arm.

He shrugged off his sister's hand and continued putting food into his saddlebags. The grim look that had been on his face ever since word reached Bridgewater that Torm and his pack of scavenger-bandits had kidnapped Unara didn't change.

"Keldar, *listen* to me!"

He turned on her, his eyes flaring with the red-gold light that usually shone when one of the Gifted was angry or impassioned. "I *have* listened to you. The ruins of Kleev are as dangerous as you say. But I can't abandon her to those savages— and that fat fool she's supposed to marry certainly isn't going to do anything about it."

"And what can you do, one guard against Torm and all of his men? You may be Gifted, but you're no wizard to descend on them and destroy them with a thought. They'll slaughter you like a pig! You don't have to do this just to prove you're a better man than Arlingson is—and that she made the wrong choice."

"You're right," he said, his voice softer now. "I don't have to do this to *prove* I'm better than Arlingson. I have to do it because I *am* better than Arlingson. Who could leave her to Torm and still call himself a man?"

He finished stuffing food and supplies into his saddlebags and headed for the door. Before he walked out he turned around and saw Vina standing near the table, angry, fearful, tears running down her face.

"Don't worry," he said with a smile. "I'll be back with Unara in a few days."

"If you're going to throw your life away for a woman who wants nothing to do with you, go ahead. But don't expect me to mourn when you don't come back." She snatched up a broom and began sweeping with short, angry strokes, her back to him.

He left the little house where he lived with Vina and her family and walked through the narrow, muddy streets of Bridgewater toward the main gate. Soon he came to the town square, where small knots of people stood around discussing the news and wondering what would be done about it. Never before had Torm and his men taken a captive so close to the town walls.

One of the groups clustered around a familiar, hated figure: Roane Arlingson, the town's richest merchant and the man Unara was to wed. Some of the people around him were his personal guards; the rest were the usual handful of people trying to curry favor with him. Keldar tried to hurry on through the square toward his destination, but he wasn't able to avoid Arlingson's observant eye.

"Keldar!" the merchant said peremptorily, gesturing to Keldar to come over. Keldar stopped but didn't bother to walk to Arlingson. With a scowl Arlingson came to him, his plump body jiggling with every step.

"Where are you going?" he asked when he got close enough to talk.

"To Kleev, to do what you should already be doing: get Unara back."

"I'm not going to throw my men's lives away on a fool's errand. She's already dead, Keldar."

"They sent word asking for ransom, didn't they? A thousand silver eagles, I heard."

"You think I'm going to pay them? Don't be stupid."

"Of course, you're not going to pay. What could I be thinking, that Unara's husband-to-be would want to get her back?"

Arlingson's scowl deepened. "Have a care, Keldar. Watch your tone with me. You're still just one of the Baron's Guard, for all your airs."

"I may just be a Guard, but at least <u>I'm</u> willing to try to save her."

"Even you aren't so stupid that you think she's still alive. But suppose she is—what can *you* hope to do against Torm and his bandits?" Arlingson sneered. Captain Darrson and all the rest of you Guard have never brought him to bay."

"I'll do whatever I can. I'd rather die trying than wonder if she was killed because I wasn't brave enough to try to get her back. Stay here and cower behind your guards' shields. I'll get her back myself, without your help, and when I do she'll see who truly loves her."

"She is betrothed to _me_, not you, and I will decide what's to be done!"

"You have no say over me, Arlingson. I'm not one of your lapdogs." Keldar turned his back on the fat merchant and continued walking.

"Captain Darrson will have something to say about this!" Arlingson shouted after him. Keldar ignored him.

Bridgewater wasn't a large town; it took him only a few more minutes to reach his destination: the guardhouse at the eastern gate. He went inside, passing by several of his fellow Guards on the way. Seeing the expression on his face they didn't try to talk to him.

He put on his brigandine and his helmet, then got down his crossbow. It was never possible to predict when raiders or monsters out of the Wildlands might attack Bridgewater, so he always kept his weapons in good repair. The crossbow's mechanisms were well-oiled so the trigger pulled smoothly and didn't throw off his aim.

With armor on his back, his sword and dagger at his hip, and the crossbow and a quiver of quarrels in his hands he went out to the stables to get his horse. He led it out into the courtyard and began packing for his trip.

He was putting the saddlebags on his horse and adjusting the saddle when Captain Darrson came storming in. "Guard Berrenson, what in the name of the Dead Gods do you think you're doing?"

Blade of Fire

Keldar turned to face him. Darrson was a tall, broad-shouldered man, past his prime but still strong and confident. He was used to intimidating people, but Keldar had never felt any fear of the man, which only made Darrson dislike him. The feeling was mutual.

"I'm making ready to ride to Kleev. I'm going to try to rescue Unara daHelanor. Torm and his bandits kidnapped her from one of Arlingson's coaches a few hours ago. They killed three of his guards, too. They only left one alive to bring back their demand for a thousand silver eagles to return her unharmed."

"No, you're not. It's Arlingson's woman that's been taken, and him that's asked to ransom her, so he'll handle the matter himself. Unpack your things and return to duty on the wall."

"He's not going to do a damn thing. He's already told me it's too dangerous and expensive. When he doesn't respond they'll use her until she dies and then toss her body to the carrion scavengers."

"They probably already have, you fool."

"As long as there's hope she's alive, I'm going after her."

"No, you're not, Guard Berrenson, and that's an order."

Before Darrson could react Keldar punched him in the face. The captain tottered two steps and then fell flat on his back, out cold. Blood dripped from his smashed nose.

Without another word Keldar mounted his horse, rode through the east gate, and headed toward the ancient, ruined city of Kleev.

***

It took him two hours to ride through the farmlands surrounding Bridgewater. The area was heavily patrolled by the Baron's Guard, but even so it took a hardy breed of man to live outside the town walls, exposed to raiders and monsters. But they were the lifeblood of the town; the trade coming up and down the river couldn't bring enough food for everyone inside the walls, much less the travelers that passed through from time to time.

Once past the cultivated area he entered the Wildlands. That was what folk called the wilderness regions between settlements, where the raw, wild magic unleashed by the death of the gods and the breaking of the world a thousand years ago still ran free. Unchecked by wizard's spell or the bastion of civilization, it could give birth to monsters and other horrors or warp the very land itself.

Even in the Wildlands a patrol could usually ride in safety, for few of the beasts and monsters that lived there would dare to attack an entire group of armed men. But one man alone might seem succulent prey to many of them, so he remained wary as he rode.

***

It walked slowly along a low forested ridge, moving its bulk carefully so it made as little noise and disturbance as possible. Again and again it tasted the air with its tongue, seeking something to eat.

Blade of Fire

From the ground below a welcome scent came to its nostrils—the smells of horse, and metal, and man. The smell of food.

But man and metal could be dangerous. Like many of the monstrous things of the Wildlands, it was intelligent, nearly as intelligent as a man, and it had not lived to become so large and mighty by taking foolish risks. It would attack the man and his mount from surprise, giving them no chance to resist, and then feast at its leisure.

It crept to the edge of the ridge, concealing itself in a thicket, and looked down.....

***

With little more sound than the rustle of leaves the creature sprang, its six scaly feet poised to plunge their deadly talons into rider and horse. But that slight noise was all the warning Keldar needed. Glancing upward he saw death plummeting toward him and reacted with lightning speed. Kicking his horse in the ribs to get it out of the way, he drew his sword.

The lizard landed with a thump that shook the ground and bounded after him, frighteningly quick, frighteningly powerful.

Wheeling his horse around to face the beast, Keldar called upon his Gift: the ability to enhance the weapons he wielded with elemental force. He drew forth the power of Earth to sharpen and strengthen his blade. For the briefest second it glittered brightly in the sun, but that meant nothing to the lizard. It leapt, intending to knock the man out of the saddle and crush him to death so it could sate its hunger.

But Keldar ducked beneath its leap, thrusting with his sword as the monster passed over him. The magically sharp blade cut through the thick scales on the lizard's belly and sheared off one of its legs. The monstrous thing hiss-howled in pain, a sound unlike anything Keldar had ever heard in his life.

Limping now, less sure of itself, the lizard turned back toward him—but Keldar was too fast for it. Driving his horse close to the beast he slashed downward with all his strength, shearing through the thing's spine and into one of its shoulders. His horse veered away just in time to keep him from being battered by the creature's fall.

It lay there, twitching, shrieking, unable to move most of its body. Wary of its spasmodically snapping jaws, Keldar rode close again and thrust his blade deep into the lizard's skull. It twitched and hissed a few times more, then lay still. Greenish-black blood continued to pour from its wounds for a long time.

***

Keldar spent that night in a small hollow that provided some shelter from the wind and some concealment from whatever might roam the land by moonlight. Sleeping alone in the Wildlands was dangerous, but he had no choice; he couldn't ride through the night and be in any shape to fight Torm and his men on the morrow. A campfire, a blade ready at hand, and his own tendency to sleep lightly would be his only protection.

He woke several times during the night, stirred from his

sleep by noises from out of the darkness: a howl, an owl-like screech, a strange slithering sort of sound. Once he saw red eyes staring at him from the impenetrable shadows beyond the mouth of the hollow; he built the fire back up and the eyes vanished.

The morning dawned grey and cloudy, fitting his mood. He broke his fast with a bit of sausage and cheese from his saddlebags, then mounted up and continued his journey. The road led into a forest; he became even more alert, not knowing what sort of creatures might lurk in the woodlands.

Before noon he broke out of the forest and could at last see the ruins of the ancient city of Kleev. Clustered in the center, like a gigantic forest themselves, were the metal skeletons of what had once been great towers, some of them twisted or bent at impossible angles by the magics that had destroyed the city— and that, for some inexplicable reason, had kept them from falling ever since. At night, he knew, some of them glowed with an eerie witchfire, the centuries-old remnant of the awesome forces with which the Dead Gods had fought their final battle.

Another hour's riding brought him to the outskirts of the city. Staying on horseback would make it harder to remain unseen, so he found a sheltered thicket and tied his mount loosely to a sapling. That way if Torm's men got the better of him, or some Wildlands creature found the thicket, the horse could break free and fend for itself.

Sword in sheath and crossbow in his hands he entered Kleev, every bit as wary as he'd been in the forest. Creatures as dangerous as those of the Wildlands often lived in ruins such as these. Even worse were the two-legged monsters, men as clever as himself who knew the ruins and wouldn't hesitate to kill him for what he carried—or for the meat on his bones. Any scavenger desperate enough to live in Kleev and strong or smart enough to survive there was a threat, and the worst of them all were Torm and his bandits.

His every sense alert, he crept through streets all too often clogged with rubble, underbrush, and oblong heaps of rusted metal. He kept his back to crumbling remnants of brick walls when he could; cover and protection were both desirable. As he went he marveled, and not for the first time, at the city around him. What magics must the Ancient Men have commanded, to build such greatness that the signs of it could still be seen a thousand years later? Perhaps they were so powerful they challenged the gods themselves, and when the gods sought to restrain them they fought back, and so destroyed their world and their gods with it. Not even the wisest wizards could say for certain what had happened to the Dead Gods or the world that worshipped them.

He stopped to rest and considered his position. He knew Torm's gang laired in Kleev; survivors of their attacks had heard them speak of it, and they'd been seen riding into the ruins. But Kleev was an enormous place where the rocky ground made tracking people difficult at best. The only way to find them would be to do what he did when hunting deer in the forest: hide in a likely place and wait for them to come by.

Another quarter-hour's stealthy progress and he found the perfect spot: a wide intersection where two broad roads met. Compared to most of the streets he'd been walking on it was clear and level, and thus a likely path for anyone who frequently came through this part of Kleev. He crouched behind a thorny bush growing in the shadow of a shattered wall and waited, crossbow at the ready.

Hours passed. A few times he saw furtive movements around the periphery of the intersection that might have been scavengers or large beasts; once he heard the sound of someone—or something—digging nearby. The eerie feel of the place began to wear on his nerves. He was sitting in a vast hall of the dead, and who knew what their restless spirits might do to one who lingered too long over their graves?

Then the sound of laughter reached his ears. Peering stealthily around the corner of the wall he saw two men on horseback approaching the intersection from the east. They wore mismatched leather clothes, carried swords and crossbows, and took no trouble to conceal their presence. These could only be two of Torm's bandits; no one else in this part of Kleev would be so brazen.

Messengers? A patrol? Were they going to Torm's place of refuge or coming from it? There was no way he could say for certain—though to Keldar's experienced eye they looked too rested to be returning to the gang's lair. And if they had recently left Torm's hideout, following them was too dangerous; he didn't know where they were going or how long they'd be gone. But they, or perhaps something they carried, could tell him where Torm was.

Slowly he raised his crossbow to his shoulder. As the two riders entered the intersection he took aim at the one furthest from him, exhaled, and then firmly squeezed the trigger.

The quarrel pierced the man's chest; with a strangled gurgle he fell from the saddle. Before he hit the ground Keldar burst from his hiding place, drawing his sword as he ran. The other bandit shook off his surprise, drew his own blade, and spurred his horse toward Keldar.

They met with a clash of blades that left both men unwounded. From the way the bandit wielded his sword he would be no match for Keldar in an ordinary duel—but here he had the advantage of height and mobility. That advantage had to be eliminated.

As the bandit wheeled his horse around for another pass, Keldar stood his ground. When horse and rider came close, Keldar dodged to the right, out of the way of the bandit's slash, and stabbed at the steed—not to kill, but deep enough to make it rear from pain and fear. The bandit, unbalanced by his sword-stroke, wasn't able to keep his seat.

He hit the ground hard, but to Keldar's surprise came up again swiftly, ready to fight. He was tougher than he looked it seemed, and so Keldar took no chances. He called on his Gift, imbuing his own blade with the elemental power of Water. Now his foe could no more hope to block Keldar's attack than he could to hold back an ocean wave.

The bandit came close, sword raised to defend himself or lash out to take advantage of an opening. Keldar thrust with what seemed like an easily-parried blow—but almost of its own accord his Water-enhanced blade snaked around the bandit's sword to plunge into the man's belly. With a groan the bandit toppled to the ground, his sword falling from now-nerveless fingers.

Keldar stood defensively for a moment, still wary but regaining his breath—calling upon his Gift tired him out far more quickly than ordinary combat. No other attackers appeared; he heard no sounds of alarm.

He flipped the bandit over on his back with a nudge from his booted foot. Hands clutched over his stomach wound, the bandit glared at Keldar. "Corag take you!" he cursed, spittle flying from his lips.

Keldar pinked the bandit in the shoulder, eliciting a yelp of pain. "Listen well, scavenger," he said as the man writhed in pain. "That belly wound's going to kill you slow. I could leave you here to die in the hot sun—assuming nothing comes along to make a meal of you before that happens. Or I could finish you off now, quick and easy, if you tell me what I need to know."

"What?" the bandit rasped through clenched teeth.

"Where I can find Torm."

The bandit's face contorted briefly, but like most of his kind he had no loyalty to anyone but himself. "Half a mile east. Big building with a bird on it." He lifted one hand to grasp an amulet he wore around his neck. Keldar reached down and tore it from him to look at it more closely. It had a strange angular shape, suggestive of a bird of prey.

"My thanks," Keldar said. Without another word he drove his sword through the bandit's heart. The man's body convulsed once, briefly, then fell back and lay still. After wiping the blood from his blade on the bandit's greasy leathers, Keldar sheathed his sword, retrieved his crossbow, and cautiously made his way east.

***

An hour later Keldar was crouched behind another broken wall looking at what had to be Torm's refuge. At the bottom of one of the metal towers men had used bits of rubble and scrap lumber to repair and extend some walls, creating a three-story structure and a stable. From part of the tower several dozen feet above hung an emblem that matched the amulet the bandit had shown him.

It took Keldar a long time to reach his hiding spot unseen by the guards atop the lair, but fortunately they weren't giving their duties their full attention—one leaned lazily against a metal pillar, two played at dice. He was close enough to the building to hear noises from inside, though he couldn't make out specific words. Through the grimy glass in a few windows he could occasionally see someone.

The only door was a sturdy wooden one, perhaps something the bandits had stolen from some farmer or town. No one stood guard outside, but it had to be locked—and behind it were at least a dozen men. Silently he cursed himself for not asking the bandit how many men Torm had, but there was nothing he could do about it now. He settled down to wait for an opportunity, hoping he wouldn't have to hide until they were all drunk or asleep.

An hour later he had his chance. He heard a deep voice shouting inside, then the clatter of men moving about. A few minutes later three of Torm's bandits, all well-armed, left the building, got their horses from the stable, and rode off to the east. Ten minutes later another group of three rode west—and behind them they left the door into Torm's lair slightly ajar.

Praying to the Young Gods no one would shut it before the riders were out of sight, Keldar waited, watching the guards carefully. When the one not dicing moved away to relieve himself, Keldar made his move, running as quietly as he could to the side of the building where the guards couldn't see him. He crept up to the door and peered through. Inside were at least half a dozen men. Two were sitting and eating, the others were sharpening their weapons or taking care of other chores. Of Torm there was no sight—and he had no way of knowing how many men might occupy the other floors. But he'd never have a better chance to rescue Unara than now, when six men were absent.

He drew his sword and dagger slowly so they made very little noise, took a deep breath, and kicked in the door. All the men in the room looked up in surprise; one who was walking near didn't even have time to shout before Keldar's swift slash cut halfway through his neck.

Then Keldar was in among them, calling on the elemental force of Air to fill his blades with the swiftness of the stormwinds. He slashed and ducked, stabbed and parried, a whirlwind of death that Torm's men could not stand against for all their viciousness and strength. Swept up in the frenzy of combat, he had only the briefest awareness of his actions—his sword cutting through a bandit's throat, his dagger thrusting beneath a ribcage to pierce a man's heart—and even less of the blows his enemies tried to deal him in return. Shouts and screams filled the building.

More men poured into the room: the three guards from the roof, come running down at Torm's call to kill the attacker. With battle-cries and curses they rushed down the stairs ready to hack Keldar to ribbons—only to meet death themselves. With the power of Air still at his command Keldar wove between them like a winter's wind, leaving each man marked with a deadly wound. They joined the others gasping out their lives on the floor.

In less than a minute's bloody work all his foes were dead— all save one. From the room at the top of the stairs stepped a tall, broad-shouldered, heavily muscled man, an axe in one hand and a dagger in the other: Torm the Cruel, bandit-lord of Kleev. "You must think yourself a great swordsman, to have slain so many men," he said with a sneer. "But those dogs were no true warriors. Test your skill against me, little man, and meet your death!"

Keldar backed away from the stairs, unwilling to fight on such treacherous ground, and let Torm come to him. The big man moved with surprising speed and agility for one so large, and Keldar could see from the way he held his weapons that he had both good training and experience in battle. He swallowed hard and called the power of Earth into sword and dagger.

As Torm stepped off the stairs Keldar struck, slashing downward at the bandit-lord's right shoulder. Torm didn't even raise his weapon to parry—but Keldar's blade struck him and bounced away with a jarring impact that nearly shook the sword from his hand!

Torm smiled wolfishly—and his eyes glowed red-gold with savage amusement. "Did you think you were the only one touched by magic, guardsman? You have a strong Gift, but mine is even

Blade of Fire

stronger: No blade will bite upon me, no arrow will penetrate my skin! Now you will die, helpless and stupid, knowing that Torm is your better!"

Torm swung his axe; Keldar backed away, not daring to try to parry such powerful blows for fear Torm would snap his sword in two. His mind raced—how to defeat a man who cannot be cut? The sharpness of Earth, the speed of Air, the unavoidability of Water, none of these were of any use if the target of the blow was better armored than the giant reptiles of the Wildlands.

But perhaps the power of Fire could burn him.

Deftly avoiding Torm's next attack, Keldar concentrated, imbuing his weapons with Fire. The blades burst into flame, and as Keldar maintained his concentration they went from fiery-orange to white-hot. Stepping out of the way of Torm's axe-stroke, he lashed out, hitting the big man in the neck.

Torm screamed in agony. Keldar had not cut his flesh, but the side of his neck was burned black by the blazing blade. With axe and dagger Torm slashed swiftly, viciously, trying to drive Keldar away from him. But Keldar dodged and cut, hitting the bandit-lord on arm and face, eliciting more bellows of pain.

Keldar's blade flashed again and struck Torm in the side, touching not only flesh but the bandit-lord's clothing as well. In mere seconds Torm was burning like a torch, his tunic and pants aflame. Roaring with torment and fury he charged, trying to overwhelm Keldar and drag him down to Death's realm too. Mustering all his strength and speed Keldar knocked Torm into one of the room's metal columns. Torm hit the column, stopped moving, and slumped to the cement floor.

Keldar leaned wearily against a wall, panting like a bellows, his sword dragging the ground. Of all the elements he could call into his blades, Fire was the most tiring, and he had held it in both of them. Thank the Young Gods there were no more of Torm's men to fight!

As some of his stamina returned he began to feel the pain of wounds—shallow cuts on thigh and arm, a gash in his side where a bandit's blade had bitten through his brigandine, light burns where he'd touched Torm. He used his dagger to slice the tunic off a dead bandit and tore it into strips to make crude bandages to staunch the flow of blood.

His immediate needs taken care of, Keldar began to search the building. Unara had to be here somewhere; he dared not even think of the alternative. He found a few things of value the gang had stolen in its raids, including a small wooden chest of coins, but no Unara. The despair inside him grew deeper and darker.

Eventually he came to Torm's rooms on the upper floor. There he found her, bound hand and foot, gagged, and thrown into a closet. He reached down gently, carefully, and cut her bonds, then removed the gag and helped her to her feet.

He could see relief in her face, and gratitude, but something else as well, something he didn't understand until she spoke. "I had...not expected you."

"You thought some of Arlingson's men would come for you."

"Yes. Where are they?"

"He didn't send any. He left you for dead."

"You lie! Roane would never do that. He loves me."

"He loves money more—paying the death-price to the wives

of his guards who'd die trying to rescue you would wound his heart more than abandoning you."

She slapped him then, the crack of it echoing loudly in the close confines of the room.

He didn't speak for a few moments as he stared at her. The fury in her expression was born half of the insult he'd just given her, half of the knowledge that he was right. But it didn't change things. He could see that she still preferred Arlingson's money and prestige to his own lowly position. Finally he said, "Are you ready to go now?"

She nodded, still too angry to talk to him. He turned to go and she followed.

***

It took less than an hour to get back to his horse. He knew the way now, and the greatest danger facing him, Torm's gang, was greatly diminished. He could have gone even quicker, but he had to watch over Unara to make sure she didn't hurt herself, and that slowed him.

They rode, she sitting behind him, until it was fully dark so they could put as much distance as possible between themselves and the perils living in the ruined city. They camped for the night near a wooded copse. Unara said little, rarely looking at him or getting close to him. They slept fitfully, each standing guard while the other snatched a few hours' rest.

In the morning they continued, Keldar walking while Unara rode. The uncomfortable silence between them continued, broken only rarely by some curt instruction or warning from Keldar that Unara obeyed without responding to.

By mid-afternoon they reached the outskirts of the settled lands around Bridgewater, where untamed forest and field began to give way to plowed ground. Keldar brought the horse to a halt and began removing the saddlebags.

"Why are we stopping?" Unara asked. "We're almost home."

"You are," Keldar said. "But I'm heading north. If I walk fast I can reach the next settlement before it gets too late. Tell the Baron what happened, and have him pay the bounty for Torm to my sister. Give her this chest of coins as well."

"But...but why? Bridgewater is your home too."

"There's nothing for me there. My sister has her husband and children; she doesn't need me. You have Arlingson, much good may he do you. All there is for me is a career in the Guard taking orders from that fool Darrson, and I'm through taking orders. I'll find my own way in the world, one where I answer to no man I do not respect."

"You can't go off alone! You'll be killed before nightfall."

"I went to Kleev and rescued you all on my own, didn't I? I'll be all right. I've got my sword and my crossbow, and plenty to eat in these saddlebags. Go on, now." He smacked the horse on the rump and it took off at a slow trot. He stood and watched until Unara was nearly out of sight, then turned and began his journey north.

The End

Waist Deep

by Bill Blume

A trail of smoke in the distant sky gave Dale the closest thing to hope he'd seen since his travels had brought him back into the Ice Lands. He'd lost track of time, so he couldn't say when he'd last seen another man or woman. There were no more seasons to mark the end of one year and the start of the next. The four seasons had given way to the Three Deserts which never changed.

Pain stabbed into his toes with each step. The snow, which came up to his knees, had invaded his boots like a tiny army of daggers. The smoke promised a fire and warmth, so he pushed forward.

Then he heard the howl.

He stopped and readied his rifle. Whatever had made that noise sounded big. Even worse, it had come from the direction of the smoke. He couldn't say how close, though. The forest was full of trees, but they were all leafless timber. Sound travelled like the wind in this place.

His stomach ached, and that reminder of several days

spent eating nothing but handfuls of snow pushed him forward. That howl meant food. The only question was which of them would get eaten, him or whatever monster had made that noise.

The sun was moving low, barely visible behind the overcast clouds, when he reached the source of the smoke. He'd hoped to find people and shelter. What he found was disappointment.

Small patches of flame still burned on the bones of what had been a house. Whoever had called this gutted wreck home must have been here a long time. They'd built a wall out of ice. The ingenuity to make the ice bricks impressed him, but it didn't stop whatever created the gaping hole in the wall. Four men, lined up shoulder-to-shoulder, could have walked through that opening.

He waited, with his rifle in his hands, behind the trunk of a large tree. Whatever creature had cried out earlier, it had stayed silent since. Chances favored it was busy gnawing on the former occupants of the cremated house. A trail of red dotted the snow heading north from the opening in the icy fence.

Deciding he was alone, Dale trudged through the snow to the opening. Up close, he couldn't decide if the tracks belonged to one large animal or many smaller ones. He wasn't sure which was worse, and "animals" was being optimistic. About the only thing man shared the Desert of Fire with was the Wraiths. Only the sky and the dead homeowner knew what creature had spontaneously spawned from the ice in this place.

He'd hoped there might be enough of the house left to give him a place to stay the night, but that hope died fast. The house's charred skeleton didn't look likely to survive the night.

Waist Deep

Sunset was minutes away. He wouldn't survive the night without a fire, but the light might call back whatever had ruined this place. The chimney still stood, like a middle finger salute to the gods and the home's destroyer. He decided to take his chances and use the fireplace for its intended purpose.

As he came closer to the chimney, he realized there was fresh smoke coming from its top. A faint glow emanated from the mouth at its base. The warmth called to him, and he ran the rest of the way.

He expected to find a fire, but the only thing that occupied the inside of the chimney was that warm glow. The light was coming from below the ground.

The floor of the house had burned away to reveal a stone foundation. If there was a lower level, then he didn't see a way to it through the stone. Against his feet's wishes, he stepped back into the snow and circled the foundation. He found a door leading down into the ground on the far side of the chimney. It had to be a storm cellar. The house where he'd grown up had one of these. When the earth tilted, his family had survived the first few weeks in their storm cellar. As the oceans and land masses shifted, they'd been forced from their home. Only within the past few years, at least he assumed it had been that long, did the world seem to settle.

Dale slung his rifle over his shoulder to free his hands. He touched the door and was shocked to realize it was made of metal. The builder must have found it somewhere near here. An entire city might be hidden beneath the snow in this mountain range. The surface of the earth was rewritten too much to know where any nation or city had stood.

He pulled the door open and jumped back in time to avoid taking an arrow in the chest.

The unexpected attack sent him sprawling into the snow. He scrambled to get his rifle back in his hands, but he knew he didn't have a chance. "Stop! Wait! I'm human!"

Two figures darted up out of the ground and stared down at him along the shafts of their drawn arrows.

"It can talk?" the smaller of the two said.

The big one next to him didn't say anything. He just held his bow and arrow ready with a pair of arms as thick as some of the tree trunks in this forest.

"Please, don't." Dale gave up on his rifle and held up his hands in a show of surrender. "I'm not an 'it.' I'm human, same as you."

"If you're human, then why is your skin so dark?" The smaller one seemed to be the only one who did any talking.

"You never seen a black man?"

"What's a 'black man'?"

Wasn't that just his luck? These ignorant hillbillies were probably going to kill him. The only thing that had kept him alive this long was that they spoke the same language.

"Listen, I'm human, same as you. I just have a different skin color. I'm guessing you ain't ever seen any Latinos either?"

The confused look on their faces answered that. Actually, only the small one looked confused. The big guy didn't seem to know any expressions beyond dull intensity. Despite the difference in size and demeanor, they looked a lot alike, down to the same scraggly, red beards. Probably a safe bet they were related.

"I'm just looking for some shelter for the night," Dale said. "Wasn't expecting to find anyone in there, not with the state of things up top."

The quiet one looked at his little brother and shrugged. Nice to see there was a brain in there, even if he didn't say much. The small guy nodded, and they lowered their arrows.

"What's your name?" the little brother asked.

"I'm Dale. You two?"

"I'm Tor." Then he pointed to his big brother. "This is Zalm."

Zalm offered a hand and yanked Dale up.

"Just you two?" Dale asked as he picked up his rifle and slung it over his shoulder.

Neither answered. One look at Tor said it all. They were it, as of a few hours ago.

Dale pointed to the cellar's open door. "Why don't we go inside, get warm, and——"

A howl echoed from the North. He didn't need to say anything else to get them back in the cellar. Wasn't the biggest space, especially with "Paul Bunyan" in there, but then it definitely wasn't built for comfort.

"You boys build this?"

Tor busied himself with the fire. "Our parents built it. Mom was a construction worker before the world broke."

That explained a lot about the place. Dale wished he could've seen it before everything burned. Now that he wasn't worrying about getting impaled by wooden arrows, he realized these two guys looked young. They probably were born after the world shifted.

"Where did you come from, Dale?"

"Texas, originally." The blank look on Tor's face was a mirror of Zalm's and added to the family resemblance. "I've been all over. Was born just five years before everything went to shit. My parents stuck mostly with the ocean, but my stomach never took well to life on a boat."

Tor stared at him with wide eyes. "Is it true? The stories about the leviathans?"

"I've only seen one. Was on a boat that was part of a small fleet. What I saw looked like a sea serpent. Split the biggest ship right down the middle. Only two ships out of five got away. Crew of the ship I was on mutinied, killed the captain and sailed for land." He decided it might be best to leave out the part where he shot the captain in the back of the head with the same rifle that was in his lap. "Ship wrecked on some coral a mile short of the coastline. My parents didn't survive that. Only a handful of us reached land. We must have landed smack in the middle of the Desert of Fire. Damn well-named place, too."

Tor offered him a water skin. Must have thought he was thirsty by the way his voice cracked. Just the memory of that place roasted him.

"Man came through here about a year ago," Tor said. "Claimed there were creatures made of flame. We weren't sure whether to believe him. He wasn't a good man."

"Desperation can make a man do bad things."

Waist Deep

"He hurt our mother." Tor didn't need to say more than that. His tone said plenty. Dale remembered more than one man getting tossed overboard for trying to force himself on a woman.

"Well, he wasn't shittin' you. The wraiths live in the lava. One climbed out of a pool right in front of me." That was the last night he'd seen any of the shipwreck's survivors. They scattered when the wraiths attacked. In his dreams, he still heard the wraiths' wails, the sound they made when they chased him up the rocks. For all he knew, he was the only survivor.

Dale took another chug from the water skin and handed it back to Tor. "Barely any water to be had down there. Had to drink my piss just to stay alive long enough to get out of that place."

Tor glanced down at the water skin with a sudden look of disgust. "Here." He handed it to his brother, who didn't seem to share his apparent concerns about backwash.

"Anyway, was a long time ago." A howl to match the feeling in his soul sounded from beyond their hidey hole. "So what is it you two have planned? You gonna rebuild or you gonna move on?"

Tor looked up at the cellar door.

"Gonna kill it." Wasn't Tor who spoke, though. That answer came from the big guy, Zalm.

"Damn, didn't think you could talk."

Zalm didn't answer. He took a chug from the water skin and gave it back to his brother.

"He can talk." Tor put the water skin away. "Just doesn't make a habit of it."

"So what was it that tore through here?" All Dale could think was how much food a beast that big might provide.

"We didn't get a good look at it, but it had black fur." Tor stabbed the logs with a poker. Fire was fine. The boy was probably hiding his tears. "Was as big as the three of us combined. Mom and Dad had gone hunting. She didn't come back. Dad said it killed her. He got us in here just as it broke through the fence. Dad slammed the door shut to save us."

Dale pointed at the bows and arrows they'd propped against their chairs. "You really think you can take down something that big with those?"

Tor didn't answer. Zalm shrugged without a hint that he had any doubts.

"Haven't seen much food up here." Dale's tone made it clear he was making a proposition.

Tor looked back at him and crossed his arms. "There aren't a lot of animals, but Dad taught us how to hunt what there is."

Dale patted his rifle. "Let's just say this baby has some serious punch, lot more than those arrows you're using. If I help you kill that thing, you willing to split the meat?"

The brothers exchanged a look. A shrug from Zalm settled their silent debate.

"All right," Tor said. "We'll head out in the morning."

The thought of meat warmed Dale almost as much as the fire as he went to sleep.

***

Keeping up with those two boys about killed Dale. His clothes weren't as well-suited for the snow, and the brothers weren't half-starved. Their parents had somehow carved out a life in this place. Killing this thing wasn't just about a single meal. Dale needed to convince these boys he was worth keeping around. He wasn't dumb enough to think he could survive in this place by himself. His rifle had caught more than one meal since coming into the Ice Lands, but his ammunition wasn't limitless. Unless he found a fresh supply of ammo, he was going to starve. He'd already considered taking his chances back in the Desert of Fire. At least that place had some lizards a man could kill for food.

A clear sky helped. They'd been spared any fresh snow overnight, so the tracks were easy enough to follow. Dale just had to keep up with these two kids who were keen to pay back the thing that killed their parents. That they kept going uphill didn't help.

About midday, they stopped. Dale had fallen behind, so he was glad to have a chance to catch up. The two kids weren't resting, though. Something had them bothered.

Dale planted the butt of his rifle into the snow and held onto the barrel while he caught his breath.

"What's the problem, juniors?"

Tor pulled off a knit cap and wiped some sweat from his brow. "No feeding site." He pointed to the tracks in the snow. The spots of blood had stopped, so he guessed their dad had either run out of blood or maybe the blood had frozen. The drag marks were clear enough.

"What's that mean?"

"There's no sign that it stopped to feed." Tor hesitated on

that last word.

Dale was too tired to put his brain to work. "So why is that bad?"

Big dude Zalm answered. "Feeding babies."

"What?"

Tor put his cap back on. "We're worried it's dragging the body back to its lair. If it's doing that, then it might be to feed babies."

"In other words...?"

"We might be dealing with more than just one of these things."

"A pack of giant, black-furred monsters." Dale hung his head down. "Well, on the bright side, that's more food for us. Who knows? If they're young enough, maybe we can try to domesticate them, cultivate a herd."

The quiet one's eyebrows pushed together as he stared down at Dale. He didn't need Tor to translate the look on his brother's face.

"Yeah, I know, but it's fun to dream." Dale groaned as he stood straight. "So what are we thinking here? We calling it quits?"

Tor glared at him, his body shaking with his anger. "Are you scared, old man?"

"Hell, yes." Dale laughed, but there was no hiding the edge of fear behind it. "We're talking about a bunch of big, hairy monsters! If you aren't scared, you're a damn idiot."

Zalm grunted, his gaze shifting between the two of them. With a simple roll of the eyes, he walked between the two of them and continued to follow the trail in the snow.

Waist Deep

"We've sacrificed more than half of our daylight." Tor shook his head. "Too late to turn back, and there's no adequate shelter between here and our homestead. We have to move forward."

Tor followed his brother. Dale leaned on his rifle and took a deep breath. He'd allied himself with a pair of teenaged maniacs. What was worse was that it really was too late to turn back.

***

The path turned steeper and moved into the mountains. All feeling had fled Dale's feet, and his face, wrapped in a long scarf, felt as if it might crack if he touched it. Muscles ached as he struggled to keep up with the hell-bent youths.

To make matters worse, snow started falling. Their clear trail in the snow was vanishing. Dale realized that even if he did try to turn back on his own, he'd be lost. The sun was hidden behind the clouds, and the brightest part of the sky was vanishing behind the taller mountains to the west.

"I'm gonna die following these fool boys," Dale muttered to himself. He tasted blood coming from his chapped lips.

The only good news was that the brothers had stopped again. Tor waved for him to catch up. What the devil did this boy think he was doing, looking for a good spot to do snow angels?

Tor took a few steps towards him and shouted over the wind. "There's a cave, a little higher. Spotted it earlier, before the snow started. If we can make it there before sunset, we can—"

A howl shook the mountain. Tor raised his bow and arrow. Dale drew his rifle.

"Goddammit! How did it get behind us?"

"It must have circled around to trap us." Tor canted his head for Dale to get behind him. "Follow Zalm. We have to make for the cave."

Dale didn't move. "What if the cave is this thing's home?" He searched through the snow for something to shoot, but all he saw was a shifting veil of grey. Their visibility was little more than twenty yards.

"Doesn't matter." Tor walked backwards, not bothering to wait for Dale. "We're too exposed out here. At least the cave might give us some cover."

"I'll bet its last meal thought the same damn thing."

Dale didn't try to go backwards. He'd fall on his ass doing that. He turned and ran, not that it was much of a run. He was fighting uphill with half of his legs sinking into the snow with each step.

A low growl vibrated through the ground. Dammit, it was close.

The only other thing Dale heard was his panicked breaths. His heart pounded, and his chest ached. He cursed God for his life in one thought, and with the next, prayed for Him to save it.

A crosswind struck him from the east. The same snow that slowed him also saved him from falling, but he had to stop to regain his balance. Tor struggled past him.

"Here! Hurry!"

Zalm's shout was answered by the unseen beast's growl. An arrow shot past Dale and Tor and into the void behind them.

Dale looked over his shoulder. A shadow loomed behind

them. A second arrow flew into that dark shape, and a sharp roar of pain and rage ripped through the descending night.

He turned, pressed the butt of his rifle into his shoulder, aimed and pulled the trigger.

The shot thundered loud enough to drown out the wind. The shadow retreated, disappearing without any hint as to which direction it had moved.

Tor shouted after him. Dale couldn't decipher what the boy was saying. He just responded to the urgency in his voice and ran for the cave. The black maw in the mountain's side beckoned. Just before he reached it, a light flared within the black.

The light revealed Tor's shape by the edge of the entrance. His bow and arrow were held ready. Dale ran past the boy. As soon as he made it inside, his feet betrayed him. He fell on his back and slid deeper into the cave. How he managed not to crack his skull open, he didn't know.

When he stopped sliding, he realized the floor of the cave was a flat sheet of ice. He wondered how that could possibly occur naturally.

He whimpered as he rolled over to get back on his feet. The brothers guarded the cave's entrance. Their breath trailed into the darkness beyond. A torch, which Zalm must have lit, was stabbed into a pile of snow.

Tor's head bobbed as if searching for a different line of sight to help him see the monster hidden in the snow. "Did you hit it?"

"Not sure." Dale fumbled with the rifle. He dug a shell from his bag and loaded it like a blind man without thumbs trying to play "Pin the Tail on the Donkey."

As soon as he loaded the shell, everything went to hell.

A black shape shattered through the opening. The beast slammed right into Tor and dragged the boy deeper into the cave with him. Zalm fell without shooting an arrow. The torch skidded across the ice. Somehow, it managed to stay lit. Dale shot at the dark shape. The blast deafened him.

His shot missed. The entrance, weakened by the monster's entrance and his stray gunfire, collapsed.

Tor gasped under the weight of the animal. Blood ran down from his mouth and a wound hidden beneath the beast's paws on his chest. The creature snarled at them, giving Dale his first good look at it.

The shape of the thing resembled a wolf, but even on all fours, it was taller than Zalm. Wet, dark fur covered most of its body. Its stench was less like a wet dog, and more akin to rotten meat. Mange had reduced the right side of its face and snout to open wounds coated in bloody, pale yellow puss swimming with maggots. The eyes didn't match. The left was big with a yellowish-brown iris that seemed perfectly natural for a beast of this kind, but the right was more like a human's with a small, pale blue iris floating in a seat of white.

The eye resembling a wolf's exploded into a bloody mess. One of Zalm's thin wooden arrows buried deep into its socket. The shot didn't kill it. The beast yelped, but didn't retreat. Its massive body lunged at the larger brother.

Zalm didn't get a chance to shoot another arrow. The collision of their two bodies shattered his bow. The string snapped with a comic "boing."

Dale scrambled to reload as he ran to Tor. The boy wasn't as bad off as he'd looked. The cuts to his chest looked superficial. The blood coming from Tor's mouth gave him a manic look as he stared dumbstruck at the battle between his brother and the beast.

The two slid across the icy floor. Zalm's left hand held onto its throat by a thick patch of fur. The giant wolf's rear paws scrambled back and forth, unable to get a good footing on the ice with Zalm's weight keeping it off-balance. The beast shook its head, but the boy refused to be shaken loose.

Dale forced his attention back to his rifle and kept muttering the same two words to himself, "Shoot it."

Tor launched a volley of arrows. The slender shafts stabbed into the wolf's side. They drew blood, but they didn't slow the wolf's assault on Zalm.

Dale hesitated. The wrestling was too chaotic, and he didn't trust himself not to shoot Zalm. He needed just one opening.

Zalm punched the side of its face with his free hand. The repeated strikes made a sickening squishy sound as his fist smashed into that diseased flesh. A strike to the semi-human eye startled the animal, and gave Dale his opening.

He pulled the trigger, felt the kickback into his shoulder and watched as the side of the wolf's throat burst open. Blood sprayed out, but the wolf wasn't finished. Zalm lost his grip. The beast bit down at Zalm's head. Blood covered the boy's bearded face, and it was difficult to tell how much of it was his own.

The wolf's grunts and growls turned to a gurgle as Zalm's thick hands grabbed the top and bottom of its snout. He screamed and the muscles in his arms shook as he stretched the snout open far wider than its jaw was ever meant to. Bones cracked. A desperate sound bubbled out of the wolf's throat and then went silent as the jaw surrendered with a loud snap to Zalm's strength.

The mangy corpse collapsed on top of its killer.

Tor ran to his brother. He screamed his brother's name, but Zalm didn't answer.

Dale retrieved the torch, which had somehow managed to stay lit through all this. He carried it over to where the others were. Tor was struggling to shove the beast off of his brother, but the corpse wouldn't budge. He was about to offer his help, but as he brought the firelight closer to Zalm, he saw it was too late.

The side of the boy's throat was ripped open. Blood flowed out in a tiny stream and joined the tributaries coming from the wolf's to form a red, frozen lake around their bodies.

"Tor." Dale touched the boy's shoulder, but he jerked away from his hand.

"Help me get it off!"

Dale stepped back. "He's gone." He lowered the torch so that the flames were closer to Zalm's face and that open wound. The eyes were empty, the body too still.

Tor screamed and pounded at the side of the beast that had robbed him of his family. Dale wanted to say something to help, but there weren't any words for it. He'd taken it little better when his parents died. How many times had he asked himself if his parents might have lived if only he'd stood by their ship's captain instead of blowing out his brains? If they'd had the captain, could they have avoided that deadly crash on the reef? He'd never know.

Death never made sense to those left behind.

Dale left Tor to work through his grief. He raised the torch for a better look at the cavern. No sign of any giant wolf cubs. He didn't see the bodies of Tor's father or mother either. They didn't find the body while following the wolf here, so what happened to it?

A groan echoed through the cave. Dale looked at Tor. The boy's sobs had stopped, and he was turning in a slow circle, looking just as confused as to what had made that noise.

Tor drew an arrow. Dale shoved another shell into his rifle, none too simple a task with a torch in one hand.

Could it be the wind? He looked back at the collapsed entrance. It was sealed. Then they heard the groan again, as if someone was straining to do something.

"That doesn't sound like an animal," Dale whispered as he walked back to Tor's side.

Tor pointed to the far end of the cavern, a place where their torch's light hadn't reached. As they drew closer, the light reflected off the icy surface to reveal a narrow passage.

Dale led the way with the torch. Only after they were deep into the tunnel, did he realize he should have let Tor go first. If they ran into trouble, he couldn't shoot his rifle and hold the torch at the same time. Nor could Tor shoot past him.

Nothing to do now. All they could manage was to press forward and pray nothing attacked.

The grunting grew louder. Whoever it was sounded in

pain. Was it possible this was Tor's father? Could the man actually still be alive? Dale didn't dare voice the hope for fear of being wrong. Instead, he moved faster, to get to the source of the grunts even faster. More than once, he nearly fell on the icy floor.

The passage widened into a vast grotto. The ceiling was so high, he couldn't see it. There were several other tunnels scattered throughout the space. The walls were all ice carved into a variety of images. One resembled a snake and another a wolf. A third image contained fire in the rough shape of a man.

The strangest thing was in the center of the room. A man.

He wore nothing from the waist up. The man's muscular, bare back was to them. The skin, riddled with scars, was so pale that it blended into the cave. Long black and grey hair flowed down just past the shoulder blades. Pained grunts continued as the body jerked slightly. His movements suggested something encumbered him, and as more of the torchlight reached the man, Dale realized the bottom half of his body was missing. No, not missing. Closer still, and he saw what this truly was, a man trapped in the ice from the waist down.

Just before Dale could think to say anything, a loud scream came from the man in the ice. He was hunched forward, as if trying to pull himself free. Something snapped, and the noise reminded Dale of how it sounded when Zalm had split the wolf's jaw apart. Then a rip formed through the man's body where it touched the ice. Flesh and bone snapped and cracked but didn't bleed.

The strain in his cries heightened as his body cracked in half. The top half pulled free from the bottom, but no blood or foul matter spilled out. The place where he pulled apart was frozen.

A sigh of relief moaned from the half-man. He crawled forward but then stopped. He went still and silent, like a deer who knows it's in the sights of a hunter.

The head turned. The hair hid most of the face, but a single eye could be seen glancing back at them.

"Don't mind me." His voice was deep and smooth, not at all rough like all else about him. He grinned in a show of bright teeth. "Ah, you resemble my wolf's gift."

The strange half-man wasn't talking to Dale. The words were directed to Tor.

"Here, you can have this part back."

The stranger flung something big at them. Dale scrambled to his left and ducked as an arm flailed just over his head.

Tor screamed. "Father!"

Dale turned and looked down at what the half-man had thrown at them. It was the top half of another man, only this one hadn't survived losing the bottom half of his body. Even dead and frozen from his drag through the night, the family resemblance was unmistakable. The half-man had just thrown the upper portion of Tor's father at them. Black blood and other dark gore oozed from the bottom of the half-corpse.

"What the Hell is this?" Dale shouted.

The half-man didn't answer. Instead, he was busy lining up his body with the bottom half of Tor's father. His spine snaked out from the frozen bottom of his body and reached into the waist. The spine went taut after it hooked onto something within the other body. Then he pulled together, and a long luxurious moan issued from the half-man who was now whole.

"Oh, that is so much better."

Dale had already dropped the torch in his shock. He held up his rifle and aimed at the new monstrosity before him. He wasn't sure if he should shoot. Part of him didn't want to, because the decision to shoot this thing was too much like accepting what he'd just seen had actually happened.

The stranger stood, and as he turned to face them, it was clear the bottom half of Tor's father wasn't exactly a perfect fit. The upper half's flesh had to bend inward like a shirt tucked into a pair of pants that were two sizes too small.

"What are you?" Dale asked. "What the hell is going on here!"

The stranger smiled at him, and for a moment, the flesh on his face seemed to move. Then Dale realized what he was really seeing. Two more pairs of eyes were opening. Two were on its forehead and two more on its cheeks.

"I'm sorry, but I thought my coming was something explained to your kind long ago." He stalked towards them. "I am the Trickster, and this is the time of Ragnarok!"

The torch burned out, plunging them into darkness. Dale fired his rifle. The shot provided a brief flash of light to show him the man with six eyes as he lunged forward. Then the darkness fell again. There was pain, and for Dale, the world finally ended.

The End

Ben

by Darra L. Hofman

The young mother put one foot in front of the other. She no longer believed in salvation, or even a future. But there was today, and the child who still lived. If they were fortunate, they would find another home, move the dead, and eat what they'd left behind. Perhaps the dead would include a child his size, and she could find him shoes and long enough pants. They might sleep in a bed or a couch, depending on where the dead lay, but at least they could sleep with walls and a roof. She pulled the child in close for a moment, burying her face into his curls. She marveled at his perfect black lashes, and at how much he looked like his siblings. She held her tears; she was too tired, too thirsty, too sunburnt to spend time mourning. It was a distraction she couldn't afford. This son, spared from the flu and the flames, would live. And she had to live to make it so. She put one foot in front of the other.

Ben wondered, occasionally, if he would have been given his gift in a sane world. He burned with bitterness when people called him "lucky." Lucky men have never clung to their mother, listening as she said kaddish over bones she couldn't bury.

Lucky men don't wake up with the smell of burning flesh and the screams of the dying suffocating their memory. Lucky men don't hide their names, their talents, their entire selves from the world, hoping merely to live. But, he was alive. Perhaps that was a piece of luck.

Sighing, he willed himself awake. "Can't really say 'out of bed' these days." Despite fancying himself an outdoorsman, Ben had never gotten used to sleeping on palettes, in clearings, or, if lucky, in haylofts. He stretched, and packed his few belongings. Soon, he was finally going to meet her.

If Ben made headlines, she sold papers. Stories of the Dark Avenger ran through the land. He'd heard farmers and refugees whisper her exploits. He knew the "governments," such as they were, feared her. And he had little doubt the True Church spoke of her "consorting with demons and the reawakened Dark Ones" because they knew her power. He wasn't certain how he would pick her out; he'd heard so many conflicting tales. She was tall, she was short; she was beautiful, she was hideous; she was a savior, she had brought the Plague, the Darkness, and the Purging. The only things the talebearers agreed upon: she was dark, and she was terribly powerful.

Ben trudged on. Two days, perhaps three from here, she was waiting. Ben shifted his pack. "A horse, a horse, my kingdom for a horse." He laughed at his own joke. When his mother would tell him stories of knights and dragons, all those years before, "adventuring" had sounded romantic. Exciting. A life away from the complications of modernity. Damn, how he missed modernity. He missed cars, and air conditioning, and walking into a store and buying food. As he humped another mile, he fantasized about laying on the couch, eating Doritos, drinking soda, and fighting his sister for the Xbox. Poor Rachel. She'd been only nine when they murdered them all. More Jews as burnt offerings. Sometimes, Ben wondered if he was the only Jew left. He'd been certain he was the only person with a gift until he heard about the Dark Avenger. Another fifteen miles directly, perhaps another thirty keeping his trail away from the main paths. Two more days, and he wouldn't be alone. Not the only one.

Ben ran a hand through his hair. It was hard, being hungry, being cold, being sunburnt and sore and tired every minute of his life. But it was excruciating being alone. Ben had been the eldest of seven children. With grandparents, aunts, uncles, cousins, and family friends, their farm had always pulsed with life. Even after the Plague, even after the Darkening, even after losing Nana and losing little Sarah, Ben's family had been loud and joyful. True, a certain sadness clung to his mother after Sarah died, but still, she sang blessings and chased the little ones and ruffled his hair and called him "buddy." Now, he faced days of silence. He'd grown used to callouses, oozing blisters, and the dizzy irrationality that came before the hunger stopped gnawing. He'd grown used to his own stench. He'd never grown used to silence.

As the light slanted, stretched, and settled in for its own rest that evening, Ben considered. He'd never met this woman; he didn't know anything other than the fact that she, too, had a gift. Or, at least, that other folks thought she did. What would they share? Anything? Had someone found out about him, about his gift? He thought of the set-up; how Dan, in unfamiliar whispers, told him that he knew someone who wanted to meet him. He trusted Dan. Dan had always been goofy, solid, and honest, even when honesty could cost him. Surely this wasn't a set-up? What did he want from her? What on earth did he really think would come of all this? Ben sighed, and stared at the stars. Soon, the sun would reach across him, and bring him one day closer to meeting her. He began to doze. Suddenly, a rustle in the underbrush made the hair on his neck stand up.

"It's okay. It's okay." Ben pulled himself up slowly, crouching, his knife in his hand. A pair of yellow eyes met his; slowly, a ragged grey body joined the eyes in the bush. The coyote had not yet dared enter the clearing. Backing up, Ben felt the presence of two more behind him. "It's not okay." The first coyote sidled into the clearing; its heavy frame belied the coyote face. "A coywolf? Shit. It is definitely not okay." The coywolves crept closer, slavering, starving. The Plague had done a number when it jumped down to the lower species. Ben felt his heart pulsing in his eyelids. Sweat rained into his boots. Feeling their breath on his skin, he swallowed.

He turned and ran like hell. Ben hated coyotes, he'd never met a full-on wolf, and he was sure that a coywolf, much less three, would enjoy Ben-jerky for days. He felt every step jarring through his body; unfortunately, he didn't feel the tree root until his foot tangled in it. Gasping, shaking, Ben watched them come closer. He thought briefly about dying. He took another deep breath.

Ben chose.

Ben

He dropped his knife, and slowly stood up. Closing his eyes, he sought the silent well within himself, and prayed that no one was nearby. It all began to pour out, with that hot, soggy feeling of a summer afternoon. The animals didn't wait until he was done; they sniffed the foreign, the powerful, and fled. Ben felt them leave, but couldn't stop. Feeling his body empty of magic, he managed a half-smile. He was grateful they fled. It pained Ben to kill the small animals that kept starvation at bay; he ached at the thought of actually having to hurt one of the coywolves. Finally, though, the shivery gooseflesh crept over him. He felt the familiar weariness gnawing at him. Sighing, he gathered his things. Travelling at night was dangerous; staying here would be worse. Greater beings, more powerful beings, would know what had been done here. Ben's control over his gift was little at best. No, it was best to move on.

Dawn came much too early. Ben looked like shit and felt worse. But, he'd slept safely. That was something. He still had half a squirrel and some wild greens. That was something else. In fact, as the sun began to warm his limbs, Ben felt something rising underneath the exhaustion. He felt...excited? He wasn't sure. Life had been so hard for so long that he'd forgotten what excitement felt like. But, as he walked on, he felt the thrill of anticipation. For the first time since his mother had died, he thought of the future. Not just of surviving, but of living.

"I hope it isn't a trap!"

Eight miles away, Je'Rhonda willed herself not to pace, not to look nervous. She weeded the front beds, milked the goats, and swept the walk. She chatted with the neighbors about rain, about the livestock, lied to them about her "nephew" whom she had just learned had survived, and who was coming to see her. She watched the road. She took in some vegetables, watching out the kitchen window as she chopped. She slowly brought the soup-pot to a boil. Once upon a time, she would've wondered if her guest would be hungry. These days, there was no such question. In her past life, as a pediatrician, Je'Rhonda would've called social services given the state of the kids she saw. Of course, now there were no social services, and the parents were, like everyone else, just trying to make it through. Je'Rhonda did what she could. She doctored where she could, she left milk on doorsteps, and she did what she could to make the land more bountiful. Her next door neighbors' crops were finally successful. But she knew she couldn't do too much. Couldn't draw too much attention. Scavengers would be the least of her concerns if anyone noticed that her land gave as generously as it did.

Finally, she spotted him. A sad, dingy figure darkening the road was nothing new. But she knew him immediately. She could feel his presence as soon as his shadow crossed the path. She shuddered. When she'd heard about him, from Dan, she'd wondered if he was the right one. She'd wondered if he was powerful enough. Dan had assured her he was brave enough. Now, she wondered if he had any idea how terribly powerful he was. She had a direct connection to Elohim; she never doubted that her power could be severed at an instant. He was different. The power seemed to pulse from him, and Je'Rhonda suddenly understood the running and hiding that Dan had described as his life. She shook her head. There would be no safe refuge, not even here, where she'd put so much time and work into protections. She went inside to dress, to pack, and to wait.

Ben startled as a hand grabbed his arm.

"Nephew, you've made it! Come on in, sweetheart. Let your Auntie Je'Rhonda have a look at you!" The woman steered him into the cottage, silencing his questions and protests with her eyebrows. She sat him in a plain pine chair in a clean, modest kitchen. Ben looked her over. To Ben's young eyes, she was old, about 45, with a sprinkling of freckles and wide, honest eyes. As the old woman bustled about the kitchen, Ben felt sorry for her. She was not the first person he'd met who believed him to be a lost son or nephew, driven to mad hope by the grief of losing everyone.

"I'm sorry, um…Auntie Je'Rhonda, but I have to meet someone. I know we were going to have dinner tonight, but I'll come back soon, okay?" It was usually best to play along with the crazy. Ben pulled himself out of the chair, and began towards the door.

"Lucky, right?" Ben jerked back around.

"Excuse me?"

"You're the one they call Mr. Lucky, because you somehow escape from every narrow danger." She wiped her hands on her apron. "But you're not really lucky. You're powerful. Somehow, you've tapped into the old powers that have awoken. And now, you're looking for me."

"You're…you're the…."

"The Dark Avenger? Yes, that's the name that's apparently stuck."

Darra L. Hofman

Ben looked her over again. He'd been expecting her to be East Indian, or maybe Filipina. But, he guessed that an African American woman, even one as light as Je'Rhonda, would still be dark to many eyes. And as he watched her moving through the kitchen, he realized how straight, strong, and fast she still was. She flitted about, calmly preparing for their journey. Age had apparently not yet taken a step from the woman. Perhaps she was who she claimed.

"If you're her, then who sent me?"

"Dan, of course. None like him, with those curls and that beard."

Ben pressed his lips together. He gnawed the side of his finger, then sighed.

"Well, then...okay. What do we do now? How did you get to be what you are? How did I get to be what I am?"

She shook her head.

"We'll talk as we walk. Come on." She shoved a sandwich—a real sandwich, with bread, meat, cheese, and vegetables, such as he hadn't seen since boyhood—in his hands. She led him through the back garden, and into the woods. Ben gaped at the verdant garden, and then gasped when he felt the tingle of power when a branch brushed his face. She'd worked magic into the land itself? Ben was pulled from his wonder by Je'Rhonda's voice.

"This area is pretty quiet. I've not found anyone else with the gift here, and I've worked hard to obscure mine. You, though...." She wrinkled her nose. "You have so much magic on you, it's like blood in the water."

Ben

"Me?" Ben was surprised. "I'm, like, totally inept."

She stopped a second and looked at him.

"Lucky, how long have you known about your gift?"

"Um…I don't know. I guess since before Ma died."

"How many others have you met with the gift?"

"Count you? One."

"Are you…are you serious?"

Ben nodded. Je'Rhonda rubbed her temples, then shook her head.

"Lord have mercy on my soul." She grabbed his arm. "Come, we need to move faster."

"Why?"

"If you haven't been working on it, and you smell so strongly…. Yikes. It's amazing the Church and its half-wit denizens haven't already hunted you down. Come on, young man, move it!"

They half-hiked, half-ran through the night. Finally, when the sky blotted out everything but the trees, they stopped. Je'Rhonda paused, and prayed, and Ben felt the magic coming off her. It didn't pour off, in torrents, but simply trickled out. When it was done, she seemed little troubled for her efforts. Instead, she took him by the elbow. "This way, there's a cave. We can rest safely there for a while."

Ben watched as Je'Rhonda set up camp. A small, but comfortable fire, and real cooked food. Ben couldn't get over his luck. First a sandwich, now a real meal. He'd won the lottery as far as random strangers went.

"Where'd you learn to be out in the world like this?"

"Doctors without Borders, back when there were, you know, doctors and borders."

Ben nodded. He ate. He didn't notice Je'Rhonda observing him.

"You remember the before times, don't you?"

"Yeah. Not a whole lot. The Plague came when I was still pretty little, but even after the Darkening, we were okay. My parents were preppers."

"Really?" Her eyes widened. "But you're still alive? Did you not get found?"

"We did. My mom and I had gone to visit one of her friends who was sick. I was pretty pissed at getting dragged out, but it was an obligation, apparently." He looked at his feet for a while. "They were done by the time we got home. We couldn't even find everyone's bones." Je'Rhonda watched him, watched the muscles pop up in the corner of his jaw, watched how he stared at the sky, showing only the whites of his eyes, until the tear passed. "So, yeah. We started south."

"How on earth did you live?"

"We ransacked houses. I mean, there were so many dead people by then, it was pretty easy to find the houses that were empty, or only had dead people in them. So we'd close off the rooms with the dead, and take clothes and supplies, and live in a house until we'd eaten everything there was to eat. Mom would read me whatever books they had. It was alright. I missed my dad and my brothers and sisters, but I had Ma."

They sat silently. Ben thought about his family, on the strange and lonely paths of his life. He stared at the fire, chewing and grunting in satisfaction. He even hummed, softly and tunelessly. He couldn't get over a plate of food filling his hands. He wondered idly if he would've grown into his hands had he had enough to eat. Abruptly, Je'Rhonda walked to his side of the fire. She knelt down in front of him, and took his face in her hands.

"Listen, child. There is so much you don't know, it's breathtaking. But here's what you need to know. You are strong beyond your wildest imaginings, and together, we will help restore things to order. You can do it. We can do it. But you must learn and listen, and you must trust me. You listened to your mother, and trusted her, and she kept you safe. I will do the same, but you must listen to and trust me. Do you think you can do that, Lucky?"

Ben swallowed. He didn't understand this woman, nor her intense interest in him. He certainly didn't understand how she could promise to keep him safe. But her eyes screamed truth. He pulled back, but nodded.

"Very well. Sleep now, child. I'll take the first watch."

Morning came with a bite. He stretched, and looked at the forest. It stretched out into the mist at the bottom of the mountains. In the far distance, he thought he glimpsed the valley. Taking the cup of chicory Je'Rhonda offered, he marveled. It had been very rare that Ben had seen the forests; he spent most of his life under the canopy. The world was vast. He looked out over his knees. A sudden realization struck him.

"The True Church is in the valley."

"True Church." She snorted. "If we say we have no sin,

we deceive ourselves, and the truth is not in us." She shrugged, then offered Ben a half-smile. "Eventually, yes, that valley, and one who dwells within the True Church is our goal. But not yet. You're not ready. And I alone...." She gestured vaguely.

"Ready? What are you talking about? You've been talking in riddles since I met you."

"We fix our eyes not on what is seen, but on what is unseen. For what is seen is temporary, but what is unseen is eternal. You, Ben, are very, very powerful. I don't know where your gift comes from—my God tells me it doesn't come from Him, or from any of the gods."

"The gods? Plural? Look, I'm a Jew. Not a particularly good Jew, but a Jew. We say every day, <u>Shema Yisrael, Adonai Eloheinu, Adonai Echad.</u> Hear, Israel, the Lord is our God, the Lord is One. One. Singular. Not a frickin' party of gods."

"But the commandments say, 'You shall have no other gods before Me.' The pagans who worshipped other gods were not fools, even if they did not understand the greatness and glory of Our Lord. There are other gods, and they're back. Don't you understand? There are much greater forces at play than you or I, or even God." She again leaned in close, so close he could feel the contours of her nose, with that same fervor in her eyes. "You have found some other way into the power, but you can't deny it's there. You can't say you don't feel it on me, and you can't pretend that it doesn't all make sense."

Ben set his cup down and rubbed his eyes. He wanted to dismiss her, to tell himself she was crazy. He wanted to believe that he was mad, that this was all some hallucination. But he couldn't forget his mother clawing through what had been their home, desperately praying that someone had lived, shrieking silently when she found Avi's body, his little hand still grasping his beloved doll. He'd felt her every day of his life, looking for pieces of the ones they lost in him, and he couldn't lose her grief. He couldn't forget the stench of the plague victims' bodies whose homes they'd shared, their bloated bodies and staring eyes. He couldn't ignore the tingling power within him, or the beings he sensed, at the very edge of consciousness, whenever he used it.

She could have been wrong, of course. But, given the state of the world, he doubted that she was crazy. Ben laid his head in his hands, and then gazed out to the side for a moment. He pushed his fingers through his hair, his head and neck sinking against his chest. Even though he was a man, even though it had been years since his mother had passed, he wanted her. She'd always been a good judge of people, and wise in her own loud way. If she were alive, Ben knew she would ruffle his hair, and then lead him to the best answer, patiently repeating, "Well what do you think?" Ben felt like Je'Rhonda was good, but what did he know about the ways of people? He chewed his thumb. What the hell. She hadn't tried to kill him yet. And damned if he wasn't lonely enough to take the risk that she would.

"So, these other gods? Who are they? What are we up against? What's the plan?"

Je'Rhonda smiled. "My young friend, so impatient. There is a time for every purpose under heaven; whatever is has already been, and what will be has been before." She patted his shoulder. "Things will be revealed as necessary."

Ben tried not to roll his eyes. He felt like he was ten years old again, listening to his parents discuss what to do about the zealots murdering anyone who hadn't reverted to living like a medieval pissboy. He'd known, of course, that he wasn't supposed to listen outside their door. But he needed to know what was happening. He needed to understand how and why the world had fallen even further apart. Yet his questions, "What's an EMP? Why do people blame us when they didn't prepare? Where will we go if we leave the farm?" were always met with pats on the head and a "We'll talk about it later." And here he was, once again, being there-there'd and dragged along with what the grown-up wanted. Ben tried again.

"So, right now, what are we going to do? We can't stay here."

"No, we can't. We can't stay anywhere. At least not until you can match...them." Je'Rhonda glanced behind her; Ben felt the heaviness of their presence.

"What are they? They've followed me since I got my gift. I feel them in my dreams, but they don't seem to...I don't know... do anything. But still. I haven't been able to sleep a night since." Ben shivered.

"I guess the closest word we have in English is demons, though that's not quite accurate. They are...." She shook her head. "I don't really know. They're dangerous, though. They feed on the power, and you...you're lucky you're as powerful as you are. Otherwise, they'd have devoured you, down to the last pieces of your soul."

"Wait. So why haven't they? I'm really, like, unpowerful.

I couldn't even stop a guy from mugging me."

"Didn't. Not couldn't."

"Look, I don't know what Dan told you, or what you think you know about me. I'm really not some uber-powerful wizard guy. I can do some parlor tricks. I can do enough, like, telekinesis to not totally die." Je'Rhonda smiled.

"You don't know what you can do until you have to."

"So why haven't they gone after you, then?"

"I have my Lord at my side, to guide me."

"Oh. Yeah. Of course." Ben couldn't stop the eye roll this time. "I mean it, though. This doesn't make any sense. First you say we can't stay still, because they'll devour me, and then you say that they haven't devoured me because I'm oh-so-very powerful. This is all ridiculous. Ridiculous!"

Je'Rhonda sighed. "If you were to stay still, they still wouldn't go after you directly. If something ever makes you truly feel your power, you'll understand why—you could kill so easily. Even a demon would be lost against you, much less our mortal enemies."

"Never. I don't even like killing rabbits. I am not...I do not kill. I know what murder costs. That is not who I am, or ever will be."

"Fine. Regardless, the demons are not stupid beings. They know how to get into a man's heart, to wear down his soul. They would take you slowly, indirectly, but they would take you."

"And what's stopping them now? I don't have a heart and soul because I sleep in the damn woods?"

"You don't have connections. You don't have anyone left

that you love. Your loneliness keeps you safe."

"Great. Fantastic. Exactly what I wanted to hear." Ben kicked the dirt.

"Come on, young man. We have a lot of ground to cover."

They trudged on. Je'Rhonda babbled about the wonders the Lord had wrought, how fortunate they were to have been chosen be part of His great plan. Ben offered the occasional "uh-huh," and wondered why he'd thought he so badly needed company. But, as he watched Je'Rhonda use the gift throughout the day—skillfully, consciously—he remembered why he wanted to be with her. He didn't want to be "lucky," his magic saving his ass at the last second and leaving him drained for days. He wanted to be skilled. He wanted to be able to feed himself easily, know what waited around the corner, find the soft and silent places to wait and watch the world. He wanted to be able to use his magic without suffering. And, while he wasn't about to jump in the river for a baptism, he could learn what Je'Rhonda had to teach. He doubted he'd ever be able to defeat his demons, but maybe he could stop running for a little while.

They broke from hiking to eat. Ben chewed slowly, listening to the forest, and…the road? Surely Je'Rhonda wouldn't take them this close to a road? But Ben was certain he heard hooves, wagon wheels, and maybe even children shrieking. He leaned in, and hissed in her ear, "What are you thinking?"

"What am I thinking about what?" Her voice was steady and normal. No attempt to whisper, even.

"About what? About getting this close to the road!"

"What about it?"

Ben

"What if someone…finds us?"

"What if they do? Neither of us has enemies, at least, not enemies who know what we look like."

"But…people can tell. They'll know."

"How?"

"You could tell."

"Because I was chosen by Elohim. Because my Lord has given me the insight to see those with power like His, like that which he shares with me. Trust me, to the average person, you're just another skinny young man."

"But, but…."

"Young man!" She grabbed him by the shoulders. "You cannot live your life ruled by fear. You must be prudent, yes. But you cannot be afraid. You have important work ahead, and you must steel yourself for it. Be strong and courageous. Do not be afraid; do not be discouraged."

Ben stared at her. <u>Prudent</u>, he thought, *got everyone I loved dead.* Though, he had to admit, scared hadn't done him a lot of good either. Mostly, it had won him a life of near-starvation in the woods. Ben shook his head, finished his lunch, and shouldered his pack. Weary and wary, he trudged on.

Ben knew about three Jewish songs total, if you counted the sabbath blessings. He couldn't get over Je'Rhonda, who happily sang hymns and Christian rock the entire afternoon and evening as they walked. Ben couldn't decide if he was more annoyed at her blowing any cover they might've had, or at the fact that he'd had to hear "Our God is an Awesome God" on loop. Ben walked, and waited, and wondered what the hell they were doing.

Every time, though, that Ben thought he would leave if he heard one more performance of Rock of Ages, Je'Rhonda did some small, subtle thing, reminding him that magic could be a gift, rather than a curse. She simply had to wait, and she knew where to find a bridge to cross the river. Unlike Ben, who survived with crude traps and cruder hunting, she simply captured a rabbit, using her intuition to feel it out, and her magic to soothe, subdue, and kill it. But she put him off whenever he asked her to teach him, to show him.

Finally, after two days of seemingly pointless travel, Ben asked, "What are we trying to do out here? Are we looking for something, or someone? Are you going to help me learn to...you know...control it?"

"We're waiting for an answer, for guidance. And you will learn as the time comes."

Ben laid his forehead against the heels of his hands, willing himself not to pull his hair out. The years of running and hiding to live had probably been equally pointless, but at least hope hadn't been dangled in front of him then. Ben kicked a stump. Je'Rhonda continued on.

Ben probably wouldn't have paid attention to the man on the road. Small and weather beaten, the man seemed innocuous. But as he gaped at Ben, Ben felt the hairs on his neck rise. He stared back, trying to place him.

The man reached a hand towards him, and whispered, "Mark? But...but you're...."

"Dead." Ben spat. Recognition began to dawn on him. "You've mistaken me for my father, a man you murdered for the crime of being better prepared than you." Ben stalked forward. Underneath the grime and age, Ben recognized the cold blue eyes of his one-time neighbor. Ben recalled the whispered conversations and looks. He remembered the man's envy of their little farm, his ill-concealed ambition to run the lives of the survivors in the area. Memory crowded and jostled him; he lurched. Ten years of hard-won numbness crumbled. He would have collapsed had he not caught the glint of triumph in the man's eyes. Ben pulled himself back up. He swung an accusatory finger towards the man; the man shrieked as Ben's rage hit him in the chest.

"Perhaps we should look at your crimes." He swung the finger again, sweeping the man with it. A dull <u>thud</u> as he slammed against a tree. Ben's voice broke higher.

"Maybe, we shouldn't just talk about my father. After all, his crime of putting aside for his family was well known. Maybe we should talk about my safta." *Slam._*

"After all, she had numerous bad acts to her name. Cutting up pasta for little children, tucking in their shirts, pushing them in the hammock in the backyard. Or maybe you want to talk about Rachel." *Slam._*

The man began spitting blood. Ben didn't notice; he was watching his parade of murdered family and the lives they should've had.

"Nine-year-old girls are a great threat." <u>Slam</u>.

"Do you know she still played with dolls? Or how about Simon. He was six." *Slam.*

"Maybe the fact that he always sang with our mom, or helped Dad with the milking, was his problem." Ben couldn't see anymore through his tears. He bellowed and gesticulated. The man's body followed the wild paths of his hands, arcing between trees. "Liza and Leah were four, you know. Those terrible, terrible four-year-olds, singing their ABCs and playing in the mud. They definitely deserved to be burned to death in their own home." Ben fell to his knees, slamming the ground with his fists.

"And what about Avi? What the hell did he ever do to you people? Nothing! Nothing! He never did anything to anyone, because he was two! He was a baby! You know what it's like to watch your mother rocking her dead baby, and to watch little charred pieces fall off of his body?" Ben lay on the ground screaming. "They're all dead. They're all dead!" He descended into inchoate mutterings. Slowly, he pulled himself to his knees, heaving, and then rocking himself silently for a while, his eyes unfocused and his breathing ragged.

He didn't know how long he'd been sitting when Je'Rhonda thrust herself into his vision.

"Lucky?"

Ben looked at her, bewildered. "I…I…the guy. Where is he? Did he run away? Why didn't he kill me, too?"

Je'Rhonda knit her eyebrows, and pointed.

It took Ben a moment to understand. At first, he thought the man might've left his clothes. As he drew closer, he realized that the destroyed pile in front of him was the man. It was hard to believe it ever had been a man. It was pulverized, pieces and lumps of what had once been a man. Muscle, sinew, skin, bone, and blood, no longer knit together into a person, but left in a brutalized pile. Ben recognized a finger, a foot. He retched. He vomited until his body felt inside out. Shaking, he gaped at Je'Rhonda.

"What did you do?"

"Me?"

"Of course you! Who else could have done…this?"

She gave him a pointed look.

It took Ben a minute to understand. As understanding came, he staggered. He clung to a tree, trying to stop the world from spinning out from underneath of him. Again, his body broke with sobs.

"I don't, I don't, I don't understand?"

Je'Rhonda sighed. "I told you, you're powerful."

"How? I didn't…mean to do this. Try to do this." He looked up at her between his fingers. "I killed someone. I'm a murderer. A murderer!" A hysterical note warbled in his voice. "I'm like them, Je'Rhonda!"

"No, not like them."

"What? How?" Ben shoved her away. "Nevermind how. It doesn't matter! I'm the one thing I swore I'd never be." He pawed at his eyes, trying to stop the tears. "My mother lived, so I could live. And now, I'm no better than…than that." He pointed to the pile of flesh. "I'm…I don't mean anything, anymore. Why am I alive?"

"Why is any of us alive, Ben?" Je'Rhonda smiled; as her eyes crinkled, Ben was reminded of his initial impression of an old woman. "Because the Lord so chooses. This is part of His plan. This is His plan. You are part of His plan, Lucky."

Ben scrambled backwards on his hands. He shook his head. "No. This…that…." He pointed to the wreckage of the man, "I did that. Not some god somewhere. Me! There is no plan here, no higher purpose! Just…murder."

Je'Rhonda heard none of his arguments. A faraway look had settled on her face. She nodded, and mumbled, "Okay." To Ben's horror, she started walking towards the corpse. Ben rolled over to his hands and knees. The exhaustion of his magic had begun to set in; he felt the heaviness of his bones as he forced himself to his feet.

"Je'Rhonda!" He stumbled after her. "Je'Rhonda! What… what are you doing?" She shrugged, and pulled a pair of gloves from her pack.

"Bloodborne pathogens." Ben dry heaved as she began digging through in search of the man's pockets. "We need what he was carrying, but I don't need Hep C." She grimaced. "Or worse." Ben wiped his mouth.

"How can you…do that?"

"My original specialty was emerg…. I retrained as a pediatrician when I had my kids. ER hours aren't good for a family. Admittedly, I never saw anything like…this…but the pieces are the same."

"You're robbing the dead." Ben struggled to find the strength to protest further.

"As I understand it, robbing the dead is the entire reason you are still alive." Je'Rhonda paused, and smiled as she pulled a small case from the putrid pile. "There it is!" Ben had to content himself with a disgusted face.

"Can we…go? We shouldn't stay here, and I can't…I can't hold on much longer."

Je'Rhonda took in his pale, drawn face, the tremors in his hands, and nodded. She offered him an arm. Ben pushed her arm away. They moved on, she walking, he hobbling. Ben stumbled and dragged himself. He held on about half a mile before taking Je'Rhonda's arm. Slowly, they made their way further. As the sun's rays grew longer, he laid more weight on her. Finally, as she'd done every night previously, Je'Rhonda stopped, and consulted some inner voice, and led them to a quiet clearing.

She set up camp on her own; Ben lay shuddering. He'd been exhausted from magic before. Never had he felt like this. His body shot with pain, and his mind roiled. Guilt, disgust, fear, and anger threatened to overwhelm him, but fell silent, over and over again, against the wall of sheer physical exhaustion. While Ben battled himself silently, Je'Rhonda spent some time over their small fire, seasoning and working on a meal in a small steel tin. Finally, she brought the tin of broth to Ben. She held the cup to his lips, holding him up at the shoulders, and remembering the countless times she'd fed chicken soup to her own children when they were sick.

Je'Rhonda tucked Ben's blanket around him, watching over him as the sun's light slanted from the west. He fell into the heavy, dreamless sleep of the drugged. The faces of the dead and the taunts of demons both left him in peace. Je'Rhonda sat quietly, listening to his steady breathing, and to the quiet murmurs of the forest at night.

Ben woke up in the middle of the night. The moonlight filtered through the trees, clear and strong, and the fire had died down to embers. A flick of light caught his eye; Je'Rhonda, in a trick he had to learn, created a small light out of her fingertip, not too dissimilar from a flashlight. He watched her open the leather case and pull out a piece of paper; she read along, nodding and muttering to herself. Ben tried to sit up, to ask about it, but sleep washed over him again.

He awoke somewhere in the orange of dawn. He pulled himself up, feeling rested in a way he couldn't remember having felt since his mother had died. The joy of being rested quickly subsided as he recalled the events of the day before. He gathered his things, shaking his head. Je'Rhonda started from her unwilling sleep; she'd nodded off sitting against a tree.

"Lucky, you're awake."

"Don't worry, I'm not staying."

"What? Why?"

"I'm a terrible person. You…you're not…you don't seem like. You're not like me."

Je'Rhonda raised an eyebrow. "Young man, we might be more alike than you think."

"What? What are you talking about?"

"You don't think they named me the Dark Avenger for simply tending to the injured, do you?"

"What have you…who are you, really?" Ben realized with a start that he'd been walking for nearly a week with, and had committed murder in front of, someone about whom he knew almost nothing.

"It's a long story. Come, I'll tell you the whole tale in due time. We have a long way to go, and much work yet to do."

They spent the morning walking in contemplative silence. Ben charged through the forest, as if physical distance would let him escape the fears attacking him. Je'Rhonda kept steady pace behind him. Ben slowed as the morning wore on, finally trudging behind Je'Rhonda, lost in self-pity and grief. Finally, Je'Rhonda broke the silence.

"Lucky?" She looked back at the young man, his face still swallowed in sorrow.

"What?"

"You cannot expect yourself to be an angel. You're a human."

"Yeah, a pretty shit one too." He fixed her with a sidelong glance. "There was one thing I swore I'd never be, and I became it."

Je'Rhonda sighed. "Maybe it's because you're so young." Ben gave her his eyes for just a moment; she leapt into the opening. "The things that you've suffered are terrible. What was done to your family was terrible."

"And I've done the same thing to some other family."

"But not for the same reasons, Lucky. Intentions are important, child. You acted…well, rashly, honestly. But not from greed, or selfishness, or blood-lust. You acted from a place of pain, but that pain was born from the best of you, from love."

"So? I killed someone out of love. That makes it so much better. I had good intentions? The road to hell is paved with good intentions! And if there were such a place, that's where I live, and where I'm doomed to end up." He choked back a sob. Je'Rhonda shook her head, and put an arm around his shoulders. Together, they continued on towards the valley, towards a destiny yet unseen.

"Despite it all, you are still a good person, child. The Lord is a god of mercy, as well as justice."

The End

Story's End

by Nathen Gallagher

The old man jerked awake with a surge of disoriented panic, surprised to find that he had fallen asleep with his back to a log in front of their small fire. His hand strayed to the sword at his side and he halfway tried to stand before his senses caught up with his instincts. No sound disturbed the sheltered hollow except the low crack of their fire and the soft popping of trees in the dead forest beyond. Save for the claustrophobic pool of light around them, dark and stillness had swallowed the world entire.

"It's all right," said the girl across the fire. The light revealed only the dim suggestion of a face within the deep hood of her cloak, drawn up to ward against the night's chill and other things. She sat beside their packs, legs folded beneath her and hands tucked in her small lap. "I would have woken you, but the forest is quiet."

"The forest is quiet because the trees have died," he told her, "but there may be other dead things that step as softly." Still, he sat back down, though he did not lean again on the fallen log, grey as old ash and beginning to crumble around the edges. *Just like me*, he thought. The air in the hollow was mercifully still, but the ground held no heat and cold was starting to settle through his old bones. He had nearly forgotten what it was to be warm, to be truly warm, but he dared not risk a larger fire. There were things that sought heat, and there were worse that followed.

"You are so tired," she said, and something in her voice, some kindled spark of care and compassion, reminded him how very young she was. The girl was hardly more than a dozen years old, and it was a very cruel thing he did to her. "You should sleep," she continued. "Only for a little while. It would be all right." The eyes buried within the hood looked down. "I promise not to run away."

The old man believed her, but it didn't matter. It didn't even matter whether or not she knew he believed her. "I will be fine," he assured her. "We're getting close now. I will be dead before I need to sleep again, one way or another."

She said, in a small voice, "That is an awful thing to say." She was right. But the old man cared about her life more than he cared about his own, and he had never considered that she might not feel the same. He didn't consider it now, either. He simply bowed his head and focused his attention inward, briefly running through the familiar routine of sleepskin.

It was not magic, thank the god. It was merely one of many techniques taught to those of his order, far away and long ago before the walls fell and the world wept. His hair, thin from lack of care and more grey than black now, dropped down before his eyes. He drew carefully on the energy within his body, the rush of blood, the beat of heart, the void of gut, the flame of mind. This was energy that could be bent to any number of purposes by one who knew the patterns of his own soul. Breathing the energy back into his bones, the old man sighed as sleepskin fell over him and his weariness washed away like dust before a flood.

It had been two years since he'd last slept more than a handful of minutes at a time, two years of hard travel and harder choices. No one had ever extended sleepskin so long without rest, as far as he knew, but of all the things in the world that frightened him, the long-term effects on his own body could no longer be counted among them. The old man had forgotten what it felt like to dream.

He looked up, renewed and ready to keep watch through the long darkness. Sometime before sunrise they would make once more for the edge of the dead forest, through which they had been traveling for fifteen days. Beyond there had once been a town, a place of pilgrimage, though what remained he could not guess. Beyond the town lay the mountain. And inside the mountain....

"Tell me again," said the girl. She had been watching him from across the fire, from the darkness inside her hood. "Tell me how the world ended, and why we have to die."

The old man had told this tale many times, but she always needed to hear it again. He couldn't blame her. "Then listen," he said. "For it started in the days of your birth."

***

It was not long ago as the god measures time, but the world was younger then by far than it is today. You are too young to remember, but the world in those days was blessed by the god and his gift. The world was a place of magic.

No one knows where the prophets came from, nor how long it has been since the god first granted them access to his power. Some say they rose from the waves of the inner ocean, while some say they fell from the sky. But for hundreds if not thousands of years they spread the god's light across the land, founding the wealth of nations in the west and in the east. It was they who laid the great rivers across the deserts and brought life where life had fled.

With their magics in hand, the power of the god, the prophets built all that mankind could ever need. They built shining cities and warm homes wrought from the spirits of the air. They caused the land to give up food, and fashioned wondrous implements of farming and hunting so that none would ever want. This may sound of dream or myth, but we lived it and we know it was true.

So great and so surrounding were the creations of the prophets that mankind grew to depend on them completely, and abandoned whatever crude tools or simple learning their ancestors had devised. For countless generations mankind prospered and continued in its own kind, while the prophets continued in their own kind as well, and grew ever more powerful in their uses of the god's great gift. In those days the prophets grew proud of their works and their power, and asked not what more good they could do, but asked instead what greater wonders they could craft, what deeper secrets they could learn.

So it came to pass that in the days of your birth the

prophets, in their folly, reached too far. They took too much of the god's gift, and the god, unprepared, was broken. Tortured and lost in his own shattered mind, the god lashed out against the world he had long treasured and against the prophets who had been his favored children.

The earth trembled on that day, from east to west and from north to south. The air itself was cracked asunder, and the demons and the wild storms of magic came forth to tear down all that the prophets had built, all that mankind had loved. The god's gift grew tainted and many of the prophets flew into fits of rage and destruction that torched the land and smote all around them. Mankind was forced to destroy them, and as they fell during the ten years of war between man and fallen prophet, so too fell the world and all its walls, all its shining cities and warm homes, all its wondrous instruments of farming and hunting, all its ingenious tools and trinkets. The world was ended.

But the god's madness was permanent, and still the storms came and the world grew dark. Mankind huddled together and hoped only to be insignificant enough to escape the end. Yet still there was hope. For in the world's final days, the last of the prophets devised a plan....

***

"You haven't finished yet," the girl prompted after a few moments of silence. "There's more."

The old man did not reply. He had been staring into the air above the fire, where the darkness drew down upon them, and he only slowly realized what he was seeing. The small thread of smoke that rose from the stunted flame had ceased ascending straight upward and uninterrupted out of the hollow; now it drifted sharply to the south. His skin went colder than the air around it, and he held his hand up to the smoke. A soft wind rippled just above the hollow. The old man's eyes followed it to the south, out into the endless night.

"You have to tell it all," she continued. "If you don't tell it all, it's not a real—" She cut off as she followed his gaze.

"Get your things," he told the girl, refusing to let the slow fear reach his voice. "We're leaving. Now."

***

They hurried through the dead forest with neither star nor torch to guide them. The great storms had stirred up so much dust from the land that even here, at the edge of the world, no one had seen a star for years. Each of them carried a pack with what remained of their meager supplies, the old man's much larger than the girl's. They had rope, sparkstone, blankets, water, a little soap, less salt, no food. The girl had not eaten in two days, the old man in five; neither had complained, though hunger gnawed at the old man's bones. Once he could have hunted in a forest such as this, before the walls fell and the world wept.

Now the forest was dead, and it was dark. The two travelers kept close as they marched through brittle, fallen branches and the occasional carpet of dry mulch, coughing with the dust of years beneath their feet. The darkness was nearly absolute, but after a time their eyes began to pick out the shadows of trees like grey ghosts in the night, though only when they were almost close enough to touch. It was dangerous to travel in the darkness without a light; one missed step could mean a stumble into a hole or down a slope, if not worse.

The old man remembered stars, and he remembered the moon. He recalled nights many years ago when one could ride freely until dawn, the sky bright enough to light the way. Now there was only the shroud of dust and ash that sometimes fell like snow. The remaining prophets had tried to reassure the people that it was only temporary, but then the people had burned the prophets from their towers and slaughtered their children, both from self-defense and in an effort to appease the god. It had not been enough.

He could still feel that damned wind.

He was uncertain whether or not it was diminishing, but he steered them directly into it, stirring little flurries of dust and grit into their eyes. The girl kept her head tucked low, her hood tight around her, and trusted the old man to stay close to her. They made their way down a small hill, across a long-dry creek bed where smooth stones clacked unseen beneath their feet, and then came up against a steep wall of hard, dead earth on the far side, rising out of the dark as they came upon it. The old man cursed and led them to the east purely out of instinct. He looked for a way up so that they could continue into the wind, but the top of the bank was lost in gloom.

"What was that?" the girl asked.

She had fine ears, so the old man stopped to listen. He

heard a voice, through the trees back to the south but not directly behind them. Another voice followed, a sound only, no words to be heard at this distance, and the old man tensed. Normally he would hide them from the approach of others, but the darkness would do so just as well if the two of them remained silent. Yet they could not remain still; the wind in his hair was a reminder of the great need for pressing forward. And if the voices were shouting, that might mean....

"Come," the old man said. He turned them around to walk the opposite direction down the creek bed, to the west and away from the brief sound of voices.

"You're worried," she told him. She had always been able to see through any calm facade he placed between them. "It might still be far away. I could—" She hesitated.

"No," he said, his voice pitched low but firm. "We can't risk drawing it closer, not even in exchange for greater speed." Still, he considered. "Faster. Watch your footing."

They hurried along the edge of the creek bed, the old man watching the dark bank beside them and the girl watching their feet. They risked falling and twisting an ankle in the black night, but there was nothing for it. The wind was growing in strength, gusting bits of dirt off the bank at them, and there were more shouts now, to the east down the creek bed behind them. Then the old man heard it—the last thing in the world he wanted to hear, the thing he had feared, the thing he had known in his gut was coming.

A faint ripping sound reached them through the dead forest, a sound like the tearing of thick fabric under strong hands, like threads breaking against their will, edged with a softer sound like shattered glass. It came from somewhere to the east, and the wind abruptly changed to flow in that direction so that it once again blew directly into their faces.

The girl swore, and the old man looked back over his shoulder, a futile gesture of habit given the complete darkness around them. The voices were growing louder, behind them in the creek bed. Whoever was out there had evidently run into the same steep bank further down. He could hear at least three voices, all shouting and getting much too close far too quickly.

"Run," he told the girl.

"I can't see," she protested, voice strained.

"Run!"

They ran, the old man keeping pace with the girl, both of them almost stumbling, almost falling as they pitched forward through the blackness. A jagged spear of light crept into the sky behind them, casting the landscape in harsh shadows and a bright purple glow for a brief moment before it vanished, leaving them more blind than ever. It appeared again and the old man chanced a look behind, ignoring the spiderweb crack of light in the air and focusing back down the creek bed. He could make out the owners of the three voices, dark silhouettes fleeing madly from the source of the light, and behind them…of course.

The horrific tearing sound came again, somewhere close at the old man's back and on top of the steep bank, so loud that it felt as though it were his ears being ripped apart instead of the air and the fabric of reality. Sharp forks of dazzling violet light sparked across the air above them, revealing that there was still no escape from the creek bed to the north. The wind howled up toward the new hole torn in the night behind them, a greedy void that sucked the air from all around it, but above the wind he could hear the hoarse, grunting breaths, the claws on rock, and the unearthly shrieks.

The old man refused to die with his back turned. He grabbed the girl by the arm to stop her, and though she nearly pulled him over with the force of her momentum, he managed to swing her around behind him where he felt her hands upon his back, shaking. The old man stood in the harsh light of the spiderweb cracks in the sky, and he drew his blade.

The first demon leaped from the top of the bank with a snarl, outlined in black against the electric purple light above, a figure slightly smaller than a man but compact, muscular, and fast, with burning-ember eyes, a scarred and hairless head, sharp claws and sharp teeth. The old man caught the beast in mid-fall with one precise sweep of his blade, severing it nearly in half across the mid-section and forcing the body away from them to keep his footing clear.

They always came in threes, and the remaining two were not so brash as the first. Gibbering and growling, they clambered down the steep, dry bank headfirst on nimble hands and feet like stooped and twisted mockeries of humanity. They spread apart and hissed at him. The old man retreated slowly and the girl kept step at his back. He dragged his feet slowly through the dirt and ash as he retreated, pushing it up into a small pile.

The creeping webs of light in the sky abruptly vanished, leaving him utterly blind except for the faint glow of their eyes, which he knew from experience could see him just fine. The old man did not hesitate. He made the only move he had.

With a sweep of his leg he kicked the pile of dirt at the creature to his left, obscuring its vision both with the direct spray of detritus and with the cloud of dust and ash it formed between them, and a bare instant later he pivoted to his right and lunged at the second demon. It dodged his initial thrust and came for his arm, slashing with its short claws. He accepted the two hot slashes on his upper arm and used the opportunity to shove the creature downward. The demon fell and the old man impaled it through the chest with his sword.

Not an instant wasted, he pulled the blade free and spun to where the other monster, distracted mere moments by his cloud of dirt, flew at him through the darkness. He only had the barest impression of eyes coming through the air before he got his sword in front of him and fell to his back. He felt the creature catch on the end of the blade and used his backward momentum to fling it over his head and away.

The bright purple cracks reappeared above them to reveal this last creature struggling back toward him across the rocks, a trail of dark blood behind it. The old man took three steps forward and removed its head from its shoulders with one strong blow.

He examined his arm as he returned to the girl. The cuts were deep but not serious. He would wrap the wounds as soon as he had a chance; for now they were far from safe. In fact....

Running full speed up the creek bed came the three strangers, followed at a short distance by not three but nine demons crouched low to the ground, from three separate tears in the fabric of the world. There would be more fractures than that, spread out across the dead forest, and there would be more still before the magic storm subsided. Some storms brought more demons than others, but there were always more than you wanted, and the danger of the storm's potential collapse was far greater than any number of demons.

The old man and the girl shared a glance, though he could not see her eyes through the shadows of her hood. They had been caught in several storms over the past two years, and the best chance was always to escape their reach before things got out of hand. They might be able to run fast enough to stay ahead of the approaching strangers, leaving them to the demons, but at least here near the tear they would have light more or less until the storm faded, or gods forbid collapsed. Out in the darkness, the demons held every advantage, and there were miles still before dawn. Yet there were nine of the creatures. The small and shadowed face in her hood was asking him the question without speaking, and the old man nodded. Things being what they were between the two of them, he could do nothing else.

The old man stepped into the middle of the creek bed, rested his blade point-down on the rocks before him, and waited.

The three men, clearly near exhaustion already from their headlong flight, began to yell at him as they drew closer and saw him in the ethereal light. They yelled for him to run, to get out of the way, to hold off the creatures long enough for them to escape. He intended none of it. He barely even listened. The old man was concentrating.

Story's End

He inhaled deeply and drew energy from within himself. A man with his training and experience had vast reserves, but even these were dipping low after so long awake and so many dusty, fearful months of walking. It would have to be enough. He focused the energy back into his skin and his bones and his muscles; he breathed strength and speed into their fibers. There were many things he would give for a suit of mindplate in a confrontation such as this, but those days were over. Still, he had advantages that few if any today could match. Stoneskin tightened his muscles and skin with an effort of will, and battleskin poured speed and flexibility into his body. All of this left him barely able to maintain his sleepskin, threatening him with exhaustion, but he would see this through.

He lifted his sword and stepped between the running men, paying them no mind as they broke and scrambled around him. The nine demons advanced, keying in on him and the threat he represented. If they were more clever, they would have split apart to occupy him while sending others on to kill the girl and the three strangers, but the demons were not intelligent. They were feral, instinct-driven killers that sought to tear apart whatever they found or whoever stood in their way. No one knew where they came from, the god's realm or some other world. The storms simply brought them from somewhere else.

The demons surged at him in a fury of teeth and claws. The old man exploded into motion at the same moment, whirling to one side to fall upon their flank and force them to readjust. With a burst of strength he drove his blade through the middle of one, wrenching it free to hack into the neck of another, faster than they could react. The remaining seven then had him surrounded, and one leaped upon his back while others savaged his legs. Their claws scraped painfully but harmlessly along his fortified skin as he cut and hacked and turned, resisting their weight and their attacks as they tried to pull him to the ground.

One of the demons bit his lower leg as hard as it was able, and its sharp teeth ground their way through his skin and pierced hard muscle beneath. Gritting his teeth, the old man swiveled and drove his blade down through the thing's shoulder and into its torso. The wound would bleed badly when the stoneskin faded. One of the creatures clawed all the way on top of him, scrabbling at his face and trying to gouge at his eyes. The old man fell to one knee and used a hand to drag the demon off, driving it into the ground. His attention divided, another demon impaled itself on his sword and wrenched it away from him.

Gritting his teeth, the old man threw his fist into another demon's face, crumpling its features inward with the force of the blow. Another creature sank its teeth into the back of his neck and chewed, a feeling in his body like rocks grinding together. He fell backward on it to knock it loose, kicked another with his foot and struggled to his knees, searching about in the purple light. He found the one with his sword, dying, and pulled the blade free. He turned, weakening now, fading, but with enough strength for the handful of precise slashes it took to disable two more. Claws gouged his back again and he placed one hand on the ground for balance. He drove the other elbow behind him and connected with something solid, then threw himself around and drove the blade down again, right through the demon's

Story's End

burning eyes.

Suddenly all he could hear was his own labored breathing. His focus was falling to pieces, and both exhaustion and bleeding began to fray it further. Hot, slow blood was running down his chest from the wound on his neck, and as he stood his left leg nearly gave out beneath him. Stinging cuts burned across his body in more places than he could comprehend. The demons were either dead or dying around him.

Nearby, the three strangers had a hold of the girl and were hastening her away into the darkness. A fury rose through the old man's battered body at the thought that they would attempt to spirit her away, but then he realized what was happening. The wind had died. The spiderweb of light above had frozen in place. The storm was collapsing.

Though every physical part of him screamed against it, the old man broke into a limping run after the others, sword still in hand for he would not abandon it this side of death. Each step drove splinters of needle-hot pain up his leg, but he forced himself forward. They were near the edge of the storm, he thought. They might make it. A collapse would scour the earth clean with raging magic throughout the storm's area, burning trees and rocks and people to nothing and leaving only smooth, smoked ground, numerous patches of which they had walked through on their journey north. Storm collapse had leveled entire cities in the first weeks after the breaking.

The light above began to brighten, running quickly from purple through blue and into a bright green that bordered on blinding yellow. The old man's body faltered, and there was no more time. He threw himself forward with the last of his strength, and the world bloomed with impossible fire behind him.

***

He woke slowly, and wondered how he woke at all.

The old man was less a human being and more a collection of pains sewn crudely into skin. His head throbbed and his back and neck burned together as one. His left leg felt swollen and raw with fire, and exhaustion squeezed his every muscle. He had never felt so ruined, and if this was not death then surely death could not be so bad in comparison.

His hands were tied with rough rope behind him, and his head was pressed to a hard surface. He did not know if he had the strength to lift it. There were voices nearby. The old man closed his eyes and tried to concentrate on breathing; he reached inward to see if anything remained.

"What is it, then?" a voice was asking. "It's like a fire stick, only there ain't no fire, and there ain't no more fire sticks neither. How did he kill so many demons with it?"

"It's something new." This was the girl's voice. The sound of it sparked the old man to concentrate harder, to dig deeper. "His people have been trying to find a way without magic. This is made by melting certain rocks, as I understand it, and shaping them into a sharp weapon. I wish you would put it down."

"We ought to sell it," said a new voice, a man's like the other. The old man realized two things as his wits came together through the pain. First, he was lying on his stomach on a smooth mud floor, hands bound behind him. Second, it was daylight now, though how long he had been out he could not say. Not long enough for his wounds to do more than dry up and begin to scab over painfully, at any rate. He wondered where they were.

"Money?" said the first voice, incredulous with an edge of desperation. "What good's money anymore? Nothing here to buy, nothing anywhere. I say we keep it for protection, use it to kill red-eyes."

"It doesn't work by itself," the girl argued. She sounded tired. "You have to know how to use it. We need it to reach where we're going. Please."

"Ain't going nowhere, by the looks of it." There was a whooshing sound as someone swung the sword back and forth. "Your old dad here's all done in, ain't he? Guess you're with us now."

"He's awake," said a third man.

Discovered, the old man turned slowly onto his back and sat up, finding a wall behind him to prop his back against. He was dizzied by fresh waves of pain, but he swallowed them down and worked saliva into his mouth before he attempted speech.

The three men were all staring at him. One wore a brimmed hat, one had a jagged scar all down one side of his face, and one had a severely broken nose that jutted off at a strange angle. They were all several years older than the girl, from the look of them. "Can't be," said the scarred man, who held his blade. "We thought you were dead for sure."

The old man located the girl beyond them, sitting on a

block of wood, and he was relieved to see that she still wore her hood up over her head. He managed to swallow. "Water," he said through slow lips.

They exchanged a look. The man with the hat, who from the look of him might be their leader, stepped forward and held up a small skin bag to the old man's mouth, tilting it back, and the old man drank gratefully. The bag was pulled away after only two swallows, but it was enough. He coughed once, then held his head up straight and ignored the pain in his neck.

"Where are we?" he asked. "Did you bring us into the town? Is there anyone still here?"

Again a sharing of glances. "Lots of people," said the broken-nosed man. "Praying to the god and whatnot, right? We traded most of your rope for a room."

"Fools," the old man muttered. Whether he meant the three young men or the people who lived here, he did not clarify. "Untie me."

"Not likely," said the scarred man. "You killed three cracks' worth of demons, old man, and you're still alive. We're happy you did, but we ain't stupid."

Behind them, the girl turned her head to look at the old man, and they met eyes through her dark hood. She made a motion with one hand and tilted her head, questioning. He gave his own a tiny shake. He was trying to summon the inner energy and focus for battleskin, which would break him free of his bonds with ease, but he was injured and exhausted, drained, and he did not know if he could find enough. They had to escape the town before someone discovered the truth.

Story's End

The leader noticed the motion of his head and turned to the girl. He stared for a moment and then rounded back on the old man. "Tell us who you are," he said. "Tell us how you killed all those demons. Tell us what your weapon is and how to use it."

"The answers would mean nothing to you," the old man told him, still trying to concentrate through the pain and the desire to simply close his eyes and sleep.

He was too late. The scarred man made an angry sound and stepped quickly toward the girl. She raised her hands in defense and began to stand, but he pushed her back down and held the sword up toward her. "Enough of all this," he said as he yanked the hood from her face. "You don't tell us, I'll just start messing up this pretty—"

He never finished his sentence. He froze, his mouth open, and stared in horror at the girl's head. The broken-nosed man began to curse repeatedly, and the leader said in a low voice, "Mad god roll me under."

The scarred man stumbled away from the girl and raised the sword in front of him, where it trembled in the cool air. He stared wide-eyed at the pair of small, knob-like horns that flanked the top of the girl's head, poking up through her thin hair. It was the unmistakable sign of a prophet, and no one in the entire world had seen it in nearly two years, since the last had been hauled from its tower by a screaming mob, cut into pieces and burned.

The old man prayed for strength as he desperately tried to focus. They were too close to fail now. But he had nothing left. He tried to push himself to his feet, ready to throw his body into

269

the men so that the girl could escape, but his leg screamed with pain and he collapsed back to the floor. None of the three even noticed.

"You did this," the scarred man said, waving the blade at the girl, who sat calmly except for her eyes, which darted back and forth. "You brought those things. You almost killed us!"

"She killed the whole god-damned world!" the broken-nosed man accused.

"She did nothing!" the old man cried through his pain, struggling once again to rise. "Leave her, it's me you want!"

The leader was the only one to turn toward the old man. He stepped forward and pushed him easily back to the floor with one hand. "They're all dead," he said, a sort of wild and needy look in the edges of his eyes. "Every last one. Where did you find a prophet, you crazy old bastard, and why are you protecting it?"

The girl's eyes stopped moving. They fixed on the leader's back and she said in a slow, mean voice, "Leave him alone."

"The god," the old man managed through gritted teeth. "We've been walking north for two years. Past the Iteru and the great desert, around the inner ocean. We passed through the ruins of Mezentam and crossed the mountains into the dead forest. The god. We've come for the god."

"Kill him," urged the broken-nosed man. "Just knock his head in."

"He went crazy," the old man continued. "You know that. The prophets broke him, and then he broke us. But it's not too late. It can be stopped."

The leader hesitated. There was flame and fear in his eyes,

but now doubt as well. "What are you talking about?"

The old man was breathing heavily. "They had a plan. Before the people turned against them and the last of them went bad. They sent the remaining trueborn daughters of magic to us in secret. We each set out in separate groups. I am the last. She is the last. If we can reach the god's chambers beneath the mountain, the girl can kill him and sever the connection with magic. His torture will end, and the magic will die. The world could start again. No magic. Only let us go, and we will leave you be."

The leader seemed to consider this for a moment, but then he looked to the girl and his eyes hardened. "They destroyed the world," he said. "They all went crazy. They can't be trusted and they can't be allowed to live."

"Please," the old man urged. "She had nothing to do with what happened, and she doesn't use magic. But she can stop it, she can save us all. You can save us all, if you let her go. It's true. It's not just a—"

"Only one thing to do with a prophet," said the scarred man, his voice unsteady, and before anyone could move he stepped forward and drove the sharp blade into the girl's stomach.

Several things happened at once.

The scarred man shouted with wordless rage as he held the sword firmly inside her. The leader jumped toward him and tried to pull him away. The old man used the small bit of energy he had gathered from all his deep breathing and focusing to slip into battleskin and tore his arms free from the rope around them, his expression filled with deadly anger and disbelief. And the girl, reacting instinctively to the reality of the sudden lethal blow, flared with light and impossible, deadly magic.

A wave of bright red power threw both the scarred man and the leader back against the far wall with enough force to shatter the mud and hurl them tumbling out into the street. The sword flew from her body and stuck point-first into part of the wall. The girl's eyes began to glow a dark, uniform yellow, and she wordlessly rose to her feet. The wound in her midsection had vanished, sewn back together by her power, and red motes swirled in the air around her. Her unworldly eyes turned to the broken-nosed man, who was cursing repeatedly again, and the old man, now risen onto his one good leg, threw himself away and to the ground again as a lance of light coalesced silently from the bright specks of magic around her and pierced the broken-nosed man through his chest, pinning him gape-mouthed against the wall before it faded and he slid dead and smoking to the floor.

The girl was floating now, several hands above the ground, and she levitated softly and quietly through the hole she had made in the wall. Outside, the leader wasn't moving, but the scarred man was trying to crawl away, screaming "Prophet!" at the top of his lungs. As the girl floated out onto the street people began to shout in confusion.

The old man struggled to his feet, one of which was practically useless even in battleskin, and hobbled to the wall to yank his sword free of the hard mud. This was bad. It was as bad as it could possibly get, not only because the town would panic and attack the girl, but also because like called to like; the wild, catastrophic magic that coalesced into storms was attracted to

Story's End

her as long as she drew upon the god's tainted gift. By unleashing her powers the girl was not only going to draw the rage and madness into herself, she was also going to bring the end of the world down upon them, as had happened to every other prophet who had continued to practice after the breaking of the god.

Never one to complain when there was work to be done, the old man whirled his sword once through the air and limped outside.

The girl had the scarred man held up in the air with magic and was pulling his limbs off one by one while he screamed. A frightened, angry prophet was a terrible thing, especially now that magic was cursed. The world had seen nothing like this these last two difficult years. The girl blazed with swirling motes of power, drawn from the gift of the broken god.

The mud lane around them had cleared of people, but they were gathering to watch from a safe distance, clad in rags and shouting. The more they shouted, the more people came. The more people came, the more they shouted, working themselves into a frenzy. Soon they would mob and overwhelm the girl, tearing her to pieces so that her magic could not restore her. They had no choice if they wanted to save their town and their lives, and the old man had seen it all before—the screaming, the madness, the corpses, and the prophets in bloody, pulpy pieces on the ground.

Not now. Not when they were so close, when the mountain itself loomed above the town's northern edge, when inside it the broken god writhed in his chamber and tore the world apart. He sheathed his sword, staggered forward, and tackled the girl to the ground.

"You have to stop," he hissed in her ear. One of her horns pressed into his cheek. "None of this matters. We're so close, we have to go. You have to listen." He had his arms tightly around her, squeezing her into immobility as he tried to talk her down.

The magic momentarily disrupted, the scarred man and his pieces fell to the earth with a spatter of dead flesh. The crowds of people were edging closer down both sides of the street, shouting, a growing roar of anger.

Anger that was suddenly cut off as blazing cracks of purple light began to spread across the sky and the air began to swirl with wind.

The old man let out a tired, suffering sigh of breath, closed his eyes, and allowed himself one single moment of self-pity.

The loud tearing sounds drowned out the world and echoed off the mountain from all around while more and more webs of light spidered their way through the town. The screaming resumed, now more frightened than angry. With a surge of power the girl knocked the old man off and away, his exhausted body sliding down the smooth mud street until he rolled to a stop against a pile of stones.

The guttural cries of demons rode the wind alongside the shouts and screams of the townspeople as the old man used the rocks to leverage himself back up onto his quickly tiring legs. The girl was a blaze of red among the purple wash of light, floating now several arm-lengths above the ground. Demons were attacking the crowd, spreading panic. One ran past the old man and another stopped to turn toward him, so he drew his blade and cut the thing down. He had no time for this.

People were dying and running everywhere, and some were going for the girl, hurling stones and crowding around her. The old man hadn't seen so many demons and fractures in one place since the end of the war. The girl's continued demonstrations were drawing more and more of the wild magic about the town, and now she began to unleash her fury on all around her.

Sickles of power swept out from her, striking at demons and humans alike. She was rotating slowly as she attacked, as though given momentum by the howling winds that were pulled in every direction by the fractures. Anyone who tried to get near her was blown back by her power, but more were gathering and soon they would overwhelm her strength. His poor, quiet girl. She was lost now in a surge of power and anger.

The old man kept walking toward her, limping badly now, determinedly and deliberately cutting down demon and maddened townsperson alike when they tried to impede him. She was just ahead of him, a fire in the air that once could have blinded the sun but was not enough to match the growing, layering webs of wild magic above. If this storm collapsed, the entire area would be reduced to nothing, as had happened to so many great cities during the end of the war.

In places he could see the cracks overlapping, so numerous were they, and where they did they appeared to be combining. With a vague, distant sort of worry, he began to notice larger demons among the crowd, types he had never seen before, taller than a man and more muscled. Did larger fractures lead to larger demons? Step by tortured step, he closed the distance. He took a deep breath and boomed out the only word that could possibly reach her in this state, loud and clear and rising above the cries and the clatter—her name.

"Story!" he called.

She slowly completed a rotation and came to a stop facing him. Her skin looked red through the swirl of magic, and combined with her yellow eyes and horns she was a magnificent, terrifying sight. She stared at him, arrested helplessly by the power in her name, arrested as only a prophet could be. He would never have risked using it any other time, but it was too late now for caution.

He limped forward again, entering the clear circle around her unharmed though she continued to idly swat others away as she slowly sank back down to earth. They met together and he placed his hands firmly on her shoulders, dipping them through the swirl of magic without fear.

The old man leaned forward and looked her in the eyes, ignoring the carnage all around, in and among the mud huts and blood-stained streets. "You have to stop," he said. "It's too much. You can't hold them all off forever, and every time you do it gets worse. Stop."

There were tears in her eyes, and once again it broke the old man's heart to remember how young she was, this tiny creature who carried both the curse and the hope of mankind on her narrow shoulders. She was only a child, and none of this was her fault. Struck by the enormity of their situation, he did what he had not done in two years of hard travel. The old man wrapped his arms around the girl and held her in a long, careful embrace.

He froze as a sound filled the air, like a thousand rocks rolling down a hill, like the sky itself cracking in two and falling. He looked up to see that the fractures had continued to collide and combine around the city and were now forming a massive hole in the air high above and a little to the south, dizzying and awful to behold, bathing the town in purple light.

There was something on the other side, and it was coming through.

"Listen to me," said the old man as they watched. "There's no time. You can't stay here, and I can't go with you. You have to go up the mountain by yourself. You have to end this. You're the only one who can. Do you understand?"

She looked at him with those dark, strange yellow eyes for a long moment, too long, but at last she nodded. There was no need for further words. After two years together, they understood. She knew how the story ended. She knew why they both had to die.

The girl turned and fled up the street as fast as her legs could carry her, magic to see her safe and speed her steps, for it no longer mattered what sort of energies or dangers she drew. The old man faced the other direction, where a demon the size of a palace of old stepped ponderously from the sky, six legs shaking the earth and crushing mud buildings with their first steps. It had a face like an animal's, lumpy and brutish and full of teeth. It towered high above everything, but looked down upon the doomed town beneath its feet. It roared and the world trembled.

The old man found calm, somewhere inside, and he found peace. It was over and there was only one more task he might complete. Breathing deeply from some inner reserve that had only unlocked with this acceptance, he straightened on his wounded leg. The beast's eyes found him somehow through the chaos, as though it sensed who he was and what he stood for.

The old man smiled, and held his sword before him.

***

Far up the mountain slopes, along an empty path lined with stones, the young prophet named Story heard the terrible roaring and the crash of something enormous striking the ground, but she did not turn back to look. There was no need. All that mattered was ahead.

What would a world be like without magic, she wondered. Her own powers had been more curse than gift for as long as she could remember, but without the magic that had brought such prosperity, the world had collapsed and turned on itself until there was almost nothing left. Killing the god would shatter him into hundreds of incoherent pieces that might never be drawn back together, and it would end magic forever. People would need to find a new way, and learn from the prophets' mistakes.

Would they? Could they?

She would never know. There was a temple ahead, just a little further up the path. Somewhere deep within it lay the god

Story's End

she had waited her entire life to meet. She had to thank him for his gift.

The winds died around her, signifying the coming collapse of the storm below. Story stepped into the temple, and vanished into the darkness where she would write her final lines.

The End

Author Bios

Bill Blume

Bill Blume is a fantasy writer whose short stories have appeared in various anthologies and online magazines. He also works as a 911 dispatcher and is a former television news producer. Bill chairs the board of directors for James River Writers in Richmond, Virginia. You can learn more about Bill and his writing by visiting his website at www.billblume.net.

Deedee Davies

Deedee is a writer interested mainly in the fantasy, horror and science-fiction genres. Inspired by turn of the century fantasy and science-fiction, she wrote a great deal as a youngster, returning to it in 2012, when she finished her first draft novel. Deedee is also a cover artist, with around 20 published book covers under her belt. She lives in Plymouth, UK with her partner, 3 spiders, 3 snakes and a scorpion.

Nathen Gallagher

When he was four years old, Nathen Gallagher decided he wanted to paint houses when he grew up. One year later he came to his senses and figured he would be a writer instead. He has been a copy editor, a journalist, and a muffin man, but today he lives in Calgary, Alberta, where he works as a technical writer by day and pursues his love of stories by night. You may currently find him at http://chapterfish.wordpress.com, but if you don't, fear not. He'll find you.

Darra L. Hofman

Darra Hofman is an author and legal scholar. Her fiction focuses on questions of autonomy and individual agency, while her scholarly work is focused on the intersection of law, medicine, and ethics, with a particular focus on the ethics and policy of medical decisionmaking. She lives in Richmond, BC, Canada, with her husband two (soon to be three) children.

Magda Knight

Magda Knight is the founder of Mookychick Online, a UK feminist hub for alternative women. She writes horror and speculative fiction for assorted children, adults and changelings. She tweets and trills at @MagdaKnight, and discusses horror, fantasy. wring and YA in equal measure at http://www.magdaknight.com. When she grows up she would like to be a sword or a bear.

Steven S. Long

Steven S. Long is a writer and game designer who's been working primarily in the tabletop roleplaying game field for the past twenty years. During that time he's written or co-written nearly 200 books. In recent years he's branched out into writing fiction as well. His Master Plan for World Domination has reached Stage 61-Epsilon. You can find out more about Steve and what he's up to at www.

stevenslong.com.

Mandi M. Lynch

Mandi M. Lynch started writing stories at the tender age of six, pecking out the words on her mother's manual typewriter. Although the crayon drawings have improved marginally, the spelling has not. Now, she lives in Nashville, TN, with three cats - none of which write due to lack of thumbs - and spends as much of her time in the industry as she possibly can. You can find her or her small press (Ink Monkey Mag) on facebook.

William Ransom

William Ransom was born and raised in San Antonio, Texas. After gathering intelligence on so-called "normal life" by working as a gas station attendant and hotel desk clerk, he promptly climbed the ivory tower and earned a Master's Degree in Library Science from Texas Woman's University. Following graduate school he joined the staff of a local university library, where he wanders the stacks and yells at unsuspecting students. William has been writing longer than he has been published; his influences include China Mieville, Lev Grossman, and Nathen Gallagher. He currently lives in Corpus Christi, Texas, and can be found online at callmeransom.wordpress.com.

Desmond Reddick

Desmond Reddick waits out the apocalypse on the west coast of Vancouver Island with his lovely wife, two ferocious children, two chickens and one very affectionate duck. When he isn't writing genre fiction, he enjoys immersing himself in it in all media: film, music, literature and comics. Every week, you can find his horror genre podcast Dread Media at www.dreadmedia.com. He hopes that, despite what T.S. Eliot says, the world ends with a bang. He doesn't like to be kept waiting.

Scott Sandridge

Scott M. Sandridge is a writer, editor, blogger, freedom fighter, and all-round trouble-maker. You can find him at http://smsand.wordpress.com

Jay Wilburn

Jay Wilburn was a public school teacher for 16 years. He left to care for his younger son and to be a full-time writer in beautiful Conway, South Carolina where he lives with his wife and two sons. He was featured in Best Horror of the Year vol. 5 with editor Ellen Datlow. He has published many horror and speculative fiction stories. His first novel, Loose Ends: A Zombie Novel, is available now. Time Eaters will be released by Perpetual Motion Machine Publishing. He was a featured author with Hazardous Press at the 2013 World Horror Convention. He was included in the limited edition Best of Dark Moon of Digest. He is a columnist for Dark Eclipse and for Revolt Daily. Follow his many dark thoughts at JayWilburn.com and @AmongTheZombies on Twitter.

About the Editor

Joshua H. Leet is a native of Lexington, KY. He absconded with a degree in English Literature from Transylvania University and has co-authored 3 non-fiction books, including Civil War Lexington, Kentucky: Bluegrass Breeding Ground of Power (The History Press). He currently works as a contract scopist, and he edits novels for Seventh Star Press, working with authors like Jackie Gamber and Steven Shrewsbury. He enjoys reading, watching sports, television and movies, and playing Frisbee. When he dies, he hopes to leave the world the same way he came in, screaming with a clenched fist.

Check out the following pages to see more from

All Seventh Star Press titles available in print and an array of specially priced eBook formats.

Visit www.seventhstarpress.com for further information

connect with Seventh Star Press at

www.seventhstarpress.com

seventhstarpress.blogspot.com

www.facebook.com/seventhstarpress

www.twitter.com/7thstarpress

Begin your journey into The Brotherhood of Dwarves, the
popular YA Fantasy series from D.A. Adams. An action-
filled saga where the dwarves are not just sidekicks!

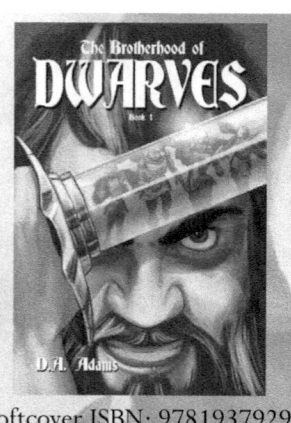

Softcover ISBN: 9781937929916   Softcover ISBN: 9781937929923

eBook ISBN: 9781937929930   eBook ISBN: 9781937929-947

Softcover ISBN: 9780983740254   Softcover ISBN: 9781937929787

eBook ISBN: 9781937929909   eBook ISBN: 9781937929770

Explore the world of Ave in the Fires in Eden Series from Stephen Zimmer! Epic Fantasy for those who enjoy authors like George R.R. Martin, Steven Erikson, and Brandon Sanderson.

Softcover ISBN: 9780982565612

eBook ISBN: 9780982565698

Softcover ISBN: 9780983108627

eBook ISBN: 9780983108610

Softcover ISBN 9781937929855

eBook ISBN 9781937929862

Enter an ancient world of heroes, blood, and steel in the tales of Gorias La Gaul from Steven Shrewsbury! Hard-hitting Sword & Sorcery in the vein of Robert E. Howard.

Softcover ISBN: 9781937929800

eBook ISBN: 9781937929831

Softcover ISBN: 9780983108634

eBook ISBN: 9780983108641

The highly-acclaimed Leland Dragon Series from Jackie Gamber! Strong character-driven YA Fantasy for those who enjoy authors such as Christopher Paolini.

Softcover ISBN: 9780983108672

eBook ISBN: 9780983108696

Softcover ISBN: 9781937929893

eBook ISBN: 9781937929817

www.ingramcontent.com/pod-product-compliance
Lightning Source LLC
Chambersburg PA
CBHW051522260626
47170CB00003B/739